The Shadow Requiem

A Shadow Concerto 3

Jill L. Ferguson

red dog press

For information, contact:

red dog press

red dog press, a division of In Your Face Ink LLC Glendale, AZ
www.inyourfaceink.com

ISBN: 979-8-9934752-8-8 Hardback
ISBN: 979-8-9934752-9-5 Paperback
ISBN: 979-8-9960568-0-4 eBook

10 9 8 7 6 5 4 3 2 1
Book design by Rick Schank of Purple Couch Creative

This book is for Dr. James Dohn and Lawrence Pech,
the series' biggest fans.

Table of Contents

$\int \wr$

Chapter 1

Aftermath

THIRTY-SIX-YEAR-OLD CELESTE MORGAN learned early that aircraft cabins were liminal spaces—neither here nor there, belonging to no country, accountable to no law except physics. Suspended above the Atlantic at thirty-six thousand feet, the world became manageable again. Distances collapsed into lines on a map. Names lost their power. Even grief, usually such a noisy companion, went quiet.

The cabin lights were dimmed to a false twilight, enough to soften edges without pretending to be night. Around her, strangers slept in small, defenseless postures with their heads tipped back, mouths open, arms flung across narrow armrests like discarded instruments. Somewhere near the galley, a flight attendant laughed too loudly at something a coworker whispered, the sound muffled as if underwater. The aircraft hummed in a register so low she felt it more in her bones than her ears.

Celeste sat upright, seatbelt fastened low across her hips, cello case wedged onto the seat beside her. She hadn't slept since New York. She wasn't tired in the conventional sense. Her body existed in a state of deliberate neutrality, like the instant before a bow touched string.

On the tray table in front of her lay her phone, screen dark. She'd turned it face down not because she expected a message but because not looking at it felt like claiming a moment of authorship. Even if it was a lie.

Her reflection wavered in the scratched oval of the window: long blond hair pulled into a knot at the nape of her neck, cheekbones too sharp when she was this thin, eyes steady in a way people liked to call calm. Calm implied absence. This was not absence. This was compression.

She thought of New York the way it had looked from the plane window; its jagged grid of light dissolving under cloud, the Philharmonic gala already receding into story. By morning it would be a column inch on page three, if that: cellist gives moving pre-performance speech; donors pleased; safety discussion trends briefly before being swallowed by celebrity divorce.

She had saved a room full of people, and the world had shrugged. That was the real victory for Eidolon: not that they could kill, but that they could fail and still vanish.

Celeste reached into her carry-on and removed the folded letter. She unfolded it carefully, aligning the creases the way she aligned sheet music—ritual as anchor. The paper was thin now, softened by handling, her mother's handwriting slanted and precise, every letter shaped as if it mattered.

You hold the bow. Remember that. The line sat in the center of the page, deceptively small for the gravity it carried. Her mother had written it years ago, not knowing for sure that her daughter would one day carry weapons through airports disguised as rosin cases, not knowing her death in Berlin would become a recruitment tool.

A car bomb doesn't end when it detonates. It migrates. It embeds itself in kitchens and courtrooms and the way a girl grips a cello too hard because it's the only solid thing in a room where nothing else makes sense.

Celeste traced the ink with her thumb, the movement so small it barely registered. "I remember," she whispered, though she wasn't sure who the words were for—her mother, herself, the part of her that wanted to believe memory was a choice instead of a wound.

Her phone vibrated. The movement was subtle, but she felt it like a shock to the system, a spike in a line she'd been trying to keep smooth. She flipped the phone face up, heart rate barely changing, pulse trained not to betray her.

Unknown number. French country code. The image filled the screen the moment she opened it: the Palais Garnier in Paris, pale stone glowing in early light, barricades arranged in neat, official geometry. In the foreground, sprayed across metal with the ugly sincerity of fresh paint: *LA MUSIQUE N'EST PAS UNE ARME*. Music is not a weapon.

Beneath it, smaller, almost intimate, like a correction whispered too late to be erased: *ELLE EST UN CHOIX*. It's a choice.

Celeste stared at the words until the cabin around her seemed to blur. She felt the corners of her mouth lift in a reflex she hadn't authorized, a smile that vanished almost as soon as it appeared.

Music is not a weapon. It was almost funny. She had spent her life turning music into exactly that, long before any quasi-governmental agency decided her marksmanship and multilingual fluency were more valuable than her ability to play Bach suites from memory. After Berlin, after the phone call that ended childhood, she'd sat alone in a practice room and pressed her bow into the string until the sound fractured, until she understood that control was something you could manufacture even when nothing else obeyed you.

It's a choice.

She locked the phone and set it down again, but the words remained, vibrating behind her eyes.

Across the aisle, a businessman in an expensive suit snored softly, oblivious to the fact that the woman beside him could end him with a pen and make it look like syncope. He had no idea that organizations existed that wrote terror into donor contracts and called it culture. He had no idea how often safety was a performance.

She envied him, not his life, but his ignorance. Ignorance was a luxury that never appeared on balance sheets.

Her thoughts drifted, as they always did when something new destabilized the internal map, to the night in Brooklyn when Volkov had said, you're bleeding, and she'd lied without thinking. *I'm fine. Stop saying that. You're too quiet. Not like this.*

She shifted minutely in her seat, easing the familiar ache in her ribs, a souvenir from that first open break with the network that had raised her. Bruise, he'd called it. Something about the word had irritated her. Bruises faded. The things that mattered left marks you couldn't photograph.

She imagined Volkov on a different aircraft, a different manifest, traveling under a name that wasn't his. Separate routes had been her decision. Safer, she'd said. He'd looked at her the way he always did when she confused control with care but hadn't argued. Volkov didn't waste energy on battles he couldn't win.

Lena would have argued. Lena would have leaned across the armrest, stolen her headphones, and demanded she drink water. Lena would have made a joke about Paris and croissants and violists in scarves pretending to understand philosophy. Lena was human in ways Celeste forgot were possible.

She pulled the phone back into her hand and opened the notes app, her fingers moving with the precision of someone who'd written hundreds of itineraries that were half truth, half camouflage.

Landing. Customs. Hotel. Instrument check. Rehearsal schedule. Venue maps. Security liaison. Exit routes. It was the skeleton of every tour, every mission, every carefully choreographed disappearance. She paused, then added a line she almost never let herself type. **What do I want?**

The cursor blinked, patient. She stared at it as if it were a trap. Want was dangerous. Want created angles someone else could use. Eidolon had always been expert at stripping recruits of their wants, replacing them with directives that sounded like purpose. That was why they watched for flinches, why they manufactured small crises in public to test compliance. It was easier to manipulate someone who thought obedience was identity.

Celeste thought of standing on the Philharmonic stage in New York, stepping forward with a microphone and turning a safety briefing into a plea for attention, not fear. She'd watched the audience scan exits, watch each other, transform into a community for ten minutes. The cameras had eaten it up. The Maestro—whoever he was, wherever he hid—would have hated it.

Good, Esra had said when Celeste told her. *Narcissists always underestimate sincerity.*

Celeste swallowed.

I want to choose, she typed. The words looked small on the screen, almost childish, but simplicity carried its own violence. Choice implied ownership. Ownership implied she would have to look at every decision she'd made and accept that duty was not the same thing as absolution.

She added a second line, her jaw tightening as she did. **I want to end the Maestro.** Not Duret—the charismatic conductor who wore influence like cologne and thought proximity to power was the same thing as power itself. Duret was a false maestro, a decoy baton waving where cameras could see it. The real Maestro of Eidolon remained unnamed, a distributed presence that spoke through systems instead of faces, who composed disasters the way others composed symphonies.

She didn't want his blood. She wanted his score.

Outside the window, the darkness held. The Atlantic had no interest in her revelations.

The intercom crackled softly. The captain announced their estimated time to arrival in Paris in calm English, then repeated it in French. Celeste understood both without effort. Languages were like fingerings: patterns drilled until the body remembered what the mind could forget. She had learned French because the agency told her it would be useful. She had learned Russian because a former instructor of hers once muttered that it mattered. She had learned Japanese because underestimation was a weapon too.

She had learned control because after Berlin, control was the only thing that didn't explode.

Her phone vibrated again. This time the name made her breathe easier. Esra.

Call me when you land. The number is real. It's routed through a ghost relay that burned itself after sending the image. Someone wanted you to see it—and to know we can't trace them back.

Celeste closed her eyes, the message echoing with the weight of confirmation. Bait, then. An invitation dressed as provocation. The Maestro wanted her in Paris, in his chosen hall, on his symbolic stage. You saved your little stage tonight. Bravo. *Now let's see how far your reach really goes.*

She exhaled slowly, not allowing the pulse spike to register anywhere visible. This was the difference between reaction and composition. She had learned, in the last months, that the moment you allowed someone else to define your tempo, you were already behind.

When the plane began its gradual descent, the cabin lights brightened, false dawn dissolving into functional day. Passengers stirred, rubbed eyes, reached for phones as if waking to themselves. Celeste folded the letter one last time and slid it back into her bag, the ritual complete.

Paris rose to meet them through layers of cloud: the river like a dark ribbon, city blocks stacked with casual intimacy, the opera house somewhere inside that map like a note waiting to be struck.

She did not know yet how the next piece would sound. She only knew she would not play it the way Eidolon expected.

When the wheels touched down, the impact reverberated through the cabin, a percussive punctuation mark that told her the liminal space was over. The door opened. The air changed. Voices layered French over English in that particular airport cadence that meant nothing was wrong.

Celeste rose with the others, cello case secure against her back, binder heavy in her carry-on, phone warm in her palm with words that had already begun to rearrange the architecture of her life. *Music is not a weapon. It's a choice.*

She stepped into the jet bridge and did not look back.

Chapter 2

Fractures

CELESTE HAD LEARNED that customs halls were theaters of micro-truths. Not lies exactly, but truths reduced to their smallest safe shapes. The shape of a passport held too tightly. The shape of a smile offered to an official who no longer saw faces. The shape of obedience performed without thought because it had been practiced for years.

She stood in line at Charles de Gaulle with her cello case strapped to her back, watching the machinery of entry grind forward. The woman ahead of her argued softly about an overweight bag. The man behind her smelled of a cologne so expensive it carried its own authority. None of them looked dangerous. That was the point.

Her passport returned to her hand with a mechanical stamp that authorized her to become another version of herself. She closed the booklet without looking at the ink, slipped it into her coat pocket, and stepped forward without turning back.

The orchestra came through in ragged waves with the strings first, then brass, then percussion, each cluster carrying the brittle camaraderie of long travel. Someone laughed too loudly. Someone else argued with a clerk about a cracked bridge. A trumpet player announced to no one in particular that he intended to eat nothing but croissants for the next week.

The binder rested in Celeste's shoulder bag with a weight that felt disproportionate to its mass. Paper should not be able to do this, she thought, not bend time, not rearrange loyalty, not turn memory into ammunition. But it did.

Volkov was not here. The absence registered in her body the way a wrong note did in a familiar chord: not catastrophic, not immediately alarming, but impossible to ignore. That silence followed her through the sliding doors and into the open cavern of the arrival hall.

Her phone vibrated. **Esra: French number originated from a terminal inside the 9th arrondissement. Two blocks from Palais Garnier. It was meant to be seen, not traced. Duret is already in Paris for "preliminary donor meetings." That is not protocol.**

Celeste read the message twice, then locked the screen. Silence was not avoidance. Silence was pressure.

Outside, Paris exhaled damp stone and diesel. The orchestra's transport coordinator waved a clipboard like a conductor with too many sections and not enough rehearsal.

"*Bienvenue!* Strings on Bus *Deux*—no, not you, brass is *Trois*—"

"*Bienvenue* to our hostage situation," Lena murmured as she appeared at Celeste's side, sunglasses shielding the bruised crescents beneath her eyes.

"I'm so glad to see you," Celeste said quietly.

"My mother asked me to bring back cheese," Lena replied. "So now I'm obligated to survive long enough to shop."

They boarded the bus. The doors sealed with a hiss that sounded like a breath finally released. Paris slid past the window in washed-out color: cafés opening like tired eyes, cyclists threading traffic with casual defiance, buildings stacked like memories that had outlived their storytellers.

Celeste rested her forehead against the glass and let the vibration travel through her bones. Her phone buzzed again. **Volkov: Hotel secured. Separate arrival as planned. Eyes on your six even when I'm not there.**

She did not reply. He didn't need reassurance. He needed consistency.

The hotel near the Madeleine wore its wealth with the practiced discretion of someone who had never worried about it. The lobby smelled faintly of citrus polish and money. A concierge greeted Celeste by name as if it were a privilege.

In the elevator, Lena leaned closer. "Security guard by the door," she whispered. "Not hotel. He scans rooms, not people."

"Yes," Celeste said.

"I thought this was a music trip."

"It is," Celeste replied. "It's just also something else."

Her room overlooked a narrow street where scooters buzzed like irritated insects. She placed the cello carefully on its stand and stood motionless, letting the space speak. Hotels had their own acoustics of pipes ticking behind walls, muffled laughter bleeding through carpet, the soft percussion of strangers closing doors on lives she would never know.

A knock came. Too light. Too careful.

She opened the door a fraction.

A young woman stood in the hall with a tablet and a hotel lanyard that looked too new, her eyes flicking left and right before settling on Celeste.

"Madame Morgan," she began, "there's a small issue with your minibar—"

"No," Celeste said and closed the door.

The woman did not knock again.

Celeste leaned her forehead against the wood for a heartbeat longer than necessary, then exhaled slowly and texted Esra a description. Don't flinch, she added.

She sat on the edge of the bed until her breathing slowed into something that could be mistaken for rest.

The first rehearsal was scheduled for ten the next morning, but Celeste was awake before dawn, staring at the narrow Paris street through sheer curtains that made everything look as if it were underwater.

Jet lag was usually a physical inconvenience with headache, nausea, and a misplaced sense of time. This was different. This was anticipatory fatigue, the kind that settled into muscle memory because the body knew something the mind refused to articulate.

She dressed in silence, donning black jeans and a soft gray sweater, concert black deferred in favor of something that looked convincingly civilian. The binder went into the bag last, as it always did, a quiet ritual of control. She left the hotel without breakfast, the doorman offering a polite nod that lingered just a moment too long on her face.

Paris before eight in the morning belonged to delivery trucks and municipal workers. A street cleaner hummed tunelessly as he guided a hose along the curb, washing away last night's evidence. Celeste walked with no destination, letting her feet choose angles her mind did not yet trust.

She had learned to love cities from the inside out, not for their landmarks but for their backstage corridors—the side streets, the unlocked doors, the invisible transitions. Music had taught her that architecture had rhythms, too. Paris was a slow waltz this early, not yet crowded enough to drown itself.

Her phone vibrated again. **Esra: I've mapped donor overlap with Palais Garnier's vendors. It's ugly. You're walking through an ecosystem, not a venue.**

Celeste typed a reply with gloved fingers. **Duret's reception tonight?**

Esra: Confirmed. Private salon, donor-only. No orchestra press. He's staging influence, not art.

She slipped the phone back into her pocket and crossed the street without looking back.

The rehearsal hall was already alive when she arrived, though it was nearly empty of sound. Musicians moved quietly through their routines: oiling valves, stretching wrists, whispering greetings that hadn't yet found energy. The conductor's stand waited at the center like an accusation.

Lena spotted her immediately and lifted a coffee cup in quiet offering. "You look like someone who's about to disassemble a religion," she said as Celeste took the cup.

"Just a system," Celeste replied.

"That's what religions call themselves," Lena said, then winced. "Sorry. Too soon?"

Celeste almost smiled.

They tuned in silence, the familiar cascade of pitches filling the room with disorganized hope. Celeste closed her eyes and let the sound settle around her, the way it always did, the way it had since childhood. Music was a language that did not ask permission.

She felt eyes on her. At first, she assumed it was just the usual awareness, the subtle shift in posture that accompanied being recognized. But when she opened her eyes, she saw the man standing near the exit doors, clipboard tucked under one arm, gaze sliding not to the stage but to the control panel on the wall beside it. He was definitely not staff, not musician, not donor.

She raised her cello, deliberately angling it so the scroll obscured her face, and watched him through the varnished curve of the instrument's neck.

He checked his watch. He looked at the panel again. Then he left.

Her phone buzzed in her pocket.

Volkov: You've been tagged. Secondary tail picked you up two blocks from the hotel. He peeled off at rehearsal. You weren't meant to see him.

Celeste's pulse steadied instead of spiking. **I saw him.**

Volkov: Of course you did.

She slipped the phone away as Maestro Duret entered the hall in a flurry of tailored fabric and deference. The rehearsal began like any other, but she felt the room differently now, as if the air itself were a medium someone else could tune.

At the break, Esra's message arrived. **Found something. There's an unscheduled "safety audit" tomorrow afternoon at the opera house. Shell company with ties to the same logistics firm that showed up in New York.**

Celeste leaned back in her chair and closed her eyes. Paris was not an interlude. It was the next movement.

The rehearsal dissolved slowly, as if the music were reluctant to release its hold on the room. Musicians packed up with the habitual efficiency of people who had spent their lives turning chaos into order with strings loosening, brass wiping condensation from bell rims, percussionists discussing where they'd stashed the good mallets.

Celeste stayed seated long after the others rose, bow resting across her lap, listening to the way the hall changed as bodies left it. The room lost something when people went. Resonance, maybe, or just the illusion of safety that came from shared purpose.

Lena touched her shoulder lightly. "You're thinking too loudly," she said.

"I don't know how to think quietly," Celeste replied.

"That's what scares people about you."

Celeste stood and slid her cello back into its case. "I don't have time to make them comfortable."

They left the rehearsal hall together, stepping into the corridor that led toward the building's backstage infrastructure. The walls were scuffed from decades of instrument cases and hurried exits, the floor patched so often it resembled a palimpsest of forgotten emergencies.

Halfway down the hall, Esra appeared as if summoned, tablet tucked under one arm, eyes sharp.

"You weren't meant to notice the man with the clipboard," she said without greeting.

"I noticed him," Celeste replied.

"That's the problem," Esra said. "He's not a watcher. He's a tester."

Lena frowned. "Tester for what?"

"Compliance," Esra said. "They don't start with explosions. They start with discomfort. Small intrusions. People who look like staff but aren't. Systems that flicker but don't fail. It's how they train environments to behave."

Celeste's fingers tightened around her case handle. "And tomorrow's audit?"

"An insertion point," Esra said. "They'll add something small enough that no one questions it. A panel here. A software update there. Chorale doesn't announce itself. It composes."

They stopped at a narrow service stairwell. Esra lowered her voice. "Duret's reception tonight is not about donors," she said. "It's about legitimizing access. The people he's invited are not patrons. They're pathways."

"Then we don't attend," Lena said.

"Yes, we do," Celeste replied. "We attend and we listen."

"You're not on the guest list," Esra reminded her.

Celeste met her eyes. "Then we change the list."

The reception was held in a private salon overlooking the Place de l'Opéra, a room that had been decorated into submission. The walls glowed with carefully restored frescoes, the chandeliers dimmed to flatter complexions and bank accounts. The invitation Celeste eventually received was hand-delivered by a man who did not look at her face when he handed it over.

She arrived wearing a black dress that belonged equally to concert stage and cocktail hour, her hair swept into a knot that signaled seriousness to people who thought discipline was a virtue they could borrow.

Lena was not invited. Esra was not invited. Volkov was not anywhere the cameras could see.

Duret greeted her as if she were a colleague rather than a commodity. "Ah, our American treasure," he said, kissing the air beside her cheek. "Paris is already whispering your name."

"Paris whispers a lot," Celeste replied.

"True," Duret said. "But tonight it listens."

She moved through the room as she did through orchestral passages, by counting beats, marking patterns. A woman from a media conglomerate laughed too loudly at nothing. A man with a defense contracting background held court near the balcony doors. The word security floated in conversation with the gentleness of perfume.

Her phone vibrated in the clutch she held like an accessory rather than a lifeline. **Volkov: Two new faces entered the perimeter. Neither on the hotel roster. Both looking at HVAC intakes, not art.**

Celeste excused herself from a conversation about donor tiers and drifted toward the balcony, the city opening below like a score waiting to be annotated.

A voice spoke behind her. "You shouldn't keep choosing rooms with exits." Aria leaned against the railing, smile thin, eyes alert. Her blue gown was a shade lighter that the tips of her hair.

Celeste did not startle. "You shouldn't be here."

"And yet," Aria replied. "Here I am. Watching Duret sell the illusion that culture is neutral."

"You're not on the list."

"I am on a different one," Aria said. "The Maestro's."

Celeste turned to face her fully. "You don't know who the Maestro is."

"No," Aria said softly. "But I know what he wants. He doesn't want your death. He wants your authorship."

The phrase hit Celeste harder than she expected.

"Music is not a weapon," Aria continued. "It's a choice. Your choice terrifies him."

Below them, traffic streamed through the square in obedient lines. "You're in danger," Aria said.

"So are you," Celeste replied.

Aria's smile widened by a fraction. "I always am."

Across the room, Duret lifted his glass, drawing attention. "To the future," he declared. "To art that shapes the world."

Celeste raised her own glass in reflex, the words echoing uncomfortably close to something true. Her phone buzzed again. **Esra: The audit team just arrived at the opera house. They're not waiting for tomorrow.**

Celeste's fingers tightened on the stem of her glass. "Time to leave," she murmured.

Aria glanced at her phone, then at Celeste. "Looks like your next movement is starting early."

The Maestro was not a man. He was a system that had just shifted key.

ƒ ₹

Chapter 3

Signals

THE PALAIS GARNIER was never quiet. Even when it was empty, it whispered. Stone remembered sound. Gold leaf trapped echoes the way old bones trapped pain, and every corridor held the residue of applause that had outlived the people who'd made it.

Celeste felt the building before she saw it. She did not enter through the public doors. Those were for cameras, tourists, and men like Duret who believed visibility was power. Instead she came through a service alley that smelled faintly of oil and cold metal, slipping past a loading bay where crates were stacked like coffins, each stamped with the insignia of a company that had existed for less than three years. Too new.

Her badge was a borrowed thing, a rectangle of laminated plastic that identified her as a temporary consultant for acoustic calibration. The name printed beneath the barcode wasn't hers. She wore it like a challenge.

Inside, the corridors narrowed. The opera house's backstage was an anatomy lesson in control: staircases leading nowhere obvious, rehearsal rooms buried under balconies, doors that opened only for people who already knew what waited behind them.

Her phone vibrated once in her coat pocket. **Esra: Audit team arrived at 22:14. They're already three levels below stage.**

Celeste slowed her pace, letting a pair of stagehands pass her, their conversation about late-night sandwiches carrying no awareness of how close the building was to becoming something else entirely.

She followed the corridor's curve until the polished marble gave way to unvarnished concrete. Here the walls were scarred with decades of frantic modifications including electrical conduit stapled into place, faded safety notices layered like geological strata.

She paused at a fire control panel recessed into the wall. Its metal casing had been buffed until it shone like a mirror. New. Too new.

Her phone vibrated again. **Volkov: I have eyes on HVAC access in west fly tower. Two techs. Neither from city contractor list.**

Celeste's jaw tightened. Two teams. Parallel operations. Redundancy was Eidolon's signature.

She continued deeper into the building, past dressing rooms whose doors were ajar, mirrors dark, costumes hanging like abandoned skins. The air smelled faintly of dust and makeup, old glue and stale roses.

A door stood at the end of the corridor, unmarked except for a small white sticker placed too carefully to be incidental. She slipped inside. The room was small, lit by a single fluorescent strip that hummed with quiet resentment. Metal cabinets lined the walls, each labeled with tidy black print: FIRE, ALARM, SUPPRESSION, MANUAL OVERRIDE.

A man stood with his back to her, shoulders hunched as he worked inside the open fire panel, a tangle of color-coded wires spilling into his hands.

Celeste closed the door without a sound. Her reflection stared back at her from the polished metal of the cabinet—blond hair darkened by shadow, eyes flat with focus. The cello player who filled opera houses with beauty had become something else entirely in rooms like this.

"Bonsoir," she said softly.

The man froze.

When he turned, she saw that he was younger than she'd expected. Late twenties, maybe. City contractor jacket. Sweat at his temples. Fear in his eyes before training erased it.

"Who are you?" he demanded.

Celeste raised her badge. "Quality control."

His gaze flicked to the name, the barcode, the lie that might have passed if she had not been standing inside a locked room at midnight.

"You're not supposed to be here," he said.

"No," Celeste replied. "You are."

His hand twitched toward the panel.

She was faster.

Her palm slammed into the cabinet door, pinning his wrist before he could close it. The sound was dull, absorbed by the building the way screams once had been.

"Don't," she said.

His breathing spiked. "You don't understand—"

"I understand everything," Celeste said. "The only question is how much you're going to tell me before I decide this conversation is over."

The man's eyes darted to the door, then back to her, calculating distances he did not yet understand. His other hand twitched toward the radio clipped to his belt. Celeste shifted her weight, just enough to communicate that every option he imagined was already obsolete.

"Take your hand off the panel," she said.

"You don't know what you're interfering with," he replied, voice cracking under its own bravado. "This isn't your building."

"That's true," Celeste said. "But it's about to become my problem."

She pressed her knee into the inside of his thigh, not enough to injure but enough to make it clear that escalation would be involuntary.

His jaw tightened, then slackened. He withdrew his hand.

"Good," she murmured.

The cabinet's interior was a small universe of intent: new fiber-optic leads threaded through old copper arteries, a secondary board grafted onto the primary system with meticulous care. It was not sabotage in the traditional sense. It was authorship, rewriting the building's reflexes so that in a moment of crisis it would hesitate instead of respond.

"You're adding latency," Celeste said. "Milliseconds."

His eyes widened. "You—how—"

"Milliseconds get people killed," she continued. "Why here?"

He laughed once, a brittle sound. "You think I'm allowed to know that?"

Celeste leaned closer, lowering her voice. "You were allowed to wire a historic opera house without oversight. That tells me someone trusts you more than they should. And you are very young to be that trusted."

Something shifted behind his eyes—not guilt, she thought, not yet. Resignation.

"They told me it was redundancy," he said. "Fail-safe improvements. They pay triple the city rate. No one asks questions when it's framed as safety."

"Who are they?"

"Chorale Logistics."

The name was a stone dropped into still water. Celeste closed the cabinet with controlled gentleness and stepped back. "You're going to remove everything you added. Now."

His mouth fell open. "I can't. It's audited remotely—"

She raised the phone she'd been palming and angled the screen toward him. The live video feed showed his face, pale under fluorescent light, her own silhouette reflected behind him.

"I've already sent your image to three separate oversight boards," she said. "Two of them don't officially exist. If you don't comply, I won't stop them from doing their jobs."

The threat was surgical. He saw it, she knew, because he turned back to the panel and began undoing his work with hands that no longer tried to hide their tremor.

Her phone buzzed softly in her pocket. **Volkov: West fly tower team just bailed. They left hardware behind. Whatever this was, it's compromised.**

Celeste exhaled through her nose. "You're late," she said to the man.

He glanced back, confused. "Late for what?"

"For being afraid," she replied. "You were supposed to be afraid before you started."

When the panel was restored to something approximating its original configuration, Celeste stepped aside. "Leave," she said. "And forget you were here."

He hesitated, then bolted, nearly colliding with a pair of stagehands at the corridor's end.

Celeste remained in the room long enough to take photographs, annotate schematics, and send Esra a silent dossier that would begin unraveling Chorale's Paris footprint.

The opera house whispered around her, no longer just memory, but warning.

Celeste closed the service door behind her and stood for a moment in the corridor, letting the normal backstage noise wash back into her senses—the distant clatter of a dropped wrench, laughter echoing from somewhere near the costume racks, the hum of air moving through ducts that were no longer quietly betraying the people who trusted them.

Her phone buzzed again before she took more than three steps.

Esra: I just watched their remote access go dark. Whatever you did, it scared them.

Good, Celeste replied. She didn't add anything else. Words were currency. Tonight she preferred silence. She moved toward the stairwell, avoiding the main arteries of the building where cleaning crews had begun their nocturnal migration. The opera house had layers the public never saw: narrow bridges suspended over darkness, doors that opened into forgotten rehearsal spaces where old pianos slumped in corners like defeated animals, control rooms sealed with locks no one remembered requesting.

Halfway up the east stairwell she paused, sensing movement before she heard it. Footsteps. Measured. Not the careless cadence of crew.

She flattened herself against the wall as two men passed below her landing. They wore black maintenance jackets without insignia, their conversation carried in murmurs that did not belong to any language she recognized at first. Then she heard the rhythm—the clipped consonants, the glottal stops. Russian.

Volkov's voice was already in her head. Don't assume language equals allegiance. But the timing was too clean to ignore.

She waited until their steps faded, then descended one level and slipped into the adjacent corridor, following at a distance that kept her in shadow. The men moved with purpose, ignoring open doors, bypassing signage, heading toward something they already knew. They stopped outside a room marked EMERGENCY RESPONSE COORDINATION.

Celeste raised her phone and sent a single word to Volkov: **Russians.** She pocketed the phone just as one of the men reached for the keypad.

The door opened from the inside. A woman stepped out, her hair pulled back tight, eyes already assessing the space behind them. She was holding a tablet, the screen alive with moving schematics of the building.

The three of them froze for a fraction of a second when they saw

Celeste at the far end of the corridor. Then everything accelerated. The woman spoke first. "She's not on the roster."

Celeste moved and closed the distance in a burst of controlled violence, her hand catching the first man's wrist mid-reach, twisting until the tendons screamed. His partner lunged, too late, momentum carrying him past as Celeste ducked and drove her elbow into the soft tissue beneath his ribs.

The woman backed into the room, tablet clutched like a shield. Celeste followed. The door slammed shut behind them. Inside, the walls were screens—floor-to-ceiling monitors displaying airflow, occupancy heat maps, evacuation routes. The opera house laid bare like a living organism under a microscope.

"You don't belong here," the woman said, breath steady despite the chaos she'd just fled.

"Neither do you," Celeste replied.

One of the men staggered in behind her, blood at his lip. The other did not rise.

The woman's gaze flicked to the fallen body, then back to Celeste. "You've already disrupted the timeline."

Celeste tilted her head. "Whose?"

The woman smiled without humor. "The Maestro's." The word landed with a weight that altered the room.

"You work for him," Celeste said.

"We work for the score," the woman replied. "And you are becoming… dissonant."

Celeste advanced slowly, the way she approached a stage before a solo, aware that every step changed the acoustics.

"Tell him," she said, "that I'm done playing background."

The woman's fingers tightened around the tablet. "He already knows."

Then the emergency lights cut out. The building inhaled. And the next movement began.

ſ ₰

Chapter 4

Echoes

DARKNESS DID NOT fall. It arrived the way silence did after a scream—sudden, violent, too complete to be an accident. The emergency lights were not supposed to fail. The Palais Garnier had been built for catastrophe: fire, riot, collapse, the occasional attempted assassination by history's less patient actors. Yet when the system inhaled, as if the building itself had braced, nothing followed. No glow strips along the floor. No guiding arrows. No calm recorded voice explaining how to leave without dying.

Just darkness.

Celeste moved before fear had time to articulate itself. She stepped sideways, feeling for the wall, trusting the muscle memory that had once guided her blindfolded through a shooting range in Colorado while instructors barked contradictory commands in German and Russian.

Behind her, something scraped, sounding like metal against marble. One of the men exhaled sharply, the sound of surprise more than pain. The woman did not make a sound at all.

"You don't belong here," the woman had said. Neither did the darkness.

Celeste counted three heartbeats, then spoke. "You brought down the house. That wasn't a test."

A shape shifted somewhere in front of her. "It wasn't supposed to be permanent."

"Nothing ever is," Celeste replied. "That's the problem with systems. They believe in inevitability. People do not."

She felt a faint draft along her left cheek, the telltale whisper of a door opened just wide enough to reframe the space.

The woman was moving.

Celeste lunged, catching fabric instead of flesh, the sound of tearing velvet swallowed by the blackout. A hand clipped her shoulder and then was gone.

Somewhere in the distance, a low-frequency alarm began to thrum, not loud enough to direct anyone but heavy enough to destabilize them. The opera house had become a lung without oxygen.

Her phone vibrated against her thigh. **Volkov: Power grid override detected. You're not dealing with maintenance anymore.**

Celeste smiled in the dark, a baring of teeth no one could see. "Good," she murmured.

The darkness forced the building to reveal its bones.

Celeste moved with one hand trailing the wall, counting door frames, letting the rhythm of the corridor replace her vision. She could hear the others now though not with her ears so much as with the part of her that had learned to read negative space. Someone's breathing was too close. Someone else was further away than they thought.

"Seal the perimeter," the woman said softly, voice amplified by the emptiness. "She doesn't leave this floor."

Celeste slipped into an alcove where an old fire extinguisher had once been mounted, its absence leaving behind a ghost rectangle of lighter stone. She lowered her pulse deliberately, listening.

Boots scraped. A whispered Russian curse cut through the dark.

Her phone vibrated again. **Esra: I just lost telemetry from half the building. They're shadow-routing emergency response.**

Shadow-routing. Redirecting help into labyrinths that no longer existed.

The building shuddered faintly as generators attempted to compensate, their failure written into the silence that followed.

Celeste eased forward until she was close enough to feel the warmth of a body ahead of her. She waited, then stepped into the sound, striking upward with the heel of her hand. The man folded without a cry, momentum carrying him into her arms before she let him slide to the floor.

She was already moving when the woman swore again, this time in French. "Don't chase," the woman said. "Herd."

Celeste turned a corner and nearly collided with a cart stacked high with costumes, silk brushing her face like the memory of touch. She ducked beneath it as something whistled past her ear, embedding itself in wood with a sound that felt final.

A dart.

So they had graduated from testing to restraint. That meant escalation had been authorized.

She reached for her phone and typed blind. **They're using sedatives.**

Volkov: Copy. West stairwell compromised. Move east. I'm rerouting external feeds.

The opera house groaned—a deep, structural complaint—as if

protesting the violence being written into it. Somewhere above her, glass shattered. Celeste closed her eyes, not to see, but to feel the space as a musician felt a hall before playing it. The corridors were no longer paths; they were measures. She chose her tempo.

When the lights came back on, she would not be where they expected.

But the lights did not return.

Instead, the opera house exhaled again, this time with a brittle crack that rippled through its old bones. Celeste felt it under her feet first: the vibration of a system forced to obey a command it had never been designed to understand.

She crouched behind a velvet-draped coat rack, silk sleeves brushing her face like apologies, and listened as the men moved past her position. Their boots no longer scraped. They had learned.

Her phone vibrated, a whisper against her thigh. **Esra: They've locked the elevators and diverted emergency power away from the fire suppression grid. This is no longer a rehearsal.**

Celeste closed her eyes for half a second. "Of course, it isn't," she murmured.

A voice echoed down the corridor, carried by a handheld speaker someone had thought to activate. "Celeste Morgan," the woman called, her French precise, unaccented. "You've proven your point. You've always been so… expressive. But you are not in control here."

Celeste leaned closer to the wall; the stone was cool against her cheek.

"You don't understand," the woman continued. "This building is an instrument. Tonight, we are tuning it."

Celeste exhaled slowly through her nose. "No," she said to the dark, knowing the woman could not hear her but needing the words to exist anyway. "Tonight, you are discovering what happens when the instrument refuses the score."

She rose and moved deeper into the service corridors, following a memory of blueprints and half-forgotten rehearsals. Somewhere in the maze ahead, an old emergency control room waited, one that predated digital oversight, that still responded to human touch.

Her phone buzzed once more. **Volkov: I've found the master breaker. It's behind a sealed panel on your level.**

Celeste's mouth curved into something that was not quite a smile. "Then let's change the music," she whispered, and vanished into the opera house's darkened heart.

The sealed panel was older than any of the systems layered on top of it. Celeste recognized the difference immediately—the way the corridor narrowed by just a few centimeters, the shift in wall texture from marble to poured stone, the faint smell of ozone that came not from electricity but from age. The Palais Garnier had been modernized a hundred times, but this section belonged to the building's first nervous system, when engineers had trusted human hands more than algorithms.

She moved without light, fingers grazing conduit seams, counting steps under her breath in a rhythm that had once guided her through a blizzard in the Carpathians while a sniper team bled out behind her. The memory rose uninvited: the way Volkov had held pressure on her arm with his teeth while she rewired a detonator by feel.

Her phone vibrated again. **Volkov: Thirty meters ahead. Panel's behind a maintenance cage. You won't like the lock.**

Celeste huffed softly. "I never do."

She reached the cage just as a door somewhere behind her slammed shut, hard enough to send a vibration through the floor. The sound was deliberate, an announcement rather than an accident. The woman was herding her.

Celeste crouched, sliding a thin blade from the lining of her coat. She had stopped carrying guns inside concert halls months ago. Too loud. Too final. Blades kept the conversation intimate.

The maintenance cage door resisted at first, then yielded with a metallic sigh. She slipped inside and shut it behind her, plunging the space into a darkness that felt thicker than before. The sealed panel was a rectangle of steel bolted directly into stone, its edges crusted with decades of disuse.

She ran her fingers over the locking mechanism, mapping it in her mind. Analog. Mechanical. No digital fail-safes. Whoever had designed this place had believed in muscle memory.

Footsteps echoed in the corridor outside.

"You can't win," the woman called, closer now, her voice carrying that same curated calm. "You can't out-run a building."

Celeste set the blade against the lock and began to work, each movement measured, almost musical. Pick, press, listen. The faintest vibration answered her touch like a string tuning itself.

"Music is not a weapon," the woman continued. "It's a delivery system. We just taught it to carry something else."

The lock clicked. Celeste inhaled. She flung the panel open and yanked down the master breaker with both hands. The mechanism protested, then surrendered with a concussion that reverberated through her shoulders.

The building screamed.

Emergency lights flooded back to life in violent strips of red, illuminating corridors that moments before had been voids. Somewhere, alarms finally found their voices.

She turned just as the woman rounded the corner with a tablet clutched in white-knuckled hands.

For the first time, fear showed on her face. Celeste didn't wait for it to settle.

The red emergency lighting washed the corridor in a color that belonged more to blood than to safety. The sudden illumination startled the men behind the woman into motion. One reached instinctively for a weapon, the other staggered, disoriented by the shift from total dark to emergency glow.

Celeste didn't hesitate.

She stepped forward and kicked the tablet out of the woman's hands before it could become anything else. The device shattered against the stone wall, sparks fanning outward like a grotesque parody of stage pyrotechnics.

"You don't get to conduct this anymore," Celeste said.

The woman recovered faster than expected, lunging with a small syringe that gleamed even in the red light. Celeste twisted aside, felt the whisper of the needle along her sleeve, then drove her elbow into the woman's jaw with the kind of force that ended arguments.

The men closed in.

Celeste pivoted, catching one by the collar and using his momentum to hurl him into the other. They collapsed in a heap of limbs and curses. She stepped back, scanning the corridor; counting exits, angles, the way the light fractured shadows into new lies.

Her phone vibrated in her pocket, but she didn't look. She already knew what Volkov would say.

This was no longer a containment operation. It was a hunt.

She crouched beside the fallen woman, who was blinking through a fog of shock, blood slicking her lower lip.

"Who is the Maestro?" Celeste demanded.

The woman smiled, teeth red. "You still think he's one person."

"Who writes the score?" Celeste pressed.

The woman's gaze drifted toward the ceiling, toward the labyrinth of cables and ducts that threaded through the opera house like veins. "Everyone who's tired of pretending culture is harmless," she whispered. "Everyone who knows beauty is just obedience with better lighting."

Then the building shuddered again, harder this time, and somewhere above them something collapsed with a thunderous crash.

Volkov's message finally came through.

Volkov: Fire suppression grid is unstable. They booby-trapped it. You need to get out now.

Celeste rose, the words echoing in her bones. She had come to stop an insertion. She was leaving with the knowledge that Paris itself had been wired like a weapon.

$\int$ $\textbf{l}$

Chapter 5

Exposure

BY THE TIME Celeste emerged onto the street, the Palais Garnier had begun to perform its own disaster.

Fire alarms spilled into the Paris night like a badly tuned brass section, red light stuttering across stone that had survived revolutions and empires but was now being asked to survive something quieter, more efficient. Police vans screeched into place at crooked angles, blue light refracting off café windows and startled faces.

Celeste moved through the crowd with the calm of someone who knew panic was contagious. She kept her head down, cello case slung over her shoulder as if this were merely another delayed rehearsal, another night when art insisted on chaos.

Her phone vibrated. **Volkov: You have less than three minutes**

before the suppression grid either dumps the wrong agent or doesn't dump anything at all.

She angled into an alley, the smell of old garbage and wet paper cutting through the adrenaline. What's the casualty model?

Volkov: Non-zero. Which is why we're not staying to find out.

She closed her eyes for half a second, then opened them to a Paris that had become a chessboard no one had asked to play on.

The Maestro had not tried to kill her tonight. He had tried to teach her something.

Celeste cut through a narrow passage between two shuttered boutiques, the crowd thinning as the sirens drew people toward spectacle rather than away from it. She pressed her back against the cold stone and forced her breathing to slow, counting heartbeats the way she counted measures in rehearsal when the orchestra drifted out of alignment.

One. Two. Three.

Her phone buzzed again. **Esra: Fire suppression grid is contaminated. They seeded the system with a delayed-release aerosol. If it deploys, it won't extinguish anything. It will incapacitate anyone still inside.**

Celeste swore under her breath. Who signed off on the system update?

Esra: Chorale Logistics. Shell inside a shell inside a trust registered in Zurich.

"Of course it is," Celeste murmured.

She stepped back into the street, moving with the crowd now, letting her pace mirror panic without contributing to it. The opera house loomed behind barricades, red light stroking its columns as if coaxing confession from stone.

A police officer shouted instructions in French. A tourist cried. Someone dropped a glass bottle and the sound shattered something brittle in the night.

Her phone vibrated again. **Volkov: I've mapped a manual override. But it's inside the west fly tower. I can't reach it without triggering the perimeter sensors.**

Celeste stopped walking. **Then I'll reach it.**

A pause.

Volkov: That's suicide.

She replied, "That's authorship," before she turned away from the chaos and headed back toward the building with her cello case bouncing against her spine like an accusation she was finally willing to accept.

Celeste did not approach the opera house head-on. The perimeter was tightening, police and fire units forming a glittering ring of authority around the chaos. Cameras were already up with news vans sniffing story like blood in water. She veered instead toward a construction barrier three streets over, ducking beneath a tarp and emerging into a service courtyard no one thought to guard because it looked like nothing.

This was what Eidolon always underestimated: the forgotten spaces. The cracks between visible power.

She moved fast, skirting scaffolding and half-finished facades, then slipped through a delivery door that had been propped open by a careless worker long before the alarms began. Inside, the smell of dust and machine oil replaced the night air.

Her phone vibrated. **Volkov: I'm watching your feed. West fly tower is three levels up. There's a maintenance ladder behind the cargo elevator.**

Celeste found the ladder and began to climb. Each rung echoed into her shoulders, the cello case bumping against metal with every movement. She counted breaths, not steps—four up, one pause, four up—refusing to let fatigue become an argument.

Halfway up, she felt it. A vibration through the building that didn't belong to alarms or generators. It was deeper, slower, a systemic shudder. Esra texted, "The contaminated aerosol is primed. You've got ninety seconds before auto-release."

Celeste closed her eyes for one count too many, then opened them and climbed faster. At the top, she reached a narrow platform overlooking the fly tower, a vertical cavern of ropes, pulleys, and counterweights disappearing into shadow. The manual override panel glowed faintly at the far end, as if embarrassed to exist.

She sprinted.

The panel was locked, its casing already scorched from an earlier attempt to access it remotely.

"Come on," she whispered, fingers flying.

Her phone vibrated. **Volkov: Forty seconds.**

The lock yielded with a scream of tortured metal. She tore open the panel and froze. Inside was not a switch. It was a choice. Inside the panel were two illuminated modules, identical except for the labels etched beneath them in clean, merciless lettering.

SUPPRESSION—MANUAL DEPLOY

SUPPRESSION—SYSTEM PURGE

They were mutually exclusive. The wiring diagram flashed between them in unforgiving simplicity. One would trigger the aerosol immediately, dumping the incapacitant into every vent on the western side of the building. The other would flush the entire system, but in doing so would permanently disable the suppression grid for the next twelve minutes while it recalibrated.

Twelve minutes in a building already compromised.

Her phone vibrated so violently it almost jumped from her pocket. **Esra: The purge will leave them blind. No aerosol, but no fire response either. You're choosing between paralysis and flame.**

Celeste stared at the two modules, the red emergency lighting painting them into caricatures of good and evil when neither deserved the courtesy.

The Maestro was not trying to kill her. He was forcing her to declare her philosophy.

"Thirty seconds," Volkov said over the line, his voice stripped of everything but function.

Celeste closed her eyes. She saw her mother standing in a hotel doorway in Berlin, coat half-buttoned, suitcase waiting. She saw herself at sixteen, holding a rifle steady enough to scare men who thought steadiness belonged to them. She saw the Philharmonic audience in New York leaning forward, not to be entertained but to be seen.

Music is not a weapon. It's a choice.

She tore the SYSTEM PURGE module from its housing. The building convulsed. Somewhere far below her, air screamed backward through ducts that had never been asked to forget their instructions. The screens across the city flickered, momentarily blind.

Her phone vibrated once more. **Volkov: Aerosol aborted. Fire grid down. You just bought them twelve minutes of vulnerability.**

Celeste sagged against the panel; her breath was ragged. She had not saved everyone. But she had refused to let Eidolon decide how they died. And that, she realized, was the first time she had ever truly conducted the ending.

The fly tower trembled around her like a giant deciding whether to stay standing. Celeste pushed herself upright, forcing air back into lungs that had forgotten the concept of cooperation. The red emergency lighting had dimmed, flickering now as if the building were struggling to remember how to see.

Twelve minutes. Twelve minutes without automated fire response in a structure threaded with compromised systems. The Maestro had not designed a trap. He had designed a thesis.

Her phone vibrated again. **Volkov: You're not clear yet. Backup teams are mobilizing. They won't wait for the grid to reboot.**

Celeste scanned the fly tower, eyes cataloging pulleys, ropes, catwalks—every improvised exit the building had ever offered someone who refused to die politely.

She clipped the phone back into her pocket and ran. She vaulted a low barrier and grabbed a descending rope, letting gravity tear her down three stories in a burn that flayed skin from palm. She hit the platform below in a crouch that reverberated up her spine and didn't wait for the pain to negotiate terms. Below her, smoke had begun to seep through grates that were not supposed to exist anymore.

The Maestro was not hiding. He was teaching.

She ran again, the opera house now roaring with the sound of evacuation. Boots pounded stairwells, shouted orders, the terrified geometry of a crowd discovering that beauty was no defense.

Her phone buzzed. **Esra: West wing electrical is spiking. Something's feeding power back into the disabled grid.**

Celeste skidded around a corner and nearly collided with Lena, who stood frozen at the edge of a corridor clutching her violin case like a child's security blanket.

"Celeste?" she whispered. "What is happening?"

Celeste took her by the shoulders. "You need to leave. Now. Follow the emergency exit signs until you're outside the perimeter."

"They said it was just a malfunction—"

"Run," Celeste said, not raising her voice but dropping every ounce of command she had ever learned into the word.

Lena ran.

Celeste turned back toward the smoke, toward the building that was rapidly forgetting the difference between performance and catastrophe.

Twelve minutes was no longer a window. It was a countdown.

The corridor beyond the fly tower had begun to warp. Not visibly, not yet, but acoustically with every footstep echoing twice, the building returning sound out of sequence the way a damaged recording did. Celeste felt the change before she saw it, a distortion in the air that had nothing to do with heat and everything to do with intention.

Her phone vibrated again. **Volkov: They're feeding the**

disabled grid from a mobile power source. Someone planned for you to choose the purge.

Celeste closed her eyes for half a heartbeat then typed, "Location?"

"Sub-basement. North utilities corridor. They're using a generator rigged into the secondary transformer. You won't like the access route."

She laughed once, sharp and joyless. "I never do." She cut down a service stairwell and into the sublevels, the opera house's elegant grandeur peeling away with every descending floor until only raw concrete remained. The air thickened, stale with the memory of decades of deferred maintenance.

Somewhere ahead, machinery whined with the unmistakable voice of something that was never meant to run this hot.

She turned a corner and saw it: a portable generator bolted into place like a tumor, cables spidering outward into systems that had not been designed to accept improvisation. Two men guarded it. They were not maintenance; they were too composed.

Celeste slid her blade free and moved before thought could become doubt. The first man never saw her. She took him at the base of the skull, her palm slamming into him with enough force to erase consciousness. The second turned in time to raise his weapon, but not in time to understand that Celeste had already decided how the encounter would end.

She knocked the gun aside, drove her knee upward, and heard cartilage fail. He folded with a sound that was more surprise than pain.

She tore at the generator's interface, fingers dancing over controls she had never been trained to use but somehow understood. Art was not neutral. It taught pattern recognition. It trained instinct.

Her phone vibrated again. **Esra: You don't have much time. They'll be inside the building again in under three minutes.**

Celeste ripped the primary cable free. The generator screamed. Then it died. The silence that followed was not peace. It was shock.

The generator's death was not quiet. It coughed once, a mechanical protest that rattled the conduit above her head, then fell into a silence so complete it felt artificial. The sudden absence of vibration was disorienting, like stepping off a moving walkway you hadn't realized you were standing on.

Celeste backed away as the rig's cooling fans slowed, the whine collapsing into an irregular clicking that sounded too much like a countdown.

Her phone buzzed. **Volkov: Power backflow just dropped to zero. You cut their spine.**

Celeste exhaled a breath she had been holding since the fly tower. The sub-basement smelled of scorched plastic and wet stone, a scent that would cling to her memory long after Paris faded into a blur of headlines.

She crouched beside the unconscious man closest to her and stripped the comm unit from his ear. It was still live, the channel humming with low-level chatter. "...north corridor compromised—repeat—north corridor compromised—"

She clipped the unit to her lapel and moved. The return route was no longer viable. Emergency stairwells had become bottlenecks, choked with panicked staff and half-trained responders who had no idea the building's internal logic had been rewritten on the fly. Celeste took a maintenance ladder instead, climbing past floors that had once housed storage rooms and forgotten workshops, spaces that existed only because someone long dead had insisted on excess.

Her phone vibrated again. **Esra: Fire grid is rebooting, but it's not clean. Expect phantom alarms and misdirected suppression bursts.**

"Misdirected is better than poisoned," Celeste muttered. She emerged into a corridor just as a fire door slammed shut behind her, sealing off a section of the building that still echoed with shouting. The red lights flickered to white, then back again, as if the system were undecided about which story it wanted to tell.

A voice crackled in her borrowed comm. "Identify. Anyone on this channel, identify…"

Celeste pressed the transmit button with her thumb. "Building integrity is compromised," she said, keeping her tone flat, official. "Pull all personnel from the west wing immediately."

There was a pause. Then: "Copy."

She allowed herself a single heartbeat of satisfaction. The opera house had tried to turn itself into a weapon. Tonight, she was making it forget how.

♪ ♫

Chapter 6

Interference

BY DAWN, THE Palais Garnier had become a crime scene instead of a theater. Yellow tape replaced velvet rope. Police uniforms crowded spaces that had once been reserved for patrons in silk and donors with political reach. The building looked smaller in the cold morning light, its grandeur diminished by the bureaucratic choreography of investigation.

Celeste watched from the back seat of an unmarked sedan parked two blocks away, her reflection fractured across the tinted glass. Volkov sat beside her, his profile as familiar as her own pulse, his presence a calibration she hadn't realized she'd been missing until it returned.

"You did not choose the easy option," he said quietly.

"There wasn't one," Celeste replied.

The city exhaled around them with news vans packing up, reporters scrolling through phones, Parisians resuming routines that had absorbed too many versions of catastrophe to linger on this one.

Her phone vibrated. **Esra: Chorale assets are burning access points worldwide. Paris was a rehearsal. The Maestro is moving to a new movement.**

Celeste closed her eyes, the weight of the night settling into places adrenaline had ignored.

The opera house had survived. Eidolon had not, at least not entirely. The score was changing. Volkov shifted in his seat, eyes never leaving the opera house even as the first crime-scene technicians began threading cables through the shattered front doors.

"You could have let the purge deploy," he said quietly. "It would have incapacitated everyone in that wing. No witnesses. No questions."

Celeste didn't look at him. "I don't work like that anymore."

He studied her profile. "That's what scares them."

"And you?"

A faint smile tugged at the corner of his mouth. "I already knew who you were."

Silence filled the car, not awkward but weighted, like a rest inserted into a phrase to make the next entrance unavoidable.

Her phone buzzed again. **Esra: I'm compiling an initial Paris damage map. Chorale's donor shell companies are dissolving faster than I can tag them. Someone is cleaning the ledger.**

Celeste leaned back against the seat, exhaustion threading its way through her muscles now that the threat had loosened its grip. "Do you remember Berlin?" she asked suddenly.

Volkov did not pretend not to. "Every detail."

"I used to think the bomb was the beginning," she said. "But it wasn't. It was just the first time I realized that violence could be designed. That it could be elegant."

"And now?"

"And now I see the ugliness in the elegance," Celeste replied. "The Maestro doesn't want obedience. He wants belief."

Volkov exhaled slowly. "Belief is harder to kill."

"Then we stop trying to kill it," she said. "We expose it."

He turned to her fully. "That's not a mission."

"It is now."

They left the car just as the sun broke through the low Paris cloud cover, pale light catching on the opera house's gilded statues and making them look almost innocent again. Celeste pulled the collar of her coat higher, not for warmth but to disappear into the movement of morning.

Inside a café two streets away, Esra waited at a corner table, laptop open, coffee gone cold. She didn't look up as they slid into the chairs opposite her. "You've just destabilized a continent," Esra said. "Congratulations."

"Show me," Celeste replied.

Esra turned the screen so they could see: a lattice of dots and lines, nodes flaring red and then vanishing. "These are Chorale shell companies," she explained. "They're not deleting. They're evaporating. Someone's triggering a distributed collapse. Whatever the Maestro is, he's not consolidating power anymore. He's shedding weight."

"Like a submarine dropping ballast," Volkov said.

"Exactly," Esra replied. "Which means Paris wasn't a failure. It was a stress test."

Celeste stared at the screen until the patterns began to feel like music with recurring themes, sudden absences, the rhythm of loss. "So where does the next movement begin?" she asked.

Esra tapped a cluster of blinking points. "Tokyo. Prague. Buenos Aires. Three performances. Three infrastructures with identical architectural signatures."

Celeste closed her eyes, already hearing the shape of the coming storm. "Then we don't wait," she said. "We go where the music is going."

The café filled around them as if nothing extraordinary had happened two streets away. A woman in a trench coat argued with the barista about oat milk. A couple in matching running shoes compared split times in low, competitive murmurs. Paris had resumed its most dangerous talent: normalcy.

Esra rotated the laptop so the screen faced only them, fingers already dancing across the keyboard. "The pattern isn't just architectural," she said. "It's cultural. Each of the three cities is hosting a performance series tied to private funding streams that don't survive basic due diligence. Tokyo's tied to a philanthropic foundation that doesn't exist outside press releases. Prague's is laundered through a heritage restoration trust. Buenos Aires is more direct; it's media conglomerate money with a shell labyrinth behind it."

"Which one is next?" Volkov asked.

Esra didn't hesitate. "Tokyo. The funding was activated forty-eight hours ago. That's their lead time."

Celeste stared at the espresso crema collapsing into bitterness. Forty-eight hours. It felt generous only to people who had never had to disappear before breakfast.

"You're not going back on tour," Volkov said. It wasn't a question.

"I am, though I'm having trouble wrapping my head around them choosing Tokyo again," Celeste replied. "But I'm not pretending that's all it is."

He studied her, weighing something she could not see, she was sure of it. He opened his mouth and said, "Then we don't travel like musicians anymore."

"No," she said softly. "We travel like witnesses."

Esra shut the laptop. "That's the problem. Eidolon doesn't kill witnesses. It rewrites them. If you keep doing this publicly—New York, Paris—you stop being a ghost. You become a symbol."

Celeste met her eyes. "Good."

Esra's mouth twitched. "You're going to make this very inconvenient for everyone."

"That's the idea."

They left the café separately. Volkov peeled off toward the Métro, already shifting into a different gait, a different man. Esra disappeared into the crowd with the fluidity of someone who belonged nowhere on purpose. Celeste walked until the opera house was behind her again, its gilded façade catching the morning like a lie too beautiful to interrogate. She paused at the edge of a bridge and watched the Seine carry yesterday downstream. Music is not a weapon, she thought. It's a choice.

And she had just chosen to follow it across three continents.

By afternoon the Paris crisis had become a narrative. Celeste watched the first headlines scroll across the muted television in a temporary apartment. Electrical Failure Forces Evacuation at Historic Opera House, Authorities Rule Out Terrorism, No Injuries Reported. The words were antiseptic, scrubbed of panic, careful not to imply intention.

She had learned long ago that absence of language was its own message.

Volkov sat on the floor with his back against the couch, dismantling a pistol that hadn't existed an hour earlier. He worked in silence, the rhythm of parts clicking free oddly comforting.

"You don't have to come with me," Celeste said.

He didn't look up. "That's not how this works."

She crossed the room and stopped in front of the window, the city stretched below like a sheet of carefully folded lies.

"Tokyo is not Paris," she said. "But if the Maestro is shedding weight…" Her voice trailed off.

"Then he'll be faster," Volkov finished. He slid the reassembled weapon into a hollow in the couch frame. "And so will we."

Her phone vibrated. **Esra: I've booked you on a flight to Tokyo.**

Official cover: special guest artist, chamber collaboration with the NHK Symphony. Unofficial reality: the funding foundation behind the event has the same structural DNA as Chorale Logistics.

Celeste closed her eyes, letting the words settle. Tokyo. The first of the next three movements.

Somewhere in the city below, someone practiced scales in an open window, the notes drifting upward in uncertain pairs.

Music was already going ahead of her.

They did not pack the way civilians packed. There were no suitcases splayed open on the bed, no whispered negotiations over shoes or hair dryers. Celeste folded clothes with the same ruthless efficiency she used onstage when a page turn threatened to interrupt a difficult passage. Everything had a function. Everything earned its place.

Volkov stood in the kitchen rinsing a coffee cup he had never used. "Tokyo puts you back in front of cameras," he said. "That was the Maestro's original architecture—visibility as leverage."

"I know," Celeste replied. "That's why we don't disappear anymore."

He turned, studying her. "You're making a rule out of defiance."

She didn't deny it. Her phone buzzed again. **Esra: I've embedded a firmware update into your in-flight entertainment system. Don't look for it. It'll open when you need it.**

"Of course it will," Celeste murmured.

By dusk the apartment was bare, reduced to the temporary neutrality that came just before departure. Celeste paused in the doorway, one hand on the cello case, the other resting unconsciously over the binder.

Paris had been a fracture point. Not a victory. Not a loss. A shift in grammar.

Volkov met her in the hall, jacket collar already raised. "You still thinking about Berlin?"

"I never stop," she said.

They took separate elevators.

At Charles de Gaulle, the orchestra was assembling again, unaware that the tour itinerary had become something else entirely. Musicians laughed, argued, complained about seating assignments. Life rehearsed itself with dangerous confidence.

Celeste watched the departure board update to Tokyo—On Time. The Maestro had written the next measure. She intended to play it louder.

Celeste stood at the gate with the cello case braced against her shin, letting the ambient chaos of an international terminal settle into something that felt almost like peace. People argued into phones. Children sprawled on carpet that had been cleaned too many times to remember what it was supposed to be. A woman sobbed quietly into a croissant wrapper.

Normal life, performed at scale.

Volkov appeared at her shoulder without announcing himself, his reflection arriving a half-second earlier in the polished steel of the boarding kiosk. "You ready?" he asked.

"As I'll ever be," she said.

Her phone vibrated. **Esra: Remember—Tokyo node is older than Paris. Different architecture. Different psychology. If Paris was rehearsal, Tokyo is the premiere.**

Celeste closed her eyes for a count, then opened them to the boarding call that now carried her name.

As she stepped onto the jet bridge, she did not think of the opera house, or the men in the dark, or the woman with the tablet whose fear had finally looked like truth. She thought of sound and how it moved invisibly through air, rearranging bodies without ever leaving a mark. Music was not a weapon; it was a choice. And she had just chosen to follow it halfway around the world.

Chapter 7

Displacement

TOKYO GREETED CELESTE Morgan with order so complete it bordered on illusion. Narita Airport did not feel like an arrival hall; it felt like an agreement between architecture and expectation, between people and systems that never apologized for being precise.

Celeste moved with the orchestra through corridors that swallowed sound rather than amplifying it. There were no raised voices, no frantic gestures. Even impatience seemed disciplined here, a thing folded neatly into posture. The cello case on her back did not draw stares. In Tokyo, objects existed to be carried.

Her phone vibrated as she passed through customs. **Esra: Tokyo node is already active. You're not late. You're early.**

The orchestra's liaison, a man this time instead of Aya, greeted them with a bow that suggested he took no credit for the perfection of the moment. "Welcome to Japan," he said. "We are honored."

Celeste inclined her head in return. She had learned long ago that respect was a dialect.

They were driven into the city in a black bus that glided rather than moved, highway lights tracing calligraphy across the windows. Tokyo unfolded with breathtaking density in neon stacked on concrete, order layered atop chaos so seamlessly it became impossible to tell which had come first.

The hotel was glass and steel, its lobby a cathedral to efficiency. Celeste's room faced a narrow side street where vending machines glowed like patient sentinels. She unpacked in silence. Volkov's room was two floors below, a concession to proximity that did not pretend to be safety.

Her phone buzzed. **Volkov: You feel it too, don't you?**

She typed back, "Tokyo doesn't flinch."

She showered, dressed, then went downstairs to meet the orchestra's local coordinator for a late dinner she had no intention of enjoying. The restaurant was a minimalist shrine to restraint with bare wood, low light, dishes that looked like philosophy.

Across the table, the coordinator explained schedules with surgical clarity. "Rehearsal tomorrow at ten. Dress rehearsal at nineteen hundred. Gala performance the following evening. The foundation hosting the series is very excited."

"What's their name?" Celeste asked.

"Mirai Arts Collective," he replied smoothly. "They specialize in future-facing cultural initiatives."

Future-facing. Celeste nodded and did not smile. She excused herself early, claiming exhaustion that did not require embellishment, and rode the elevator back to her floor with the quiet certainty of someone who had already begun mapping escape routes.

The corridor smelled faintly of cedar and citrus. Hotel silence here was not emptiness but discipline with the footsteps absorbed, voices muffled by design. Celeste paused outside her room, letting her phone slip into her palm.

Esra: Mirai Arts Collective doesn't exist in Japanese registries before eighteen months ago. The funding traces back through three nonprofit shells to a private trust in Macau. Same pattern as Paris. Different handwriting.

Celeste responded, "Who signed the board?"

Esra: The signature block is anonymized. But one of the IP addresses on the internal memos resolves to a server farm used by a defense contractor we've only seen inside Eidolon's European networks.

Celeste unlocked the door and stepped inside, closing it behind her with the softest click she could manage. She leaned her cello against the wall and did not turn on the lights. Tokyo shimmered through the window in layers of electric color, a city so alive it made loneliness feel like a choice. She rested her forehead against the glass and listened to the muted soundscape. The traffic whispered instead of roared, trains glided past with a sound like held breath.

Her phone vibrated again. **Volkov: I'm making a sweep of the lower floors. No obvious tails yet.**

Celeste typed, "Yet is doing a lot of work."

She crossed the room and opened the binder, flipping through pages that had been handled so often the corners had rounded themselves into memory. Paris was still echoing through her nerves, but Tokyo was different. Paris had been decadent, theatrical, a city that hid its sins behind beauty. Tokyo was precise. Tokyo optimized.

She found the page she'd marked months ago, a notation in her mother's handwriting she had never been able to reconcile with anything else. They don't erase people here, her mother had written after a trip to Asia. They refine them.

Celeste closed the binder slowly. Refinement was a far more dangerous word than elimination.

Her phone buzzed again. **Esra: There's a private rehearsal tomorrow morning. Not on your schedule. Attendance by invitation only.**

Celeste asked, "Who's invited?"

A pause.

Esra: You are.

Tokyo did not feel like a trap. It felt like a mirror.

The invitation arrived before dawn, slid beneath Celeste's hotel door with a discretion that felt ceremonial. The card was thick, textured, embossed with the Mirai Arts Collective logo—a minimalist spiral that suggested infinity without committing to it.

PRIVATE REHEARSAL—07:30

Venue: Shinjuku Civic Hall—Studio B

No signature. No explanation.

Celeste did not wake Volkov. She dressed in concert black out of habit, then changed into something softer, something that belonged less to a stage and more to a person who might plausibly exist outside one. The binder went into her bag last.

The elevator ride down was silent. The lobby was empty except for a single concierge who bowed and said nothing as she passed.

Tokyo at sunrise was a negotiation between darkness and neon. Streets that would soon thrum with bodies were now almost reverent, as if the city itself were holding a note too long.

A black sedan idled at the curb. The driver did not look surprised when she approached.

"Shinjuku Civic Hall," she said.

He inclined his head and pulled into traffic with no further ceremony. They arrived in seven minutes. Studio B was not grand. It was efficient. Pale wood, retractable seating, acoustic panels that swallowed ambition. A man in a charcoal suit waited near the stage, hands folded, expression neutral.

"Ms. Morgan," he said. "Thank you for honoring our invitation."

"I didn't accept," Celeste replied.

"You arrived," he said. "That is acceptance."

She mounted the low stage, her footfall barely audible. "Why am I here?" she asked.

"Because Mirai does not believe in performance without context," the man replied. "And because your context is… evolving."

The lights dimmed. A single cello sat center stage, unclaimed.

The man gestured. "Please."

Celeste did not move. "You are not auditioning me," she said.

The man smiled faintly. "No. We are listening."

Tokyo, she realized, had not invited her to play. It had invited her to be studied so Celeste remained where she was, one foot still on the stage, the other grounded in the aisle, as if unwilling to let the room decide which version of her it was entitled to. "You don't study musicians this way," she said.

The man in the charcoal suit folded his hands more tightly. "We do when the musician is also the instrument."

That, more than anything else he could have said, confirmed her suspicion that this rehearsal was not about sound.

She mounted the stage slowly, not because she was intimidated but because movement was information. Studio B was acoustically dead with no sympathetic resonance, no halo to soften mistakes. Whoever had chosen the space wanted control over every variable.

She set her cello down beside the one waiting center stage, deliberately not touching it. "What piece?" she asked.

The man gestured to a tablet on the music stand. The screen flickered to life with a single word in German. REQUIEM.

Celeste felt the word land in her sternum like a bruise. "For whom?" she asked.

"For whoever fails to evolve," he replied.

The house lights dimmed further, leaving only a tight wash over the waiting cello. From somewhere behind the acoustic panels came the soft whir of motors, of adjustments, of calibrations. Not lighting. Ventilation.

Her phone vibrated once in her pocket. **Volkov: I just lost your location feed.**

She glanced at it but did not acknowledge it.

Instead, she lifted her own cello and drew the bow across the open C string, not to tune, but to mark territory. The sound was raw, unadorned by the room, and it carried exactly as far as she intended.

"You're modifying airflow," she said. "Why?"

The man did not answer immediately. "Mirai is interested in resilience," he said finally. "In how systems respond to stress without breaking their form."

"And I am the system?" Celeste asked.

"You are the variable," he corrected.

She stepped to the music stand and turned the tablet so she could see the score, if it could be called that. It was not notation so much as instruction: blocks of text, shifting tempos, dynamic arcs mapped not to bars but to biometric markers. Heart rate thresholds. Respiratory variance. Cortisol surges.

They weren't asking her to play. They were asking her to become data. Her phone vibrated again, harder this time. She glanced at it. Esra: I'm seeing signal interference around Shinjuku Civic Hall. Your connection is being sandboxed.

Celeste looked back at the man. "You don't know me well enough to do this."

His eyes flicked—just once—to the cello she had refused to touch.

"We know your mother," he said.

At those words, the air in the room changed, not in temperature, not in pressure. Intent.

"What about her?" Celeste asked, each word placed with surgical precision.

"She believed music could interrupt obedience," he said. "We're very curious whether you still do."

The motors behind the walls rose in pitch. Studio B inhaled. The air thickened, not with heat but with something closer to texture. Celeste felt it in her throat first—the faint resistance that made every breath register, as if the room had decided to participate in her physiology.

"You're altering oxygen density," she said quietly.

The man in the charcoal suit did not deny it. "We're refining the listening environment."

"My environment," Celeste corrected.

He inclined his head a fraction. "Yes."

Her phone vibrated again, this time with a clipped urgency that told her Esra was no longer pretending to be calm. **Esra: I'm seeing internal ventilation loops rewriting themselves. They're not poisoning the air, but they are manipulating it. This is a conditioning chamber.**

Celeste did not break eye contact with the man. "You're not testing resilience," she said. "You're trying to see how far I'll bend before I fracture."

He smiled faintly. "Isn't that the same thing?"

The whirring behind the panels deepened, the sound of a system settling into a rhythm it had practiced before. Celeste closed her eyes and listened—not to the motors, but to her own pulse. They wanted her body as an instrument. They wanted to measure obedience in milligrams of breath.

Again, music is not a weapon. It's a choice, she told herself. She lifted her bow and placed it against the waiting cello's string—not her own instrument, but the one they had prepared. The wood was warmer than it should have been. "What happens if I don't play?" she asked.

The man considered this. "Then the rehearsal continues without sound."

Celeste drew the bow across the string with brutal simplicity.

The note emerged thin, almost clinical, stripped of everything but pitch. The motors adjusted immediately, responding to the frequency with microscopic recalibrations. The air grew heavier.

She played again, louder this time, watching the man's eyes track invisible data she could not see.

They were not listening to the music. They were listening to her.

She shifted key abruptly, a jarring modulation that should have felt ugly in such a controlled space. The motors stuttered. For half a second, the room lost its breath.

The man's expression tightened. "You are interfering with the test," he said.

"No," Celeste replied. "I am redefining it." She let the next note ring not for precision, but for refusal.

Studio B shuddered. Somewhere in the building, a door slammed that no one had intended to close.

The note did not decay the way notes were supposed to. It hung in the air like a held breath the room itself had forgotten how to release. The ventilation motors responded with a frantic modulation, chasing a frequency they had not been programmed to recognize.

The man in the charcoal suit stepped back, his composure thinning around the edges. "Ms. Morgan," he said, the honorific now sounding more like a warning. "Please remain within the parameters of the exercise."

Celeste did not stop playing. She shifted into a sequence that had no musical logic but every biological one with short, arrhythmic strokes designed to disrupt pattern recognition, to deny the system the continuity it needed to interpret her as data. Each stroke forced the chamber to recalibrate airflow, the room growing alternately thick and thin in a way that made the man blink, then sway.

"You're destabilizing the conditioning field," he said, one hand braced against the wall.

"Then you should stop trying to condition me," Celeste replied.

Her phone vibrated violently in her pocket. **Volkov: I've got eyes on the building exterior. You're inside some kind of sealed loop. It's not supposed to let you leave.**

She pivoted mid-phrase, driving the bow harder, faster, the sound breaking free of discipline and into something feral. The room's response lagged, algorithms tripping over themselves. A new alarm chimed, softer than the fire sirens in Paris but more insidious. A pulsing tone crept into the back of the skull and refused to let go.

The man reached for his earpiece. "Initiate fallback," he said.

Celeste dropped the bow and the silence was violent. She crossed the stage in three strides and drove her shoulder into his chest before he could finish the command. He went down hard, tablet skidding across the floor, the schematic it displayed flaring red.

Her phone buzzed. **Esra: You just broke their model. The system is trying to compensate. If you don't get out in the next thirty seconds, it will reset with you still inside.**

Celeste grabbed her cello—her cello this time—and ran. The exit door resisted, then gave way, dumping her into a corridor already echoing with raised voices. She sprinted past a startled janitor, past a pair of Mirai staff who froze when they saw her, past the polite architecture of a city that had just learned it was not immune. She didn't stop until she burst into the street, lungs burning, Tokyo roaring back into her ears with unapologetic life.

Her phone vibrated once more. **Volkov: I've got you. Get in the car. Now.**

Celeste dove into the open back seat of a nondescript sedan as it peeled away from the curb, the city folding around them like a closing hand.

She pressed her forehead against the glass, heart still stuttering in the aftermath. Tokyo had not tried to kill her. It had tried to rewrite her. And that, she realized, was far more dangerous.

Chapter 8

Contact

TOKYO AT SPEED was a lesson in controlled chaos. The sedan threaded through traffic with the disciplined impatience of someone who understood that rules were not moral structures, but tools. Neon signage smeared across the windows in incomprehensible kanji, vending machines blinking like tiny lighthouses in the rain.

Celeste sat in the back seat with her cello braced against her knees, hands still trembling with the aftershocks of the conditioning chamber. The room at Shinjuku Civic Hall had not tried to break her bones. It had tried to fracture her authorship, to turn her body into a responsive interface.

"You okay?" Volkov asked from the front passenger seat, not

turning around.

"No," Celeste said. "But I'm intact."

The driver glanced at her in the rearview mirror, his expression unreadable behind tinted lenses.

Her phone vibrated. **Esra: Mirai's internal systems just went dark. They're not containing damage. They're abandoning the node.**

Celeste stared out the window at a city that did not know it had just been spared a rehearsal for something worse.

"Then we made noise," she murmured.

"Yes," Volkov replied. "And they heard it."

They did not return to the hotel. The driver dropped them at a residential block in Meguro where buildings leaned toward each other like conspirators and the air smelled faintly of wet concrete and late dinners. Volkov led them up a narrow stairwell into an apartment that looked as though it had been abandoned halfway through someone else's life. The futon was folded with geometric precision, dishes dried in a rack that had not yet learned to gather dust.

"A safe place?" Celeste asked.

"For the next forty minutes," Volkov replied.

She sat on the floor with her back against the wall, cello case still clutched like ballast. Her pulse had not yet forgiven her for the chamber, for the way the air itself had tried to instruct her body.

Her phone vibrated with an incoming text. **Esra: I'm rerouting your Tokyo itinerary. The orchestra's press team just announced your "minor illness" to explain your absence from tonight's rehearsal.**

Celeste closed her eyes. "They're rewriting the story before it exists."

"That's how Chorale survives," Esra wrote. "They don't erase events. They preempt memory."

Volkov knelt in front of her. "They almost had you."

"No," she replied. "They showed me their ceiling."

He smiled faintly. "And you broke it."

Celeste's phone lit with a text from Lena. "Are you okay?" She smiled at her friend's concern.

"I survived a test and saved what I could. Don't believe the rumors and play your heart out like you would with me beside you."

Lena responded with a thumbs up emoji.

Outside, rain began to fall with the gentle persistence of something that did not care whether it was welcome. The rain blurred Tokyo into abstraction.

Celeste watched it slide down the narrow windowpane, each droplet a temporary distortion of a world that insisted on clarity. Her muscles ached in the peculiar way they always did after adrenaline had overstayed its welcome, with no injury, just the reminder that bodies were not meant to be asked these questions.

Volkov had moved to the kitchen, dismantling and reassembling an unremarkable-looking phone with the same meticulous attention he brought to firearms. "You weren't wrong about Mirai," he said. "They weren't measuring you. They were calibrating the room to you."

Celeste closed her eyes. The memory of the chamber returned—not the fear, but the intimacy of it, the way the air itself had felt invasive. "They wanted to see how much control they could exert without crossing the line into violence," she said. "It's like… biofeedback, but ideological."

Her phone chimed. **Esra: I've got a preliminary map of Mirai's funding dispersal. They pulled out fast, but not clean. There's bleed-over into a heritage trust in Prague and a media network in Buenos Aires.**

"Three movements," Volkov murmured.

Celeste nodded. "They're composing at scale now."

She reached for the binder and flipped to a blank page, writing a single word in careful block letters. REWRITE. Not because she knew what it meant yet, but because the Maestro's language was no longer adequate. Tokyo had not tried to kill her. It had tried to claim her.

The apartment had the acoustics of someone else's solitude. Even rain struggled to make itself heard through the thick glass, as if the city itself were determined to keep its secrets. Celeste moved into the narrow kitchen, rinsing her hands under water that took too long to warm, grounding herself in sensation rather than memory.

Volkov leaned against the counter opposite her. "You didn't flinch in there," he said. "That's new."

"I wanted to," she admitted. "They weren't hurting me. They were inviting me."

"Invitations are dangerous."

"So is refusal."

Her phone vibrated again. **Esra: There's chatter about a last-minute Mirai board meeting in Singapore. It's not public. I can't see the attendee list yet.**

Celeste dried her hands slowly. "They're retreating to neutral ground."

"Or escalating," Volkov said.

She returned to the futon and sank down beside her cello, running a finger lightly along the curve of the case. Tokyo had not been a trap in the old sense. It had been an experiment in authorship.

"You know what they were really measuring?" she asked.

Volkov waited.

"Whether I'd play their cello."

Silence answered her.

Outside, the rain kept falling, as if the city had decided to cleanse itself of something it could not name.

Later, the rain stopped as abruptly as it had begun, leaving Tokyo rinsed and reflective, streets gleaming beneath streetlamps that hummed with tireless consistency. Celeste felt the shift before she noticed the silence, how the city seemed to reset itself without ceremony, without aftermath.

She lay back on the futon, staring at the ceiling, tracing hairline cracks that formed accidental constellations. Her breathing had finally slowed, but sleep remained a rumor rather than a possibility.

"They'll adjust," she said quietly. "They always do."

Volkov sat cross-legged across from her now, a dismantled device spread between his hands like a puzzle he'd solved too many times to enjoy. "Yes. But so will you."

She turned her head to look at him. "That's not comforting."

"It's not meant to be."

Esra texted again causing a low hum against the floorboards. "I've intercepted internal Mirai correspondence. It's fragmented, but one phrase keeps repeating: Subject exhibits resistance to reframing."

Celeste closed her eyes. "Subject," she repeated. "Not asset. Not target."

"They don't know what to call you anymore," Esra replied.

"That's progress."

Volkov gathered the device parts into a single, innocuous rectangle and slipped it into his pocket. "They won't try that again," he said. "Not the same way."

"No," Celeste agreed. "They'll try something quieter." She sat up and reached for her cello, opening the case with a care that bordered on reverence. The instrument emerged warm beneath her hands, familiar in a way nothing else in her life was. She did not play. She simply rested her palm against the wood, feeling the latent promise of sound.

"They think music is obedience," she said. "That if you control the environment, you control the performer."

"And?"

"And they've forgotten something fundamental."

Volkov raised an eyebrow.

"Music requires consent."

Outside, somewhere far below the apartment, a train slid along its track with a sound so smooth it felt intentional. Tokyo resumed its rhythm, unaware that it had failed an audition of its own.

Celeste closed the case and stood.

"Prague is next," she said. "And Prague won't try to invite me."

Her phone vibrated one last time. **Esra: I'll have routes and covers ready by morning.**

Celeste nodded to no one in particular. The Maestro had tried to claim her voice. Instead, he had reminded her why it was dangerous in the first place.

They left the apartment before dawn, when Tokyo was still in the act of remembering itself. The street outside had shed the last of its rain but not the scent of it. Pavement shone in long silver ribbons beneath streetlamps that hummed faintly, each light its own private island of clarity. Somewhere behind a row of narrow houses, a radio murmured a morning news cycle in polite Japanese, the cadence soothing even when the words were not.

Celeste adjusted the strap of her cello case and felt the familiar weight settle across her shoulders like an anchor that had learned how to love her back. It was the only thing she carried that had never lied to her.

Volkov walked half a step behind her, not guarding, not leading, but simply existing in the quiet geometry that had become their shared grammar. His reflection slid across closed shop windows, a man shaped by years of not being seen.

A shopkeeper raised a shutter with a metallic sigh that echoed down the block, releasing the smell of steamed rice and soy that turned Celeste briefly, painfully human. Hunger was still allowed. That fact felt like a mercy.

At the corner, Volkov slowed, the way he did when he was assembling a thought that refused to be spoken until it had sharpened itself. "If Prague mirrors Tokyo," he said, his voice pitched low to match the hour, "they won't isolate you physically. They'll isolate you symbolically."

Celeste glanced at him. "Define symbolically."

"They won't touch you," he said. "They'll touch the idea of you. They'll question your authorship. Plant stories. Manufacture discomfort. Make you expensive to defend."

She pictured her name drifting through headlines with qualifiers attached—alleged, controversial, troubled. She pictured donors withdrawing, orchestras hesitating, agents suddenly unable to return calls.

"My reputation is a fiction," she said after a moment. "They can have it."

Volkov didn't contradict her, which was how she knew he understood the cost.

They descended into the subway station as if slipping beneath the surface of a held breath. The air changed; it was cooler, faintly metallic, threaded with the ozone smell of machinery that had never learned how to stop. Commuters clustered on the platform with that particular Tokyo stillness that was not politeness but choreography. Even impatience seemed rehearsed.

Celeste stood among them, her reflection fractured across the dark glass of the tunnel wall. For a moment she looked like a hundred different women: soloist, fugitive, data point, myth.

Esra texted. "Prague is already staging narrative prep. Expect leaks, insinuations, maybe a manufactured scandal before you even land."

The train arrived with a whisper that swelled into a controlled roar, the doors sliding open in unison. Celeste stepped inside and took the nearest pole, the car filling around her with people who would never know how close they were to a story they were not meant to tell.

Music was not a weapon. But stories were. And Prague, she realized, was about to compose one with her name as the refrain.

Chapter 9

Faultlines

PRAGUE ANNOUNCED ITSELF with history. Not loudly, not in the way Paris flaunted itself or Tokyo optimized, but with the confidence of a city that had already survived too many occupations to be impressed by the present one. Celeste felt it the moment she stepped onto the tarmac, the air carrying a mineral sharpness that suggested stone more than sky.

A couple of day's later, the orchestra's arrival was unremarkable by design. No photographers. No speeches. Just a bus waiting with its engine idling like an old animal that had learned not to expect kindness.

Her phone vibrated. **Esra: First narrative injection just dropped. It's small, an anonymous blog, music forum chatter.**

Accusations of "unstable behavior" at Shinjuku Civic Hall.

Celeste exhaled slowly through her nose. "So it begins," she murmured.

The hotel overlooked the Vltava, its windows opening onto a river that had learned patience the way other cities learned ambition. Celeste stood at the glass long after the others had unpacked, watching the water erase its own footprints. Prague did not feel like a trap. It felt like an echo chamber waiting to be filled.

The rumor did not announce itself. It crept. By the time Celeste reached the rehearsal hall that afternoon, it had already found a voice; it was not a headline yet, just a vibration in the air. Conversations quieted when she passed. Someone laughed too late at a joke that hadn't been meant to include her. The orchestra's stage manager avoided her eyes. Only Lena greeted her with a hug and an invitation to get a coffee later.

Celeste unpacked her cello with the same ritual precision she always used, bow hair catching briefly on the latch before freeing itself with a soft whisper. The hall smelled of old wood and fresh varnish, a blend of nostalgia and renovation that made Prague feel like it was forever being reintroduced to itself.

Volkov texted, "They're seeding second-order doubt. Nothing traceable yet, but I'm hearing the same phrasing across three platforms."

"What phrasing?"

The response came quickly. "Brilliant but difficult. Temperamental. Prone to episodes."

She closed her eyes for a fraction of a second too long.

At the podium, Duret's replacement, an earnest Czech conductor with nervous hands, tapped his baton for silence. "Let's begin with the second movement," he said. "Please, from bar forty-seven."

The music rose obediently. Celeste played with her usual restraint, letting no inflection betray how sharply she felt the room recalibrating around her. She had always believed that discipline insulated her from politics. Now she understood that discipline simply made her easier to narrate.

During the break, she found herself alone by the side door, fingers flexing unconsciously as if to shake off a sensation that did not belong to them.

Lena appeared beside her; her eyes were troubled. "They're saying things," she whispered.

Celeste met her gaze. "Who is 'they'?"

"Everyone who never had anything to say before." Lena's voice wavered, just slightly, but it was enough. "They're saying you snapped in Tokyo," she continued. "That you refused to rehearse. That security had to escort you out."

Celeste leaned back against the cool stone of the corridor, letting the chill remind her that sensation still belonged to her.

"Did you believe it?" she asked.

Lena hesitated. That was answer enough.

"I was there," Lena said finally. "I know how controlled you are. But people are… unsettled. They don't like what they can't map."

"They don't like what can't be edited," Celeste replied.

Esra texted. "Prague node just amplified the Tokyo narrative. A private donor withdrew from tonight's gala citing 'artist volatility.' It's not about truth. It's about discomfort."

Celeste slid her cello case shut with deliberate calm. "Then we stop pretending comfort is our job."

They returned to the hall, the rehearsal resuming with brittle gentility. The conductor avoided meeting her eyes now, his downbeat fractionally delayed when she was due to enter. The orchestra did not falter, but the fault line was audible to anyone who had learned to listen for it. Strategic, cultivated silence was a weapon.

By evening, Prague had chosen its story. Wearing a navy blue silk gown and her hair in a chignon, Celeste stood at the edge of the gala reception with a champagne flute untouched in her hand, watching conversations reconfigure around her like magnets repelling a charge no one wanted to acknowledge. It was not hostility; it was worse. It was polite withdrawal, the sort that allowed everyone involved to deny participation.

Her phone buzzed. **Volkov: Someone leaked a "concern memo" to the orchestra board. It's unsigned, but the language is surgical. Mental health framed as liability.**

Celeste did not react outwardly. She had learned young that people mistook stillness for innocence.

Across the room, the Mirai pattern reappeared in new handwriting: donors with overlapping shell interests, arts administrators whose résumés aligned too neatly to be coincidence. The Maestro was not present, but his syntax was.

Esra's message followed seconds later. "They're isolating you from institutional trust. Once that erodes, no one will ask where the story came from."

Celeste set the champagne flute on a passing tray and stepped onto the balcony that overlooked the river. The Vltava moved without apology, carrying Prague's reflections downstream to places that would never be asked to remember.

Volkov appeared at her side. "They're not trying to end you," he said. "They're trying to frame you."

Celeste's gaze remained on the water. "Then I stop being available for the frame."

The city breathed around them, ancient and incurious. Prague was not a battlefield. It was a courtroom with no judge.

The gala did not end so much as it dispersed, the crowd unraveling into smaller knots of self-preservation. Celeste left before the last donor finished apologizing to himself. She descending the marble staircase with her cello case as if this were simply another evening where the music had ended too soon.

Outside, the air had cooled, carrying the faint sweetness of linden trees and the metallic whisper of the river. Prague glowed the way cities do when they have learned to survive beauty with spires lit from below, bridges outlined in gold that never asked who had paid the electric bill.

Her phone vibrated in her hand. **Esra: I've traced the memo language to a linguistics model used by a consulting firm tied to Chorale's Prague heritage trust. It's not gossip. It's authored.**

Celeste stopped walking. "So the story is the weapon," she said quietly, knowing Esra would hear her through the open com she had installed on Celeste's phone.

"Yes," Esra replied. "And right now, you're the delivery system."

Volkov joined her at the curb. "We can pull you from the tour."

"No," Celeste said. "We let them think it's working."

He studied her. "That's not a retreat. That's bait."

She inclined her head slightly. "Exactly."

The river moved beside them, indifferent to narrative, erasing its own testimony with every second that passed.

For the first time since Berlin, Celeste felt something unfamiliar stir beneath the discipline: anticipation. Prague had decided who she was. Now she would decide what it cost.

They met Esra in a bookshop that pretended not to exist. There was no sign, no display window, just a narrow door set between two tourist boutiques whose neon promises were loud enough to erase curiosity. Inside, the shelves were bowed beneath decades of unsold volumes, their spines faded into anonymity.

Dressed in a black button down shirt and black pants, Esra did not look up when Celeste entered. "They're accelerating," she said. "Your name is trending on three classical music forums. Not virally, not yet. But with enough coherence to feel organic."

Celeste closed the door behind her, the bell above it remaining stubbornly silent. "How long until it isn't?"

"By tomorrow morning," Esra replied. "They've seeded a secondary narrative with whispers of substance abuse, erratic rehearsal behavior, conflict with conductors. No sources. Just texture."

Volkov leaned against a shelf of Czech poetry, careful not to dislodge history. "Can you prove authorship?"

"I can show fingerprints," Esra said. "But institutions don't prosecute patterns. They apologize to them."

Celeste moved to the counter and rested her hands on its scarred surface. "Then we don't argue with the story."

Esra finally looked up. "We don't?"

"We let it grow," Celeste said. "And then we perform the rupture."

Volkov's eyes narrowed. "You want to out-narrate them?"

"Yes," Celeste replied. "They think authorship is theirs because they wrote the first draft. But music has revisions built into it."

Esra exhaled slowly. "This is dangerous. Maybe even more so than the previous stuff." She frowned.

Celeste met her gaze. "So is letting them decide who I am."

Outside, Prague carried on, untroubled by the idea that it was about to witness a different kind of concert, one performed not onstage, but inside the collective ear.

The bookshop breathed dust. It wasn't the mustiness of neglect, but the scent of accumulation, paper aging into itself, ink releasing memories it no longer owned. A radiator hissed somewhere behind the shelves, producing heat in small, unreliable favors. The overhead lights buzzed with a frequency just shy of irritation.

Celeste wandered the narrow aisle while Esra spoke, running her fingers across spines whose titles had faded into abstractions. *Philosophiae Naturalis. Harmonia Universalis.* The ghosts of men who had believed the world could be solved with enough notation.

"They aren't just smearing you," Esra continued. "They're introducing friction. Sponsors don't cancel contracts over rumors. They cancel them when enough people whisper the same uncertainty in different rooms."

Celeste stopped at a shelf of forgotten concert programs, their covers browned with time. The smiling faces of musicians who had once mattered stared back at her from another century. "They don't need me disgraced," she said. "They need me inconvenient."

Volkov shifted his weight, a floorboard creaking beneath his boot like a reprimand. "If they succeed, orchestras won't cancel you publicly. They'll just stop offering you the solos. You'll still play. You'll just be irrelevant."

Celeste turned, the word striking closer than the slander. "Irrelevant is a kind of death."

Esra closed the laptop and pushed it aside. "Then we give them the kind of relevance they can't launder." She pulled a folded page from her bag and slid it across the counter. It was a rehearsal schedule, not official, not printed on any orchestra letterhead. Private run-through. No press. No public ticketing. "Tomorrow night," Esra said. "St. Agnes Monastery. The trust sponsoring it is the same one laundering the Prague heritage funds."

Celeste studied the paper. The monastery had been converted into a contemporary performance space years ago with a stone nave, exposed beams, acoustics that turned even whispered notes into testimony.

"They think they're staging my implosion," Celeste said slowly.

"Yes," Esra replied. "But they also want you visible. They want a public degradation. A soloist unraveling."

Volkov folded his arms. "So you don't unravel."

Celeste lifted her gaze. "No," she said. "I perform the story they can't write."

The bell above the door remained silent as a man slipped inside the shop, pausing to pretend interest in a rack of postcards. Volkov's attention sharpened instantly, his body angling between Celeste and the stranger with unconscious precision.

But the man only flipped a card, frowned as if disappointed by its sentimentality, and left without ever making eye contact. The door closed behind him with the soft finality of a thought no one wanted to keep.

Celeste exhaled slowly. Even the bookshop, with all its deliberate obscurity, was no longer immune to attention.

"They're tightening the aperture," Volkov said. "You feel it?"

"Yes," Celeste replied. "Like a room that pretends it's getting smaller."

Esra slid the rehearsal schedule back into her bag and powered down her laptop, the screen going black with a soft click that sounded too much like punctuation. "St. Agnes isn't just a venue," she said. "It's symbolic. Deconsecrated space, postmodern audience, critics who pretend they don't believe in anything anymore but still kneel to reputation."

Celeste picked up one of the antique programs and turned it over in her hands. The paper flaked slightly at the edges, decades of performance distilled into a fragile artifact. "They're not trying to embarrass me," she said. "They're trying to make me legible. They want my discipline to look like pathology."

Volkov leaned closer, lowering his voice. "And what are you going to give them?"

Celeste looked past him at the shop's back wall, where a framed lithograph hung crookedly, its abstract lines echoing the very language Eidolon had been using to rewrite her with grids disguised as freedom, chaos that only existed inside permitted margins.

"I'm going to give them coherence," she said. "Not the kind that comforts. The kind that demands attention."

They left the shop separately, their exits staggered by minutes that had once felt paranoid but now felt like basic hygiene. Outside, Prague had deepened into evening. Streetlamps haloed the mist rising from the river, and the cobblestones reflected amber light like scales on a patient animal.

Celeste walked without destination, letting the city reacquaint itself with her footsteps. Her phone vibrated, once, then again. **Esra: The**

chatter is escalating. A music blog in Berlin just republished the Tokyo rumor. They're internationalizing the narrative.

Berlin. The word alone carried the echo of fire and shattered glass. Celeste paused beneath the statue of a forgotten saint whose stone eyes had long ago eroded into neutrality. She thought of her mother stepping out of a hotel doorway, of luggage wheels bumping down a curb, of the way loss did not ask permission before becoming architecture inside a person.

She typed back. "Good. Let them bring it home."

St. Agnes Monastery emerged from the fog like a relic that had refused retirement. Once a place of vows, now a temple to experimentation with steel walkways bolted into medieval stone, uplighting designed to flatter ruin. The private rehearsal was already being whispered about online: Celeste Morgan returns after Tokyo incident. No one had published proof. They didn't need to. Suggestion was cheaper than evidence.

She stood at the edge of the nave long after the last sound check ended, her cello case at her feet like a loyal animal. Volkov was somewhere in the shadows above the gallery, eyes on every entrance. Esra had disappeared into the building's network hours ago, hunting data ghosts through the monastery's half-modern nervous system.

The Maestro wanted a spectacle. What he would get was a reckoning.

Celeste opened the case and lifted the cello into the cool air. The wood felt alive beneath her fingers, as if it, too, had sensed the shift in gravity. She did not tune yet. She simply stood there, breathing with the room, letting the ancient walls teach her how sound wanted to behave inside them. Music was not a weapon. But authorship—true authorship—was rebellion given shape. And tomorrow night, in a place that had forgotten how to believe, she would remind them all what belief sounded like when it refused to ask permission.

Chapter 10

Distortion

ST. AGNES DID not sleep. It waited. The monastery's nave lay in twilight when Celeste returned the next afternoon, light slanting through the tall lancet windows in long, dust-filled beams that looked less like illumination and more like excavation. Workers moved quietly among cables and lighting rigs, their footsteps softened by the ancient stone that had once learned to absorb prayer.

She walked the perimeter first, counting exits the way she counted measures. She eyed the north transept, sacristy door, choir loft stair, temporary fire egress carved through a wall that had once meant eternity. Each path was a variation on escape, a footnote to the same unspoken truth.

Her phone vibrated. **Volkov: They're early. Two donors arrived an hour ahead of schedule. Not on the guest list. They're not here to listen.**

Celeste slid into a narrow side chapel that smelled faintly of damp mortar and melted wax long since removed. She responded, "Then neither am I."

The stage had been assembled at the center of the nave, a circle of pale wood raised only inches from the stone floor, as if the building itself were reluctant to elevate anyone. Above it, suspended lighting rigs formed a geometric halo that looked suspiciously like a targeting reticle if one had learned to see patterns as threats.

Esra's voice arrived in her ear through a nearly invisible transmitter. "They're monitoring biometric response again," she said. "Not as aggressively as Tokyo, but enough to build a comparative model. They think they're about to capture your fracture."

Celeste closed her eyes. She could already feel the audience assembling, the funders in tailored restraint, the critics polishing adjectives, the administrators rehearsing neutrality.

"They will not get one," she whispered.

Outside, Prague had begun to advertise the evening with the soft hunger of a city that had learned how to host both beauty and erasure.

Inside St. Agnes, Celeste Morgan was about to decide which one would be heard.

The audience did not arrive all at once. They filtered in with the slow confidence of people who believed the building existed to receive them. Scarves were unwound, coats surrendered to attendants who spoke in reverent whispers, programs accepted with nods that conveyed both gratitude and ownership. No cameras. No ticket stubs. This was not an event; it was a transaction disguised as culture.

Celeste waited behind the temporary stage, her cello resting against her shoulder, the bow cradled loosely in her hand like a question she had not yet decided to ask. She listened to the room assemble itself, the way she had once listened to the Philharmonic tune in New York. Each body was a small dissonance searching for alignment.

Her phone vibrated. **Esra: They've embedded sensors in the lighting rigs and under the stage. Nothing invasive. But enough to triangulate pulse, breathing, micro-movements.**

Celeste responded, "Then we give them noise."

A bell chimed softly, a signal that the performance was about to begin. She stepped into the nave. Applause rippled through the audience. It was not enthusiastic, not warm, but evaluative, the sound of people acknowledging a resource rather than welcoming a person. She did not bow. She stood at the center of the pale wood circle and waited for the echo to exhaust itself. The silence that followed was sharper than applause had ever been.

She lifted her bow and played a single note. Not a tuning note. Not a greeting. A declaration. Low, sustained, the sound carrying upward into stone arches that had once amplified psalms and were now being asked to accommodate something far less obedient.

The sensors responded instantly. She could feel it in the subtle shift of light, in the almost imperceptible hum beneath the floorboards. They were listening.

She began the piece she had written that morning in the hotel, a work without bar lines, without predictable phrasing. It borrowed fragments from the Requiem they had tried to feed her in Tokyo but twisted them into shapes that refused resolution. It was not violent. It was insistent.

Faces in the front row leaned forward. Somewhere in the back, a donor whispered something to a companion and was hushed by the force of the sound itself.

The receiver vibrated in her ear. Volkov's voice filled her ear drum, "They've activated the live analytics feed. Whatever you're doing is not matching their expected parameters."

Celeste closed her eyes. Good.

The room began to change its posture. It wasn't dramatic. There was no sudden gasp, no collective intake of breath, but something shifted in the way bodies held themselves, the way weight settled into seats. The sound Celeste drew from the cello did not rise and fall in the patterns they had paid to recognize. It didn't resolve, didn't flirt with climax, didn't even ask to be liked. It existed.

She let the bow travel slower than comfort permitted, forcing the audience to confront the space between intention and outcome. The sensors above her responded with faint calibrations, light intensifying, then dimming, trying to find a physiological anchor point that would allow the system to predict her next movement.

In her ear camed Esra's voice this time. "Their model is scrambling. They're comparing tonight's data to Tokyo, to Paris, to New York. You've created a statistical orphan."

Celeste almost smiled. She leaned into the next passage, not louder but more interior, as if she were playing for the building rather than the people inside it. The stone responded the way she had hoped by swallowing certain frequencies, amplifying others unpredictably. She was not performing in the monastery. She was performing with it.

A cough in the second row became a disruption that echoed too long. Someone crossed their legs and the scrape of shoe against wood sounded like an accusation.

The piece began to fracture, not in error, but in layers. Harmonics slipped free of melody, dissonances stacked without apology. It was music that did not ask permission to be misunderstood.

Volkov's voice vibrated in her ear. "Board members are leaving. They're not sure what they're supposed to be evaluating."

Celeste pressed the cello harder against her collarbone, her pulse steady despite the invisible machinery trying to map it. They had expected rupture. They had designed for collapse. Instead, she was offering them authorship in real time, showing them what it looked like when a system refused to flatten itself into compliance.

The final note did not end. It simply ceased to continue. The silence that followed was not confusion. It was vacancy. For the first time that night, the sensors above her did not adjust.

The silence after the final note was not empty. It was occupied.

Dust hung in the air like something that had been summoned but not dismissed. The lighting rigs hovered in a faint tremor, unsure whether to brighten or fade, their algorithms having lost the grammar that normally told them what human satisfaction looked like.

Celeste did not move. Her bow remained suspended above the strings, her left hand curved in a shape that no longer belonged to a scale anyone had taught her. She could feel the heat from the lights settle into her shoulders, the subtle ache in her forearm where discipline had given way to defiance. She was suddenly aware of her own breathing, thought it was not labored, not accelerated, but stubbornly present in a room that had wanted it to become a metric.

In the front row, a woman who had arrived wrapped in silk stared at her hands as if they had betrayed her. A man two seats down checked his watch, then seemed embarrassed by the act, lowering his wrist as though time itself had been rude to intrude. There was no applause. Not because they disliked what they had heard, but because the reflex had been interrupted. Applause required closure. This piece had refused to close.

Esra's voice whispered in her ear. "They've lost narrative control. I'm seeing internal communications spike with no consensus language."

Celeste finally lowered the bow. The sound it made against the wood was intimate, indecently loud in the hush that followed. It was the first thing that broke the spell, and it felt like a confession rather than an ending. She inclined her head but not a bow, not gratitude, simply acknowledgment and stepped off the stage.

Behind her, the audience began to stir. Not applause, still, but the low friction of people rediscovering how to occupy their bodies. Someone cleared their throat with unnecessary force. A chair scraped back.

In the control room above the nave, someone swore in Czech.

Volkov's voice slid into her ear like a knife finding its sheath. "They're retreating. Donors are leaving through side exits. Press liaisons look like they're trying to remember what emergency talking points feel like."

Celeste walked through the nave without hurrying, past faces that had paid to define her and now did not know where to place the definition. She passed beneath stone arches that had outlived belief systems and would outlive this one, too.

At the side door, she paused and glanced back once, not at the people, but at the space itself. St. Agnes had been a monastery, then a ruin, then a performance venue. Tonight it had been something else entirely.

Esra said in her ear, "Congratulations. You just created the first undocumented outcome in their model."

Celeste pushed open the door and stepped into Prague's night, the river carrying light away with an indifference she found suddenly comforting.

The Maestro had wanted her fracture. She had given him a void. And now he would have to decide what to write into it.

Chapter 11

Alignment

PRAGUE WOKE TO the aftermath the way it always had: civilly, with no intention of remembering what had happened the night before. Celeste watched the headlines assemble themselves on the muted television in her hotel room. They were careful, hedged, wrapped in language that suggested discretion rather than failure.

Experimental Performance Divides Private Audience

Celeste Morgan Challenges Classical Convention in Prague

Sources Question Artist's Stability Amid Unorthodox Choices

No one accused her of wrongdoing. No one praised her either. The story had been clipped into a shape that could be safely digested, drained of anything that resembled authorship.

Her phone vibrated. **Esra: They're reframing fast. The narrative pivot is already underway.**

Celeste turned the television off and stood, the quiet in the room settling around her like a held note. She had not broken their system. She had forced it to respond. And that, she was beginning to understand, was the only kind of progress that counted.

She dressed without ceremony, choosing a charcoal coat that blurred her into the early-morning fog outside the window. Prague lay beneath a low ceiling of cloud, the river smudging the city into an impressionist study of itself.

Her phone buzzed again. Volkov had texted, "They're not going to come for you directly. They're too busy containing donors. But they are repositioning assets."

"Where?" she typed.

A pause.

Volkov responded, "Buenos Aires. Prague was meant to be containment. It became proof of concept."

Celeste closed her eyes briefly, imagining another city beginning to assemble its own version of the trap, another performance hall learning how to listen to the wrong things. She stepped into the corridor and nearly collided with Lena, who stood there holding a folded newspaper like a fragile thing.

"I didn't know where else to go," Lena said. "They're saying things about you. They're calling it performance art."

Celeste took the paper and skimmed the article, noting how carefully it danced around the absence of fact.

"Performance art isn't a crime," she said.

"They don't mean it as a compliment," Lena replied.

Celeste met her gaze. "Then they've misunderstood what art is for."

They walked together toward the hotel café, moving through a lobby that smelled faintly of furniture polish and lemon, the kind of artificial cleanliness meant to suggest permanence. Outside the tall windows, Prague unspooled itself into morning with tram bells chiming with the weary patience of a city that had learned to negotiate with history rather than defeat it.

Lena carried the folded newspaper, her fingers worrying the edges as if she were afraid the words might leak out and stain her hands. She kept glancing sideways at Celeste, the way people did when they were uncertain whether proximity might make them complicit.

The café was almost empty, the breakfast rush already spent. A lone businessman hunched over his laptop near the window, earbuds sealing him inside a private geography. A pair of tourists whispered in Spanish over untouched croissants, arguing about whether beauty was worth the early hour.

They took a small table near the back where the light did not quite commit. Lena smoothed the newspaper open between them. The headline was cautious in bold print, the body text a labyrinth of euphemism and implication. Celeste noticed how often her name appeared in quotation marks, as if the article itself did not quite trust that she was a person.

"You scared them," Lena whispered. "Not with what you did, but with what you didn't do. You didn't play the ending."

Celeste stirred her coffee though she had no intention of drinking it, watching the crema collapse into itself like a small, private disaster. "Endings are promises," she said. "I didn't want to promise them anything."

Her phone vibrated against the tabletop, a faint insect hum. **Esra: I've pulled the full Prague engagement report. The monastery's analytics were forwarded to a holding server in Argentina within thirty seconds of your final note. They're not regrouping. They're relocating.**

Celeste's hand stilled mid-circle. The café's ambient noise—the clink of china, the whisper of a milk steamer—seemed suddenly louder, more insistent, as if the world were eager to drown out inconvenient revelations.

"Then Buenos Aires isn't next," she said quietly. "It's now."

Lena stared at her. "What does Argentina have to do with anything?"

Celeste folded the newspaper and slid it into her coat pocket, not out of modesty but refusal. "It has to do with who's listening," she replied. "And who's trying to learn what obedience sounds like in Spanish."

Lena's brow furrowed. "You make it sound like…like they're using concert halls to teach people how to think."

Celeste finally looked up. "That's exactly what they're doing."

Silence settled between them, not awkward but stunned, the kind that followed a truth that had never bothered to introduce itself gently.

Outside, a tram rattled past in a shower of sparks, Prague continuing its morning with all the practiced indifference of a city that had survived too many authors and editors. Inside the café, Celeste Morgan was already leaving, even as she remained seated, her mind composing the next movement in a language no one else had yet learned to hear.

She and Lena did not linger in the café. Prague was already adjusting around them, the lobby filling with people who would never know how close the building had come to becoming a node in something far larger than art. Celeste walked with Lena toward the elevators, the newspaper's weight still pressing against her ribs like a second pulse.

Volkov waited for them in the hall outside the hotel gym, dressed in a jacket that made him look like a man who belonged anywhere he stood. "They've shifted the center of gravity," he said without preamble. "Every asset I can see is sliding south."

Celeste nodded. "Buenos Aires."

"Yes," Volkov replied. "And this time they're not experimenting. They're operational."

Lena slowed. "Operational how?"

Celeste stopped walking. "They're not trying to shape me anymore," she said. "They're trying to replace me."

Lena's mouth parted, the idea too large to swallow in one piece. "With what?"

"With a model," Celeste answered. "A musician who never refuses the score."

Volkov's gaze sharpened. "You're not their proof of concept anymore. You're their control variable."

The elevator arrived with a muted chime that sounded almost apologetic. Celeste stepped inside first, the mirrored walls catching her reflection from angles she didn't trust. She looked thinner than she felt, harder somehow, as if Prague had etched itself into her without permission.

Buenos Aires was no longer a destination. It was an audition.

They rode the elevator in silence, the soft instrumental music leaking from hidden speakers like a performance no one had requested. Celeste studied her reflection in the mirrored wall, seeing herself doubled, tripled, fractured by seams in the glass that were meant to be invisible. A model, Volkov had said. A replacement.

The doors opened onto their floor and they moved as if choreographed, splitting without explanation toward separate rooms. Celeste unlocked hers and stepped inside, the scent of lavender cleaner greeting her with inappropriate calm.

Her phone vibrated. **Esra: I've uncovered something new in the Prague analytics packet. It wasn't just you they were monitoring. They were comparing your biometric resistance to archived profiles.**

Celeste asked, "Archived profiles of whom?"

There was a pause long enough to imply dread.

Esra: Of other musicians. Cellists, pianists, conductors. All of them disappeared from the international circuit over the past decade. Not dead. Not disgraced. Just... rewritten.

Celeste sat on the edge of the bed, the room suddenly too small for the shape of the thought. "Rewritten how?"

"Personality shifts. Behavioral softening. Loss of signature style. They return to public life technically intact, artistically compliant."

The Maestro wasn't creating assassins. He was manufacturing obedience. Celeste closed her eyes, the hum of the minibar vibrating faintly through the floor. She had not escaped the system. She had been measured against it.

The room felt newly hostile, not in any way that could be photographed or filed, but in the quiet way spaces became accusatory when they had overheard something unforgivable. Celeste crossed to the window and parted the velvet curtains just enough to fracture the reflection of her face across the glass. Prague waited below, all towers and river light, a city that had perfected the art of standing after being told to kneel. She watched a tram slide across a distant bridge, its interior lights flickering like the pulse of something that refused to be counted.

Her phone buzzed softly in her palm. **Volkov: I'm seeing movement on a private charter registry. Mirai affiliates just booked a flight out of Vienna to Buenos Aires under a cultural exchange trust.**

She closed her eyes for a moment and let the words settle into muscle instead of memory. *Cultural exchange.* A phrase that had once meant scholarship and symphony halls and students who believed that beauty was something they were allowed to inherit.

"They're not just running operations," she murmured to the empty room. "They're exporting doctrine." The word doctrine hung there, heavier than gunfire. It implied theology. Belief. The slow laundering of intention into tradition.

She turned back to the desk and opened the binder, its spine giving with a sound that had accompanied too many sleepless nights to count. The pages inside were an archaeology of her life—flight numbers, aliases, contingency diagrams—but buried in the back was a thinner section she had only shown to Volkov. Her mother's handwriting.

When systems refuse to listen, do not shout. Interrupt their grammar.

Celeste traced the indentation of the pen with her thumb, feeling the imprint of someone who had never believed obedience was synonymous with peace. She remembered her mother standing in the kitchen in Berlin, humming fragments of Bach while packing a suitcase, explaining that translation was not betrayal, that it was survival.

Her phone vibrated again, this time with Esra's signature staccato urgency. **Esra: If Buenos Aires is next, they're going public with the model. I'm seeing a pilot program attached to a youth conservatory. Students. Teenagers.**

The room constricted. Students. Children whose wrists were still learning what instruments could weigh. Children who had not yet learned how it felt to be calibrated by something that did not care if you survived the process.

"They won't stop with me," Celeste said aloud, not for Volkov or Esra, but for the walls, for the river, for whatever in the building might still be listening.

She closed the binder and crossed to the cello case, unfastening the latches with hands that had learned steadiness at fourteen when panic had been presented as curriculum. She did not remove the instrument. She simply laid her palm against the curved maple back, grounding herself in grain and varnish, in the reality of something that could not be digitized without losing its soul.

This was no longer about outrunning the Maestro. It was about outliving him.

Inheritance, she realized, was not what you received. It was what you refused to surrender.

Chapter 12

Presence

THE FLIGHT TO Buenos Aires departed before dawn, the airport still half-asleep in the way only European terminals managed with lights dimmed to a conspiratorial glow, coffee machines hissing like small animals waking too early.

Celeste stood in the check-in line with her cello case propped against her leg, watching travelers negotiate the mathematics of luggage and fatigue. A child cried somewhere behind her; the sound was partially swallowed by the terminal's engineered acoustics that turned human urgency into polite noise.

Her phone vibrated. **Volkov: Two seats behind you, left side. Not following you. Watching around you.**

Celeste didn't turn. She shifted her weight slightly and watched the reflection in the polished metal of the baggage scale. A man in a gray blazer glanced at the departure board too often. A woman in oversized sunglasses pretended to scroll through her phone while never letting her thumb touch the screen. They were not Eidolon operatives. They were plausible.

The plane itself was an aging wide-body with seats that carried the ghosts of better decades. Celeste settled in by the window, tucking the cello into its paid-for seat with the tenderness of someone who understood that objects could feel abandoned.

Her phone buzzed again as the engines came to life. **Esra: The youth conservatory in Buenos Aires is called Instituto Aurora. Their new director took the position three months ago after working briefly for a consulting firm in Zurich. No public résumé before that.**

"Aurora," Celeste murmured. "Dawn. They're not even hiding the metaphor anymore."

As the plane climbed, Prague flattened beneath them into cartography with bridges becoming lines, spires surrendering to abstraction. She closed her eyes and let the vibration of flight bleed into her bones.

Buenos Aires was not a city. It was a generation.

They landed in Buenos Aires beneath a sun that felt too generous for the secrets it was about to illuminate. Ezeiza Airport opened into heat and sound, voices ricocheting off tiled ceilings in overlapping Spanish that made no effort to slow itself down for visitors. Celeste breathed it in—the tang of jet fuel, the sweetness of strong coffee drifting from a kiosk, the faint undercurrent of something floral that suggested a city unwilling to forget pleasure even when it was being watched.

Her phone vibrated. **Esra: Instituto Aurora is less than four kilometers from Teatro Colón. They're embedding doctrine at the source.**

Celeste slid into the crowd, letting the cello case become her passport. In South America, musicians were not anomalies. They were currency.

Outside, the city pressed in with unapologetic life with yellow taxis weaving between buses painted with political graffiti, vendors hawking empanadas from carts that steamed with cumin and beef. A woman argued into a phone in rapid-fire Porteño Spanish, her laughter detonating between syllables.

Volkov joined her at the curb. "This place doesn't know how to whisper," he said.

"No," Celeste replied. "But it knows how to sing."

They rode toward the city center with the windows cracked open, Buenos Aires unspooling in murals and balconies and trees that refused to be pruned into submission. Celeste watched a boy kick a battered football against a wall scrawled with protest slogans, each impact sending dust into the air like punctuation.

Esra texted again, "The conservatory's performance wing was renovated last month. Ventilation overhaul. Sound isolation panels. Behavioral analytics software disguised as acoustic optimization."

Celeste closed her eyes, the rhythm of the road syncing with her pulse. "They're not conditioning adults here," she said. "They're rehearsing the next generation."

Instituto Aurora occupied a block that had been scrubbed into neutrality. The jacaranda trees lining the street were in bloom, their violet petals drifting down onto pavement that looked too recently power-washed to be accidental. The building itself was a lesson in restraint with three stories of pale glass and limestone, modern without declaring allegiance to any era, as if it had been designed to survive whatever ideology followed the current one.

A banner fluttered above the entrance. *FORMA EL FUTURO.*— SHAPE THE FUTURE.

Celeste paused beneath it, the cello case pulling at her shoulder like ballast. Words had weight. Whoever had chosen that phrase understood how much.

Inside, the air shifted. It wasn't cold, but it wasn't warm either. It was climate controlled into an emotional blankness that erased urgency. The lobby was open and luminous, sunlight diffused through a ceiling of etched glass that softened shadows until everyone looked like a version of themselves someone else had approved. They wore uniforms. Not identical, but coordinated: charcoal blazers, slate-blue shirts, soft black slacks or skirts. Subtle distinctions of rolled cuffs or mismatched shoes were permitted just enough to suggest individualitywithout ever allowing it to become disruptive.

The students were young. Twelve to sixteen, perhaps. Old enough to understand ambition, too young to recognize indoctrination when it wore the costume of opportunity. They were beautifully varied with skin tones spanning continents, accents sliding between Spanish, English, Portuguese, and something Eastern European Celeste could not quite place. Diversity as design.

A receptionist smiled too smoothly, her accent flattening into neutrality when Celeste spoke. "We are honored to have you, Ms. Morgan. The students are very excited."

"Are they?" Celeste asked.

The woman blinked once, too quickly. "Of course. Your career is… inspirational."

Celeste's phone vibrated in her palm and she glanced at it. Esra: Facial recognition cameras just tagged you. You're live across internal systems.

Down the hall, a door stood ajar. Sound drifted through though it was not music, not quite. Scales, yes, but flattened, de-emotionalized, stripped of the hesitations that made children human. Celeste followed it, each step echoing in a corridor designed to erase echoes.

The rehearsal room was a perfect rectangle. Twenty students sat in disciplined semicircles, instruments raised in parallel arcs. Violins, violas, a lone bassoon whose player was too small to carry it without help. Their eyes were not on the conductor. They were fixed on a screen mounted high above the chalkboard.

On it, a waveform pulsed in luminous blue, rising and falling with algorithmic precision. Beneath it, numbers scrolled of heart rates, respiration intervals, neural compliance indexes disguised as "focus metrics."

The children played to the waveform. Not listening to themselves. Not listening to each other. Listening to permission.

No one noticed Celeste at first. She stood in the doorway and watched the children calibrate themselves to a line of light that had replaced the idea of sound. The conductor, a young woman barely out of graduate school, stood rigidly at the front, baton raised but unused, her eyes flicking nervously between the students and a tablet mounted to the stand in front of her.

The waveform spiked.

A boy in the second row, who was freckled, all elbows, stiffened visibly and corrected his posture without being told. His bow arm adjusted by fractions that no teacher would have time to request.

Celeste felt something old and volatile uncoil in her chest. This was not instruction. It was training.

Her phone vibrated and she looked down. **Volkov: Building security just reclassified you as Tier Observational. You're not a guest anymore.**

The conductor flinched. She hadn't meant to. It was the involuntary twitch of someone whose body had learned to answer before the mind had time to argue. Her eyes darted to the doorway, caught on Celeste, and held there a beat too long.

The waveform wavered. A murmur rippled through the students but it was not sound, not quite, more like the collective intake of breath that happened when twenty young bodies realized something unscripted had entered their room. Several of them glanced at the door, curiosity briefly breaking through the discipline that had been poured into them.

"Please," the conductor said, too brightly, stepping away from the stand. "This is a closed session."

Celeste did not retreat. She walked into the room instead, the sound of her shoes on the polished floor slicing cleanly through the antiseptic uniformity of the scales. Every step distorted the waveform slightly, like static intruding on a broadcast.

"You're not teaching them to play," Celeste said, keeping her voice calm so it wouldn't echo in a way that made this feel like a confrontation. "You're teaching them to comply."

The conductor's smile didn't fade; it tightened. "We use adaptive focus metrics to optimize performance."

A girl near the front with dark hair braided too tightly and fingers already calloused despite her age hesitated before her next note, eyes flicking between Celeste and the screen. The waveform dipped. A sharp chime sounded from the tablet. The girl straightened instantly, shoulders snapping back into position, bow resuming its arc as if the lapse had never happened.

Celeste felt her jaw harden. This was what Tokyo had been: a rehearsal for a system that didn't wait for adulthood to begin rewriting people. She opened her cello case. The click of the latches was louder than it should have been in that room.

Several students froze outright, the discipline unraveling in the face of something not on the screen. The conductor took a step toward her, then stopped when the waveform spiked again, confused by a variable it had not been trained to process.

Celeste lifted her cello and placed it against her shoulder. "This is what you're erasing," she said softly, not to the conductor but to the children. "The space where you decide what a note means before someone else tells you."

The waveform flattened into an anxious shimmer.

Somewhere in the building, an alarm began to learn her name.

The alarm did not scream. It chimed, politely, the way this place did everything with an almost musical tone meant to reassure rather than alert. But Celeste had learned the language of danger well enough to hear what lay beneath the courtesy.

The waveform above the students began to fracture, its perfect geometry breaking into erratic pulses as her presence destabilized the model.

"Ms. Morgan," the conductor said, voice trembling now beneath the professionalism. "You are disrupting a sanctioned session."

Celeste drew her bow across the open C string. The sound was not loud. It was true. It bypassed the algorithm by refusing to be interpreted, vibrating the stone floor, the wooden panels, the rib cages of the children who had never been asked to trust anything that wasn't measured. Several of them gasped—not because it hurt, but because it was the first note that had not asked permission from a screen.

The waveform spiked wildly, then stalled.

A boy in the back, whose hair was shaved into military neatness, lowered his instrument without realizing he had done it. He stared at Celeste as if she had spoken a language he had forgotten he knew.

The polite alarm chimed again, this time closer.

Her phone vibrated. **Esra: Security override triggered. You've got less than two minutes before they lock the wing.**

Celeste met the children's eyes, one by one. "You don't need this," she said, voice steady. "Music is not something that happens to you. It's something you choose."

The girl with the braided hair swallowed hard. "We're not allowed to choose," she whispered.

Celeste felt the words land like a confession.

"Yes," she replied softly. "You are." She played again—not the piece from Prague, not anything with a name, but a fragment she remembered from childhood, something her mother used to hum while packing lunches before school. The melody wove between the students, simple enough to be remembered, wild enough to resist capture.

A violin answered her. Tentatively at first, then with growing certainty.

The waveform went dark. The alarm stopped chiming. And for the first time since she'd entered Instituto Aurora, the room was not listening to a system. It was listening to itself.

For a moment, no one breathed. The children stared at the blank screen as if waiting for it to scold them back into obedience. When it didn't, a strange electricity moved through the room that was not rebellion yet, but recognition.

Another violin joined the first. Then a viola.

The conductor stood frozen, baton slack in her hand, watching as the sound reorganized itself without her permission. She glanced down at her tablet, tapping it twice in quick succession. Nothing happened.

The melody was clumsy, unscored, born in real time. A boy on bassoon came in on a note that didn't quite fit, then found a way to make it belong. Laughter bubbled up from somewhere near the back, startled and instantly smothered, but the damage had already been done. They had remembered themselves.

The alarm chimed again, no longer polite. Footsteps thundered in the corridor outside, authority arriving with the impatience of something that had not expected to be challenged by children.

Celeste lifted her bow one last time and let the phrase resolve into silence. This time a silence that had been earned.

Her phone vibrated. **Volkov: You've got thirty seconds. I'm pulling fire doors, but they'll override.**

Celeste closed her case and slung it over her shoulder, moving to the door. "Keep playing," she said over her shoulder to the room. "Not this melody. Yours."

The braided-haired girl met her gaze and nodded once, solemnly, as if accepting a charge she did not yet understand.

Celeste stepped into the hallway just as security rounded the corner, their uniforms a darker shade of the students', their faces carrying none of the uncertainty that had cracked the rehearsal room open. She didn't run. She walked, fast enough to be inconvenient, slow enough to make them think twice about grabbing her in front of witnesses who had just learned how to listen.

Behind her, the music did not stop.

They didn't touch her. Not in the hallway filled with echoing notes that no longer belonged to any curriculum. Not as students spilled from doorways, instruments clutched like contraband, eyes wide with something too alive to be disciplined back into silence. Security formed a corridor of authority around her without ever closing it. Their radios crackled in clipped Spanish, each instruction contradicting the last. Detain. Observe. Do not escalate. Who authorized this?

Celeste walked straight through them.

Outside, Buenos Aires was waiting with all the uncontained appetite of a city that had never pretended obedience was virtue. A street musician across the way was tuning a battered guitar, the imperfect notes drifting through open windows as if the world were trying to harmonize with what had just been released.

Her phone vibrated. **Esra: I'm scrubbing Aurora's internal feeds. They're bleeding control protocols everywhere. This won't stay local.**

Volkov appeared from behind a delivery truck, his eyes sweeping the entrance, already mapping exits from memory that didn't belong to him. "They won't close ranks fast enough," he said. "You turned their pilot program into folklore."

Celeste paused at the curb, the conservatory's glass façade reflecting a hundred fractured versions of herself: soloist, saboteur, teacher, rumor.

Inside the building, a violin rose again, unaccompanied, then was joined by another. The music did not have shape yet. It didn't need one. It was contagious.

Celeste stepped into traffic and let Buenos Aires carry her away.

Behind her, a generation had just been reminded that sound was not something you survived. It was something you created.

Chapter 13

Threshold

THE STORY DID not break in Buenos Aires. It bled. By morning, the conservatory incident had become a mosaic of amateur video clips, blurry uploads with captions that contradicted each other just enough to feel real. A girl crying into her violin case. A security guard shouting in the background. The sound of children playing a melody no one could identify, but everyone seemed to recognize.

Celeste watched it unfold on a muted screen in the back of a moving train, Argentina sliding past the window in broad sweeps of farmland and forgotten factories. She had not slept. Neither had Volkov, who sat across from her pretending to dismantle a phone while monitoring the city's digital pulse.

Her phone chimed with a message from Esra. "They're calling it The Aurora Breach. No central narrative yet. That's good. That means they don't own it."

Celeste leaned her head against the window, the glass cold and steady beneath her temple. The Maestro had wanted a model. What he had received was a contagion. And now, finally, the world was beginning to listen.

The train clattered through the outskirts of Buenos Aires with a sound that belonged to labor rather than elegance. Grain silos rose like unfinished monuments beyond the windows, their rust streaked with the same red dust that coated the rails. Celeste felt the rhythm of the tracks settle into her bones, not as music but as momentum forward whether she was ready or not.

She toggled her phone to airplane mode and back again, watching notifications stack like unread confessions. The Aurora Breach was already fracturing into dialects: Spanish threads arguing over whether the girl with the braid had been brave or reckless; English think-pieces speculating about Celeste's mental state; a German forum resurrecting her Berlin past with the curiosity of people who believed grief was a qualification.

Volkov, who sat next to her, broke the quiet. "They're not sure how to respond."

"That means they're afraid," Celeste replied.

He glanced up. "That doesn't make them less dangerous."

Across the aisle, a woman hummed softly to herself, a melody that had nothing to do with the headlines but everything to do with a child sleeping against her shoulder. The conductor's voice crackled faintly over the intercom in Spanish, announcing a minor delay that no one appeared to mind.

Another text arrived from Esra. "There's chatter inside Eidolon channels. Not command-and-control anymore. It's argument. The Maestro isn't issuing directives. He's trying to regain authorship."

Celeste closed her eyes. For the first time in years, she did not feel pursued. She felt answered.

They disembarked in a town whose name never appeared in guidebooks. A place where the platform was little more than poured concrete and a faded timetable that listed arrivals as aspirations rather than facts. The air smelled of diesel and orange blossoms, a contradiction Celeste found oddly comforting.

Volkov led the way through a narrow exit that opened onto a street lined with low stucco buildings whose balconies sagged beneath too many potted plants. A boy chased a loose dog down the sidewalk, laughter echoing off walls that had learned to keep secrets.

Her phone vibrated. **Esra: I'm rerouting your digital footprint through half a dozen abandoned arts nonprofits. You're becoming a rumor.**

Celeste adjusted the cello strap on her shoulder. She had spent years trying to be untraceable. Now she was learning how to be everywhere.

They took rooms above a bakery that perfumed the entire block with sugar and yeast. Celeste stood at the window and watched people begin their afternoons with no awareness that a story was being written around them. For the first time since Berlin, the quiet did not feel like exile. It felt like rehearsal.

The bakery below them began work before Celeste learned how to sleep again. She woke to the sound of metal trays clattering against tiled counters, the rhythm irregular but persistent, a domestic percussion that reminded her of mornings in New York when she had pretended that the world could be reduced to practice rooms and stage doors.

Sunlight filtered through gauze curtains and pooled on the floorboards in thin golden bars. The room was spare with an iron bed, a chipped dresser, a single framed print of a tango dancer mid-turn, frozen in a moment of impossible balance.

Her phone vibrated. **Esra: Overnight metrics: the Aurora clips doubled in viewership. Most reposted version has no commentary just the raw sound. That's not an accident.**

Celeste swung her legs over the side of the bed and let her bare feet find the cool wood. She leaned out the window far enough to catch the scent of fresh bread, a smell that made hunger feel like permission rather than need.

Volkov knocked once and let himself in. "You're becoming a movement," he said.

She met his eyes. "I never wanted followers."

"Good," he replied. "They're harder to control than targets."

Her phone buzzed again. **Esra: I've traced a counter-operation. They're mobilizing something called Project Maestro. It's not a kill order. It's an overwrite protocol.**

Celeste closed her eyes. They had stopped trying to end her story. They were trying to outperform it.

The bakery's shutters rolled open with a metallic groan that reverberated through the thin walls like a signal the building itself had been waiting to send. Celeste stood at the window, watching people line up with the hopeful impatience of those who believed the day could be made manageable with sugar and coffee.

"Project Maestro," she said aloud, testing the words the way she tested a difficult passage before performance. "They're naming it after the thing they don't understand."

Volkov leaned against the doorframe, jacket slung over one shoulder. "Names are how they make systems feel human."

Esra texted, "They're recruiting. Conservatories in three countries just received anonymous funding offers tied to 'behavioral optimization curricula.' Buenos Aires was the proof. Now they're scaling." Celeste read it aloud before she turned from the window, her reflection briefly splitting in the glass between past and present versions of herself. "Then we don't counter the protocol," she said. "We rewrite the audience."

Volkov frowned. "That's not a plan. That's an idea."

"Music doesn't move because of the performer," Celeste replied. "It moves because someone else decides to listen."

She opened the binder and flipped to a blank page, writing a single phrase in her mother's handwriting, not because it was legible but because it felt necessary.

Interrupt their grammar.

Outside, a delivery truck backfired, the sound echoing down the street like the punctuation of a sentence no one was supposed to hear.

The Maestro had named his countermeasure. Celeste was about to name hers.

They spent the afternoon building something that could not be diagrammed. Volkov cleared the small table by the window and laid out burner phones like chess pieces, each one already singing softly with intercepted data. Esra's voice lived inside Celeste's ear now, a presence as constant as the hum of the bakery ovens below.

Esra said, "I've mapped the first wave of Project Maestro rollouts. They're not announcing anything publicly. They're seeding pilot grants. Strings attached, but invisible ones. Psychometric software framed as learning aids, attendance incentives tied to biometric compliance."

Celeste sketched lines across the blank page in the binder, not notes, not code but patterns. "They're trying to build obedience before students learn to resist it."

"Yes," Esra said. "And they're doing it in the language of opportunity."

Volkov glanced toward the door. "Someone's coming."

Footsteps sounded on the stairs that were slow, careful, carrying the faint scent of cinnamon from below. Celeste closed the binder and reached for her cello, not to play but to make a statement with presence.

A knock sounded, hesitant.

She opened the door to find the bakery owner, a woman in her sixties with flour on her forearms and a cautious warmth in her eyes. She held a paper bag that breathed heat.

"You are the musician," the woman said in Spanish. It wasn't a question.

Celeste nodded.

"My granddaughter sent me a video," the woman continued, offering the bag. "From the conservatory. She says it's the first time she's ever heard students sound like they were choosing the notes."

Celeste took the bag, the warmth bleeding into her palms. "What did you hear?"

The woman smiled, the kind that arrived without permission. "I heard children who remembered they had mouths." She turned and descended the stairs without waiting for thanks.

Celeste closed the door and leaned against it, feeling the weight of the exchange settle into her chest more deeply than any headline ever had. "That," she said, "is the audience."

Esra's voice shifted, lighter, almost disbelieving. "I'm seeing something strange. Independent music teachers are sharing the Aurora clips in closed groups. No commentary. Just the sound."

"They're doing it themselves," Volkov said. "You didn't start a rebellion. You started a method."

Celeste opened the paper bag and broke off a piece of still-warm bread, the crust flaking onto her fingers. She ate without ceremony, the taste grounding her in a way no data ever could. "Project Maestro wants to replace performers," she said. "So we stop being performers."

"And become?" Volkov asked.

She looked at the binder, at the empty page waiting for a name that would never quite fit.

"Composers," she replied.

The room filled with the sound of typing, of whispered coordination, of ideas that had not yet learned how to behave. Esra's presence expanded across their screens and phones, her voice threading through layers of encryption that had once been the sole property of people who believed information was a privilege. "I'm deploying a ghost network," she said. "Nothing centralized. Nothing traceable. Think of it as… sheet music without a conductor."

Celeste leaned over the table, the warm bread still heavy in her stomach, the smell of yeast and cinnamon anchoring her in something older than any system she was about to dismantle. She began sketching notations that weren't notes but were small arrows, slashes, clusters of words in different languages: play wrong on purpose, teach by unteaching, refuse optimization.

Volkov watched her hands. "You're not writing a plan," he said. "You're writing an instinct."

"That's the only thing they can't model," Celeste replied.

Esra said over one screen, "First conservatory in Córdoba just declined the Maestro grant. They cited misalignment with pedagogical philosophy."

Celeste closed her eyes. A refusal. Small, quiet, but real.

They worked until the afternoon light turned amber and the bakery's second shift began, trays clattering in a rhythm that had become their metronome. Outside, the street filled with children released from school, their voices bouncing off walls in disobedient harmony.

"Look," Volkov said, tilting his screen toward her. A video was trending—not viral yet, but gathering momentum. A classroom in São Paulo, students playing scales out of sync with their teacher's metronome, laughing as they tried to recover something no one had ever told them they were allowed to lose. The caption was in Portuguese. We choose our mistakes.

Celeste felt something like laughter press against her ribs, unfamiliar and dangerous.

They weren't waiting for her anymore. They were writing themselves.

Chapter 14

Reframing

THE MAESTRO DID not issue a statement. That was how Celeste knew they had crossed a threshold.

By the third day in Argentina, the silence had become louder than any press conference could have been. Funding announcements froze mid-cycle. Cultural ministries postponed grant ceremonies without explanation. Conservatories that had once competed for anonymous "innovation packages" quietly withdrew their applications, citing staffing changes, scheduling conflicts, even the weather.

Celeste watched the cancellations ripple outward on Esra's live map like fractures in ice.

"They're not retreating," Volkov said. "They're consolidating."

Her phone vibrated. **Esra: Project Maestro has gone dark.**

No new deployments. They're burning nodes instead of reinforcing them.

"Because they've realized control doesn't scale once the audience becomes the author," Celeste said.

Outside, the bakery's door opened and closed in a steady rhythm, customers drifting in for comfort that required no explanation.

The Maestro had wanted obedience. What he was getting was improvisation. Improvisation, Celeste was learning, did not look like chaos. It looked like people reclaiming small, stubborn decisions. A teacher in Rosario refusing to submit attendance analytics. A violin instructor in Lima letting her students choose their own warm-ups and posting the result without commentary. A conservatory in Córdoba hosting a "wrong notes recital" where applause followed courage instead of accuracy.

Esra's map flickered with new data points every hour with green dots replacing the red ones that had once marked Chorale's reach. It wasn't a takeover. It was a migration.

"They're losing the room," Volkov said, leaning over her shoulder.

Celeste didn't correct him. "They're losing the audience," she replied.

Her phone buzzed. **Esra: There's something else. High-level chatter in Eidolon channels is referencing a contingency. Not a kill protocol. A reveal.**

"A reveal of what?" Volkov asked.

Esra hesitated with the telltale three dots making the pause before she texted, "Of you."

Celeste turned slowly and said aloud, "They can't rewrite what they don't understand."

Esra's voice ricocheted through Celeste's phone. "No, but they can try to define it first."

The reveal came disguised as gratitude. It surfaced first as an editorial in a European arts journal that had not mattered for a decade and then suddenly mattered everywhere. **Celebrating the Unorthodox: Celeste Morgan and the New Improvisational Era,** the headline read, its tone reverent enough to feel sincere until the footnotes began to accumulate.

By afternoon, translations appeared. Spanish. German. Russian. Japanese. They praised her courage, her "emotional volatility," her refusal to conform to "institutional restraint." They named her not as a musician but as a movement, a convenient shorthand for something no one yet understood.

Celeste's phone vibrated with a text from Esra. "They're canonizing you. Turning you into a brand they can sell without you."

Volkov read over her shoulder. "They're not smearing you anymore. They are appropriating you."

The bakery television, normally tuned to local telenovelas, was now showing a panel discussion about the "Morgan Effect," a circle of commentators speculating on whether the global surge in experimental pedagogy could be traced to her "psychological breakthrough."

"She didn't start this," one of them said earnestly. "She just gave it a face."

Celeste shut the screen off. "They're trying to make me safe," she said.

"Safe things are easy to replace," Volkov replied.

Both of their phones lit with an incoming text from Esra. "The Maestro's fingerprints are all over the editorial's metadata. They're shaping the narrative from inside admiration."

Celeste picked up her binder and flipped to a blank page. "Then we don't let them finish the story."

The bakery smelled different when the television was silent. Without the constant chatter of daytime programming, the space filled instead with the sound of dough being kneaded somewhere behind the counter, a thick, deliberate rhythm that carried more honesty than any panel discussion ever could. Celeste sat at the small table near the window with her binder open, the blank page staring back at her with the uncomfortable patience of something that knew it would not be filled gently.

Outside, the street had begun to take on the muted gold of late afternoon. Children drifted home with backpacks too large for their frames. An old man watered potted plants with a care that felt ceremonial. Buenos Aires, unlike Prague, did not seem inclined to pretend it was not alive.

Her phone chimed again, as did Volkov's. **Esra: I'm intercepting internal memos tied to the editorial. They're using phrases like curated rebellion and controlled divergence. They're packaging you as proof that the system allows freedom.**

Volkov leaned against the counter, arms folded, watching a customer debate between two pastries as if the decision might define the rest of her day. "They're selling a narrative where the cage pretends to be optional," he said aloud.

Celeste closed the binder and pressed her palm flat against the cover. "They want to own the meaning of what happened," she said. "They want to reduce it to temperament. To charisma. To a story about me." She stood and crossed to the door, looking out at the street as if it might answer her. "But this was never about me."

Both of their phones vibrated again. **Esra: I've found a second wave of editorials queued in five languages. They're reframing your resistance as a personal journey of trauma, healing, redemption. Very marketable.**

Celeste turned back to the table, her reflection in the glass overlaid with headlines she hadn't yet read but already understood.

"They're writing me as a person," she said. "So, they don't have to talk about the system."

Volkov's gaze sharpened. "Then you stop being a person."

The words landed with unexpected clarity. Celeste opened the binder again and began to write not prose, not music, but directives that refused to behave like either.

No central voice.

No fixed origin story.
Share the method, not the myth.

Outside, a bus roared past, rattling the window just enough to blur the lines she had written. Good. The Maestro wanted to reveal her. What he would get instead was her disappearance into everyone else.

They stopped using her name that night. Esra stripped "Celeste Morgan" from every internal thread that had begun to echo the bakery's address, replacing it with something deliberately unspectacular: Open Source Rehearsal. No founder. No biography. Just instructions that looked like games until someone tried them and realized the room had changed.

Celeste's phone vibrated constantly now, not with alerts but with proof. A conservatory in Montevideo was hosting a "no-screen evening," asking students to describe what they heard instead of what they played. A quartet in Oslo uploaded a piece that consisted entirely of the spaces between notes. A high school band in Oakland refused to tune to the same pitch, letting dissonance become architecture.

Volkov watched it unfold from behind three layers of anonymization. "You're dissolving into the audience."

"That was always the only way to survive a system that thinks people are prototypes," Celeste replied.

Esra interrupted with a text. "The Maestro just lost a major sponsor in Zurich. They cited 'reputational instability.' He's being framed by the same narrative logic he built."

Celeste leaned back in her chair, the bakery's ceiling fan stirring the scent of sugar and yeast into something almost holy. They had tried to canonize her. Instead, she had become unquotable.

The backlash arrived wrapped in flattery. A documentary crew from a Scandinavian network requested an interview, praising Celeste's "cultural courage." A Parisian gallery offered to mount an exhibition titled The Morgan Method. An American podcast promised an episode that would "humanize the algorithm." Celeste declined all of it without ceremony. She no longer trusted anything that required a spokesperson.

And still her phone vibrated. **Esra: I'm seeing panic behavior. Eidolon proxies are leaking counter-narratives with claims that Open Source Rehearsal is unsafe, destabilizing, psychologically harmful.**

Volkov laughed softly. "That's new. They're worried about consent."

Celeste looked out the bakery window at a man teaching his daughter to ride a bike, his hand hovering just behind the seat, refusing to hold it unless she truly needed him to. "They don't understand what they're afraid of," she said. "They think it's noise. It's actually choice."

Her phone buzzed again. **Esra: There's a deeper layer. I've found references to something they call Coda. It's not about you. It's about ending the method entirely.**

Volkov's amusement vanished. "Ending how?" Celeste typed his question.

Esra's reply took longer this time. "By making it lethal to participate."

The word lethal changed the room. It wasn't panic that followed. Celeste had long since exhausted the vocabulary of fear, but a narrowing, the way focus sharpened when the stakes stopped being theoretical.

"They'll stage an example." Volkov's voice was barely above a whisper "An accident. A student hurt. A teacher blamed. The method becomes the villain."

Celeste felt the air grow heavier; the bakery was suddenly too small to contain the consequences of ideas that had escaped it. "Then we make sure there are witnesses before they write the ending."

Another text arrived from Esra. "I'm triangulating chatter around three conservatories flagged as high-risk adoption nodes. Berlin. Toronto. Seoul."

Berlin. The name carried more than geography. It carried

unfinished grief. "They won't go where the story is loudest," Celeste said. "They'll go where silence still feels plausible." She stood, the chair legs scraping against tile like a decision finally made audible. "We can't protect everyone. But we can make it harder to erase them."

Volkov followed her gaze to the street, where the last of the day's light pooled at the curb like a held breath. "What does that look like?"

Celeste picked up her binder and closed it for the first time in days. "It looks like going home to the place they think already belongs to them."

Berlin was not a destination. It was a wound that had learned to speak.

They booked the flight that night under names that did not matter, slipping through Buenos Aires International with the quiet efficiency of people who no longer expected borders to be real. Celeste watched the city dissolve beneath them as the plane climbed, the river flattening into something that looked almost harmless from a distance.

Her phone vibrated as they leveled off. **Esra: I've buried your trail under Open Source Rehearsal mirrors. Whatever happens in Berlin, it won't belong to you alone.**

Celeste closed her eyes, the vibration of the engines settling into the same rhythm that had carried her across continents for most of her life. She thought of the students in Aurora, of the boy with the shaved head lowering his instrument without permission, of the girl who had whispered that they weren't allowed to choose. Choice was dangerous. That was why it mattered.

Berlin greeted them with slate-colored sky and rain that seemed to fall sideways, the city refusing to present itself without weather. The taxi ride from Tegel passed neighborhoods that still wore their histories like unfinished sentences with war-era facades beside glass towers, memorials folded into shopping districts with the casual cruelty of time.

They did not go to a hotel. Volkov led them to an apartment above a shuttered record store whose windows were papered over with posters from the 1980s. Celeste climbed the narrow stairs with the weight of her cello pulling at her shoulder like memory itself.

Inside, the apartment smelled of dust and vinyl and old electricity. The walls were bare except for a single framed photograph of a cellist performing outdoors in a public square, her hair blown wild by wind.

Celeste looked closer and realized she knew the woman in the photo. It was her mother. She rooted to the floor.

Volkov stood behind her, silent, like he was uncertain whether to speak. Esra's voice arrived in her ear piece, suddenly subdued. "I didn't know it was still here. The lease never closed after the bombing, according to my sources."

Celeste stepped closer, her fingers brushing the glass. She remembered that day, the laughter just before the photo, the promise of coffee afterward, the sound of a city still pretending it could keep its citizens safe.

Celeste's phone rang and she put it on speaker. Esra's voice was meant for both of them. "I've intercepted a coded transmission. Coda protocol is active in Berlin. They're planning something public. Something irreversible."

Celeste straightened slowly, grief transmuting into clarity. "They took my mother here," she said. "Now they want to take the method."

Volkov met her gaze. "Then they've chosen the wrong city."

Outside, Berlin thundered with rain, a city that had been burned and divided and rewritten more times than any system could track.

And somewhere inside it, the Maestro was about to learn what happened when you tried to end a story that had already taught itself how to survive.

∫ ∫

Chapter 15

Reframing

BERLIN DID NOT pretend to forget. It stored memory in architecture in bullet-pocked facades that had been repurposed into luxury apartments, in subway platforms where the echo still carried a hint of border patrol boots. Celeste stood at the apartment window long after the rain had begun, watching headlights fracture across the street like scattered punctuation. Her mother's photograph lay on the table behind her, propped against a chipped coffee mug as if the two had always belonged together.

Volkov's computer was open and Esra's face filled the screen. "I've isolated the Coda protocol blueprint. It's not an attack on Open Source Rehearsal. It's a demonstration."

Celeste did not turn. "Demonstrations don't end methods. They terrify people out of using them."

"Yes," Esra said. "And this one is scheduled for tomorrow night. Location: a youth chamber recital at the Alte Münze."

The name closed around Celeste's throat. The Alte Münze was a former mint turned cultural venue that had brick halls, vaulted ceilings, and acoustics that made even beginner ensembles sound like prophecy.

"They're going to hurt a child," Volkov said with barely disguised anger

Celeste picked up her cello case and rested her hand on it, grounding herself in wood and weight. "They're going to try," she replied.

They spent the night in rehearsal of a different kind. Esra fed them fragments of Coda's architecture: risk trees, decision cascades, conditional triggers that bloomed across Volkov's screen like invasive species. It wasn't a single event. It was a choreography: pressure introduced into a public performance, a student isolated, authority delayed just long enough for harm to become story.

"They don't need a body count," Volkov said. "They need a moment that teaches fear."

Celeste traced the map of the Alte Münze with her finger, noting exits, dead zones, the way the old mint's vaults forced sound into narrow corridors. "They'll pick a performer who's already visible," she said. "Someone praised for adopting Open Source Rehearsal."

Esra's eyes moved back and forth like she was reading something on her screen before she said, "Found them. A quartet from Kreuzberg Secondary. They went semi-viral after uploading a no-metric rehearsal. They've been added to tomorrow's program last minute."

Celeste closed her eyes. She could already hear the panic trying to write itself into the future. "We don't stop the recital," she said. "We change the audience."

Volkov looked up. "That's not enough. If Coda's active, they'll trigger something regardless."

"Then we make the trigger unrecognizable," Celeste replied. She opened the binder and began to write, not instructions, but permissions. Allowing failure. Allowing deviation. Teaching a room how to refuse a script it didn't know it had been given.

Outside, Berlin breathed through rain, a city that had learned how to live inside unfinished sentences.

Morning came without apology. Berlin's gray was not a color but a condition, flattening the city into a series of honest silhouettes. They ate standing up, bread torn by hand, coffee strong enough to feel like a dare, while Esra's voice sketched the countdown. "Security contracts were quietly amended at the Alte Münze overnight. There's a third-party vendor embedded into crowd management. They don't wear Eidolon tags, but their firmware does."

Volkov slung his jacket over the back of a chair. "So the building becomes the accomplice."

"Yes," Esra replied. "The locks. The ventilation. The lighting. Coda is less about force than inevitability."

Celeste lifted her cello from its case and played a single harmonic, letting it bloom in the apartment's stale air. "Then inevitability needs a counterpoint."

They left before the city fully woke, blending into commuters who had learned not to look too closely at anything that might ask them to remember. The Alte Münze loomed over a quiet square like a monument to transactions no one wanted to audit.

Celeste stood across the street and watched technicians load equipment through the side entrance. One of them laughed, the sound startling in its ease.

"They don't know what they're building," Volkov said.

"No," Celeste replied. "But they're about to."

They didn't enter as saviors. They entered as infrastructure. Esra tunneled into the Alte Münze's systems from a café three blocks away, her presence reduced to code moving through fiber that had once been copper coin. Volkov disappeared into the maze of temporary barricades and sponsor signage, becoming just another man in a black jacket who looked like he belonged wherever he stood.

Celeste crossed the threshold last, cello case on her back, the building's heavy doors swallowing the city behind her with the weight of history.

Inside, the hall was already warming to itself. Parents hovered near coat racks, their faces a collage of pride and worry. Students darted between them in borrowed concert black, bow cases banging against knees in a choreography that had nothing to do with Coda.

Her phone vibrated. **Esra: First lockout node is live. They're not waiting for intermission.**

Celeste paused beside a poster announcing the Kreuzberg Secondary Quartet, their smiling faces too large for the page. Four teenagers who had no idea they were about to be written into someone else's lesson plan.

"They're compressing the timeline," Volkov said in her earpiece.

Celeste moved toward the backstage corridor, every step an argument against the architecture of inevitability. She could feel the building listening, not in any mystical way, but as a network, a grid waiting for a signal that would tell it what kind of room it was supposed to become.

Not tonight, she thought.

Backstage at the Alte Münze was a study in benevolent neglect. Brick walls sweated old humidity into air that smelled faintly of rosin and cold iron. Folding chairs leaned against each other like conspirators, and someone had taped a hand-lettered sign to a door that read Quartet – Be Brilliant. It was meant as encouragement. It read like pressure.

Celeste found the Kreuzberg students clustered in a narrow anteroom, their instruments half out of cases, their conversation pinned somewhere between excitement and terror. They fell silent when she appeared, recognition rippling across faces that had only ever known her through screens.

"You're not on the program," one of them said, awe colliding with suspicion.

"No," Celeste replied gently. "I'm on the building."

Her phone vibrated. **Esra: Coda's priming sequence is running diagnostics through the ventilation grid. They're preparing to isolate a section of the audience.**

Celeste looked at the students. She didn't analyze their talent or their fear, but their potential to become a story someone else controlled. "You don't have to play the piece the way it's written," she said quietly.

One of the girls, a violist with nervous eyes, shook her head. "They'll mark us down."

Celeste met her gaze. "They're going to mark you anyway."

The words landed with the weight of betrayal, then something like relief. Celeste could feel it. So she added, "Play the room instead. If something feels wrong—if the building stops listening—stop listening to it back."

The boy with the second violin frowned. "What does that even mean?"

Celeste lifted her cello case and opened it, not to play, but to show them the worn wood inside, the imperfections no camera ever framed. "It means trust the moment you're in more than the score you were handed."

Her earpiece activated again. Volkov said, "They've locked two emergency exits. They're funneling movement toward the east vault."

Celeste closed the case. "You'll hear a sound tonight that doesn't belong to your music," she said to the quartet. "When you do, don't try to correct it. Follow it."

They stared at her, four young faces trying to decide whether this was wisdom or madness. Berlin had asked them to choose. So had she.

They were called to the stage before anyone had time to reconsider courage.

A volunteer usher opened the anteroom door with a brittle smile and gestured them forward, as if nothing in the building were currently rewriting its own intentions. The quartet filed out, shoulders squared too tightly, bows gripped like life rafts. Celeste watched them go, counting their breaths the way she once counted bullets.

Her phone vibrated. **Esra: East vault airflow just dropped by twenty percent. They're shaping acoustics through oxygen. It's subtle, but it'll trigger panic in enclosed sections.**

"Hypoxia as pedagogy," Volkov muttered in her ear. "That's new."

Celeste stepped into the shadowed corridor parallel to the hall, the one that ran behind the brick arches and let technicians move unseen. The Alte Münze was a relic of controlled value. Coins once stamped here had carried empire in their alloy. Now the building was being asked to carry something uglier.

The house lights dimmed. Applause began, polite, earnest, the sound of people who wanted to believe this was just another youth recital. Celeste closed her eyes for one beat and pictured her mother's hands guiding a bow across open strings, not correcting, just listening.

Onstage, the quartet began. They were nervous, yes, but not obedient. The tempo wavered just enough to suggest they were watching each other more than the conductor. The room leaned in.

Her phone vibrated again. **Esra: Coda trigger is tied to biometric stress thresholds. They're waiting for audience agitation.**

Celeste felt the building tighten around that expectation, doors prepared to fail politely, ventilation ready to forget its job. She slid into a maintenance alcove and traced the ductwork with her eyes, listening not for sound but for pressure.

Then it came. Not from the music, not from the crowd, but from the building itself: a low-frequency hum that didn't belong to any instrument, a mechanical note that unsettled the air rather than moving it.

Onstage, the violist flinched. She had heard it. Instead of correcting, the girl bent the next note toward the hum, dissonant, exploratory. The cellist followed, then the first violin, their harmony unraveling into something feral and unscored.

The audience stirred.

Her phone vibrated, urgent now. **Esra: Coda's thresholds are spiking. They didn't design for resonance feedback.**

Volkov's voice cut in, breathless. "Fire doors are trying to close. East vault only. They're forcing a crowd migration."

Celeste stepped into the open. She didn't go onstage. She stood in the aisle where parents turned to look at her with startled recognition. She raised her cello and played—not loudly, not heroically—but into the hum, bending her tone until the mechanical vibration had something human to answer to.

The building hesitated. She could feel it: the lag between instruction and execution, the half-second where software waited for permission it had never learned to ask.

Onstage, the quartet was no longer performing. They were conversing with the room. People began to stand, not in panic, but in attention. Phones came out. Someone laughed, disbelieving. The east vault doors stalled mid-close with a groan that sounded suspiciously like surrender.

Her phone vibrated one last time. **Esra: Coda aborted its own cascade. It can't distinguish the threat from the art.**

Celeste lowered her bow.

For a heartbeat, no one applauded. Then the room exhaled, not as approval but as recognition that something had been attempted here and had failed to become the story it wanted to be.

The Maestro had tried to end the method. Instead, Berlin had just taught it how to defend itself.

Chapter 16

The Cost of Echoes

BERLIN DID NOT erupt; it absorbed. The Alte Münze emptied in a hush that felt less like relief and more like collective denial. People did not run; they drifted, clutching children, murmuring to phones that were already uploading their own incomplete truths. No one had language for what had just happened. They only had footage.

Celeste stood in the loading corridor, cello case pressed to her thigh, the brick still humming faintly around her. The quartet had been ushered past her by staff who could not meet her eyes. The girl with the braid mouthed *thank you* as she disappeared into a swarm of parents and journalists, the word fragile enough to feel stolen.

Volkov reappeared from the shadows near the soundboard, jacket unzipped, eyes calculating. "This wasn't supposed to fail," he said. "Not cleanly."

Celeste didn't answer. The building was still listening, still trying to decide whether it had malfunctioned or been re-authored.

Esra's voice sounded in Celeste's ear. "Something's wrong. I'm pulling Eidolon telemetry now. This wasn't an aborted cascade. Coda was rerouted upstream twenty seconds before full activation."

Celeste's fingers tightened around the handle of her case. "Rerouted where?"

Esra hesitated, which was a rare, dangerous thing. "Nowhere public. It vanished into a dark subnet. Someone wanted this version to happen."

Volkov's jaw set. "He staged his own failure."

The realization did not come with anger. It came with dread. The Maestro had not miscalculated. He had composed this.

They emerged into the street where rain misted the night into reflection. The press had already assembled behind barricades, cameras hunched like mechanical birds waiting to feed. A reporter shouted Celeste's name, pronouncing it carefully, as if language itself were being auditioned.

They did not stop.

In the apartment above the shuttered record shop, Esra's voice arrived thin but insistent through the burner phone on speaker. "I'm decrypting the blackout packet. It's enormous. This wasn't about sabotaging you. It was about mapping them."

"Who?" Celeste asked.

"Every institution that didn't comply tonight. Every orchestra, school, foundation that shared your method in the last thirty days." A breath. "Berlin was a sieve."

Celeste sat on the edge of the narrow bed, the city's noise leaking through cracked windows like a poorly mixed track. Her mother's photograph hung crooked on the wall, the cello under her chin frozen forever in public courage.

"He wanted to see who would choose us," she said.

Volkov stood with his back to the door. "And now he knows who to burn."

Celeste's phone vibrated again, but it was not Esra this time. Unknown number. No encryption. Just a line of text, perfectly punctuated.

You turned obedience into a spectacle.

Now watch what spectacle does to the innocent.

Celeste did not reply.

Outside, Berlin thundered with rain, a city that had been rewritten too many times to believe in coincidence. Berlin had not been a victory. It had been a census. And somewhere in the dark, the Maestro was already composing.

Sleep did not come. Celeste lay on the narrow bed staring at the cracked plaster ceiling while Berlin worked its way through the early hours. Somewhere below, a truck idled too long. A door slammed. A couple argued in a language she half understood but completely recognized.

Her phone rested on the nightstand like an accusation. *You turned obedience into a spectacle. Now watch what spectacle does to the innocent.* She replayed the message again and again, not searching for threat but for signature. It was not rage. It was pedagogy.

Volkov moved quietly through the apartment, checking windows, listening to the building like it might betray them. Esra remained on the line, breathing just enough to remind Celeste that silence could still be inhabited. "I found the sieve protocol," Esra finally said. "Berlin wasn't a test of systems. It was a test of loyalties."

"Explain."

"Every institution that amplified Open Source Rehearsal was fingerprinted. IP overlays, metadata drift, donor-channel leaks. The Maestro didn't care if Coda failed publicly. He needed to see who chose you."

Celeste closed her eyes. Her phone audibly vibrated again.

Volkov said, "Someone just died in Toronto." He was staring down at his own phone.

Celeste sat up. "Who?"

"A violin instructor. Heart attack during rehearsal. He'd uploaded a 'wrong notes' session yesterday."

Esra inhaled sharply. "I'm pulling hospital feeds—"

Volkov said, "It won't matter. The story's already being shaped."

Celeste stood, the floor cold against her bare feet. "That wasn't Coda," she said.

"No," Volkov replied from the doorway. "That was punctuation."

The Toronto footage arrived before anyone could ask for it. A student's phone, angled poorly, the frame jittering as voices in the background rose into alarm. A man collapsed just beyond the music stands, his violin sliding from his hand with a sound that cut deeper than the shouting that followed. No blood. No visible trauma. Just a body that had decided, without warning, to become an ending.

Celeste watched it once. Then she closed the file and turned away from the screen, the apartment suddenly too narrow for her breath.

"They'll call it stress," Esra said quietly. "They always do. Artistic temperament. Overwork. The tragedy of modern creativity."

Celeste's phone vibrated again from the unknown number. **One down. You have a movement now. Movements require martyrs.** Celeste read it aloud to Volkov and Esra.

Volkov slammed his fist against the wall hard enough to send plaster dust drifting down like snowfall. "This is escalation," he said. "This is him stepping onto the stage."

Celeste picked up her cello case and set it upright in front of her, pressing her forehead briefly against the smooth curve of the wood as if it could hold her steady. Then she said at last, "He isn't punishing us. He's educating us. Teaching the cost of authorship."

Esra's voice cracked slightly "There's more. I'm seeing parallel events—São Paulo, Rotterdam, Busan. Nothing dramatic enough to headline yet. Just… small failures. Panic attacks. Accidents. Enough to create a pattern if someone is looking for one."

Celeste straightened, grief hardening into something colder. "He's not trying to destroy the method," she said. "He's trying to poison it. Make participation synonymous with risk."

Volkov met her gaze, something unspoken passing between them. "You can't protect everyone."

"No," Celeste replied. "But I can stop being the story."

Esra said, "The Maestro is releasing a private brief to donors. Framing you as an uncontrolled variable, someone who is brilliant, dangerous, unsupervised."

Celeste looked at her reflection in the darkened window, Berlin smeared across the glass behind her like an unfinished chord. "Then we take the variable away," she said softly.

Outside, the city rumbled, trains threading beneath streets that had learned how to live with scars. Inside the apartment, the movement paused, not in defeat, but in recalibration.

These actions were no longer a continuation. They were a reckoning.

Morning arrived without negotiation. Berlin was all steel and slate beneath a sky that refused to be either storm or mercy. Celeste stood at the window while the kettle boiled behind her, the city's roofs catching light the way old instruments caught dust—proof of use, not care.

Esra said, "I've identified the Toronto instructor's biometric anomalies. It wasn't cardiac failure; it was neurogenic shock triggered by ultrasonic modulation. Not lethal by design but lethal by proximity."

Celeste closed her eyes. The Maestro wasn't killing. He was conducting physiology.

"They've turned the method itself into a delivery system," Volkov said from the kitchen. "Participate long enough, your body becomes the instrument."

Esra hesitated. "There's something else. The Maestro isn't routing commands through Eidolon anymore. He's using cultural institutions as relay points. Symphony boards, conservatory councils, philanthropic boards. People who don't know they're part of a weapon."

Celeste watched a cyclist skid on wet cobblestone below, recover, and continue. "He's hiding in respectability," she said.

Her phone vibrated again from the unknown number. **Every system fails eventually. Yours will fail first because it pretends to care.** She read it aloud to the others.

Celeste turned from the window, resolve settling into her posture like muscle memory. "Then we stop pretending this is a movement," she said. "Movements can be infiltrated."

Volkov met her gaze. "And what does that leave us with?"

"A language," she replied. "One that no institution gets to own."

They didn't argue about what that language would look like. They listened for it.

Esra stripped the Toronto data down to its rawest trace: frequency maps, pressure signatures, modulation drift. The Maestro's method was not software. It was acoustics tuned to nervous systems, a parasitic grammar that rewrote the body before the mind could intervene. "He's not broadcasting commands," Esra said. "He's broadcasting environments."

Celeste sat cross-legged on the floor, cello resting against her shoulder though she did not play. She traced the harmonic series of the room with her breath, feeling how the apartment responded, where sound lingered, where it died. "That means every space is a collaborator," she said. "And every collaborator can be made unreliable."

Volkov crouched beside her. "You're talking about destabilizing architecture."

"Yes." Her eyes opened. "He weaponized culture. I weaponize acoustics."

Esra cut in, "I'm detecting pre-deployment signals in three cities. He's moving from musicians to rooms. Museums. Libraries. Churches."

Celeste stood slowly, the cello shifting with her like a second spine. "Then we stop playing halls," she said. "We play fields."

Volkov frowned. "That's not metaphorical, is it?"

"No," she replied. "It's cartography."

Outside, Berlin exhaled its morning, a city that had been taught too many times what happens when spaces stop being neutral. The Maestro thought he was ending a movement, but Celeste was about to take it off the stage entirely.

They left the apartment separately, Berlin already thickening into midmorning without waiting for their permission. Celeste took the S-Bahn east, letting the train dissolve her into commuters who had no idea their earbuds were practicing a kind of private resistance. Volkov moved west toward a secure contact buried inside a cultural endowment. Esra scattered herself across fiber in a pattern that looked like failure to anyone watching too closely.

Esra texted Celeste and Volkov as part of a group chat. "First environmental test site confirmed. An abandoned botanical research station outside Potsdam. Glass domes. Resonance anomalies. He's tuning rooms where no one's listening yet."

Celeste stared at her reflection in the train window, her face layered with the ghost of passing trees. "He's building sanctuaries," she responded. "Places to teach the body how to forget."

She exited two stops early and walked, the rhythm of the city receding into birdsong and the rustle of leaves just beginning to green. Potsdam's outskirts felt rehearsed for something that had not yet been scheduled.

The research station emerged from the forest like a held breath with cracked glass ribs arching over overgrown beds, a cathedral to botany that had outlived its funding. The silence inside was not empty. It was waiting.

Celeste stepped beneath the shattered dome and set her cello down in the center of the abandoned rotunda. Somewhere inside the structure, the Maestro had already composed. She was here to erase the key.

Chapter 17

Recognition

THE GREENHOUSE SANG before she touched it. It was not sound in any conventional sense—no vibration in air, no frequency the ear could seize—but a pressure that lived beneath hearing, the way a held breath announced itself to the body long before the mind learned the word anxiety. Celeste stood inside the broken botanical dome with her cello resting against her hip and felt the architecture recognize her.

The Potsdam research station had been abandoned for fifteen years. Grant money had evaporated, specimens relocated, and yet the place was not dead. It was waiting in the patient way only structures designed for growth ever did. Cracked panes let winter light spill across iron ribs that had learned to rust in elegant arcs. Beneath her feet, the concrete floor trembled faintly, not with instability but with calibration.

Her phone vibrated with an incoming text from Esra. "You're standing inside a live acoustic test bed. He's embedded transducers in the frame, ultrasonic emitters tuned to amplify sympathetic nerve response. This isn't a trap. It's a rehearsal space."

Celeste moved slowly toward the center of the rotunda, each step changing the room's mood. When she stopped, the pressure in her chest eased, as if the building had adjusted its breath to hers. "He's teaching rooms how to conduct people," she murmured.

The forest outside rustled, oblivious. Somewhere between the trees and the broken glass above her, the Maestro had composed a place where obedience no longer needed an audience.

And for the first time since Berlin, Celeste understood the new war was not about music. It was about where music was allowed to live.

Celeste felt the space shift before she heard the footsteps. The sound wasn't loud; it was barely more than the whisper of rubber soles against wet leaves, but the greenhouse's pressure field responded instantly, rippling like a breath drawn too sharply. The building was no longer alone with her.

She turned slowly, bow still resting in her hand, and saw the woman standing just inside the arched doorway where broken glass framed the forest like a wound that refused to scab.

Aria. She had not changed as much as Celeste expected. Still slight, still carrying her percussion bag slung over one shoulder, the mallets inside clicking softly with every movement like nervous punctuation. But her eyes were different now. They looked angry in addition to weary.

"You shouldn't be here," Celeste said.

Aria closed the door behind her, the metal frame answering with a soft, anxious creak. "Neither should you."

The greenhouse tightened its posture. Celeste felt it in her sternum, a pressure like fingers learning the shape of a throat.

"How did you find me?" Celeste asked.

Aria didn't answer immediately. She moved farther into the rotunda, careful with each step, listening not with her ears but with the instinct Celeste had once recognized as genius.

"They wanted me to come," Aria said at last. "I started getting messages after Berlin. Private links. Invitations to something called Resonance Labs. They said it was for people who weren't afraid of new ways to feel sound."

The words felt rehearsed, the way indoctrination always did when it borrowed the language of courage.

"And you followed them here?"

Aria's mouth curved into something that almost resembled a smile. "I followed you here. They kept using your name like a blessing. I figured if I stayed close enough to it, I'd eventually see the truth."

The greenhouse answered her voice with a shiver.

Celeste lowered her cello to the floor and stepped closer, not wanting her colleague's nervous system to be the next instrument the building tuned. "Aria," she said gently, "this place isn't a school. It's a calibration chamber. Whatever you think they're offering you—"

"They're offering me freedom," Aria interrupted, her voice sharper than it had been in Berlin. "They're saying I don't have to perform inside rooms that already decided what I'm allowed to feel."

Celeste inhaled slowly, matching her breath to the subtle oscillation beneath the floor. "That's how it starts," she said. "They promise you space. And then they teach your body what kind of space you're permitted to survive in."

Aria's grip tightened on the strap of her percussion bag. "You talk like you're not doing the same thing."

The pressure spiked, the greenhouse testing the argument. Celeste felt it slide into her chest like an unwelcome harmony. The Maestro had chosen his student well.

The greenhouse did not like contradiction. The pressure in

the rotunda thickened, no longer subtle enough to pretend it was imagination. Celeste felt it crawl up the back of her neck, the way a migraine announced itself long before pain had permission to exist.

Aria swayed, just barely, the mallets in her bag clicking together like bones. "Do you feel that?" she asked.

"Yes," Celeste said. "That's the room deciding which of us is easier to listen to."

Aria's eyes widened in recognition. She stepped farther inside, curiosity overpowering caution. "It's like standing inside a drum," she murmured. "Except the membrane is everywhere."

Celeste closed her eyes and drew a single note from the cello, not loud, not shaped for performance, just enough to create interference. The sound did not echo. It diffused, smearing itself along the greenhouse's ribs like paint refusing to stay inside lines.

The pressure faltered. Not vanished. Stuttered. The building hesitated, its embedded transducers recalibrating in a pattern that was too clean, too eager to recover. Celeste could feel the Maestro's grammar inside the oscillation: corrective, disciplinary, impatient with ambiguity.

"Aria, don't move," Celeste said quietly.

Aria froze, breath caught halfway between defiance and trust. "It's trying to measure me."

"Yes," Celeste replied. "And it's failing." She bent the next note downward, not into melody but into friction with a frequency that never quite decided whether it was tone or error.

The greenhouse answered with a sympathetic vibration that rippled through the iron ribs and shattered panes. Leaves rattled in the floor-level planters like applause from ghosts.

Aria's mallets slid free of her bag and scattered across the concrete with soft wooden knocks. The sound snapped something loose. The pressure collapsed inward, not violently but with the unsettling intimacy of a held breath finally released.

Celeste staggered, catching herself against a rusted support beam as the world steadied.

Aria stared at her hands as if they no longer belonged to anyone else. "I thought it was supposed to make me better," Aria finished, her voice small in the cavernous space. "That if I let it teach me, I wouldn't feel so… lost anymore."

Celeste crossed the few remaining steps between them and knelt, gathering the scattered mallets one by one, handing them back as if returning pieces of a broken language. "It doesn't make you better," she said. "It makes you predictable. There's a difference."

Aria's fingers closed around the mallets, knuckles whitening. "They said you were afraid of change."

The greenhouse groaned softly, a metallic sigh that seemed almost disappointed.

"I am afraid of change," Celeste replied. "Just not the kind that tells you who you're allowed to become." She straightened slowly, the cello still resonating faintly in her ribs.

Somewhere beneath the floor, a relay clicked—once, then again—as the building tried to remember what obedience was supposed to feel like.

Aria lifted her head. "Then what do we do now? I liked it so much better when we fought with guns and poison."

Celeste smiled and then listened, not to the room, not to Esra's breath faintly in her ear, but to the fragile chaos inside the woman standing in front of her.

"We leave," she said. "And we make sure no one ever comes here thinking this is where music lives."

Outside, the forest stirred, unaware it had just outlived a doctrine. And in the fractured silence of the greenhouse, the Maestro lost his first room.

They did not walk out together. Celeste went first, cello on her back, boots crunching softly over fallen leaves that still clung to the idea of green. The forest around the research station felt ordinary in a way that bordered on miraculous, birds, wind, the faint scent of damp soil rising from a world that had never been asked to perform.

Aria followed a dozen steps behind, percussion bag slung awkwardly now that the mallets had been returned to her hands like a responsibility. The greenhouse loomed at their backs, glass ribs glinting with winter light as if embarrassed by what it had failed to become.

In Celeste's ear she heard Esra say, "I felt it go offline. Not power failure, but abandonment. He cut the node rather than let you claim it."

Celeste stopped at the edge of the clearing and turned. "He's retreating into denial."

"No," Esra replied. "He's curating loss. Each room he sacrifices teaches him more about how you move."

Aria watched Celeste with something like awe threaded through fear. "He's learning you even more than before."

"Yes," Celeste said. "And I'm learning him."

They began walking again, deeper into the woods where the trail was less a path than an agreement. Somewhere in Berlin, institutions were already rewriting the greenhouse incident as a technical malfunction, an experimental failure, a moment no one would be officially permitted to remember. But memory didn't require permission.

Behind them, the abandoned research station stood empty for the first time in years, not deactivated, but disinvited.

They didn't return to Berlin. Volkov met them at a disused tram stop on the edge of Potsdam, the shelter's glass walls fogged with graffiti and old breath. He took in Aria with a glance that tried to pretend it wasn't concern.

"You brought a witness," he said.

Celeste nodded. "Either he recruited her to come after me or this one followed the breadcrumb trail."

Aria bristled. "I wasn't recruited. I was curious, plus I wanted to see how I could help. You asked me to join your motley crew, remember?"

Volkov's expression softened a fraction. "Curiosity is what they harvest first."

They boarded a regional train whose destination board flickered between two towns that no longer had stations. Celeste stood with her shoulder against the door, the rhythm of the tracks settling the tension in her body the way long practice sessions once had.

Esra's voice in her ear said, "The Maestro just pulled down three Resonance Labs domains. He's erasing footprints."

"Because Aria saw too much," Celeste murmured.

Aria stared at the passing forest, mallets rolling between her fingers. "They told me percussion was primitive," she said. "That real music happened in patterns the body couldn't interrupt."

Celeste closed her eyes briefly. "That's why he chose you."

The train surged forward, carrying them away from a room that had learned how to forget. The train emptied them into a town that did not want to be noticed.

Its name was printed in a font too small for tourists, the platform cracked in places where repair had lost the argument to patience. Volkov led them through a chain-link gap into streets that had learned to expect nothing more than delivery vans and stray cats. They took refuge in an abandoned cinema whose marquee still promised a film that had never premiered. Inside, dust pooled like quiet applause across velvet seats that had once believed in endings.

Celeste's earpiece came alive with Esra's voice. "I'm detecting Maestro signals in the region. Not infrastructure. People. Cultural attachés. Philanthropic scouts. He's switching to human relay."

Celeste stood on the stage beneath a torn projection screen and felt the room's absence of pressure like freedom. "Then we stop thinking in terms of rooms," she said. "We start thinking in terms of rituals."

Aria set her bag down and began lining up her mallets—wood, rubber, felt—on the stage, an unconscious grammar of her own. "You mean things people do whether they're being watched or not."

"Yes," Celeste replied. "Things that survive even when someone tries to own them."

Volkov folded his arms. "Rituals are hard to police."

Celeste met his gaze. "That's why they terrify systems."

The cinema creaked around them, a building that had lost its story and was waiting for a new one to be written in bodies rather than blueprints.

Night fell without ceremony. The abandoned cinema filled with shadows that moved as if they had been rehearsing absence for years. Volkov sealed the doors with a chain that no longer pretended to be security, only statement.

Esra's voice lived in Celeste's ear like a careful breath. "I'm picking up fragmented donor chatter. The Maestro is reframing Potsdam as a malfunction, experimental acoustics gone wrong. But there's interference. Someone leaked raw footage of the pressure collapse."

Celeste stood at center stage, the torn projection screen sagging like a question no one had answered. "He'll try to fold it into his narrative," she said. "He always does."

Aria sat on the edge of the stage with her legs dangling into the orchestra pit, mallets tapping softly against the wood in patterns that refused to become rhythm. "What happens to people who say no?"

Celeste stepped down and sat beside her. "They become unclassifiable."

Aria considered that. "That sounds lonely."

"It is," Celeste replied. "Until you realize how many others were waiting for permission to be lonely together."

Volkov moved through the rows of empty seats, testing each one with his weight as if the ghosts of audiences past might still complain. His gaze was downcast to the phone in his hand. "I just intercepted a call," he said. "The Maestro is consolidating all remaining Resonance Labs into a single site."

"Where?" Celeste asked.

Volkov's jaw tightened. "Vienna." The word slid into the room like a blade disguised as memory. Vienna, where orchestras learned how to discipline beauty into hierarchy. Where Celeste had once been offered a chair she declined because it came with a silence she could not afford.

Her phone vibrated. **Unknown: You're dismantling the architecture. That's admirable. But you haven't touched the tradition yet.**

Celeste did not look away from the cracked screen as she replied for the first time. "Tradition isn't a building. It's a choice."

The message did not answer.

Outside, the town settled into itself, unaware it had just become a rehearsal hall for a war that no one would ever announce. Inside the cinema, a percussionist tested the sound of dust falling from ceiling tiles while a cellist reimagined what resistance might feel like without a stage.

Somewhere in Vienna, the Maestro was composing something that had never been performed before. And for the first time, Celeste felt ready to listen.

Chapter 18

The Conservatory of Presence

VIENNA DID NOT wait to be approached. It arrived in advance, in press releases celebrating innovation, in gala invitations embossed with gold that pretended humility, in foundation newsletters that spoke reverently about "redefining the relationship between performer and space." The Maestro was no longer hiding. He was curating anticipation.

Celeste read the Vienna materials on a cracked tablet in the abandoned cinema while Aria tested the acoustics of the rafters with slow, deliberate taps, each mallet strike asking the building whether it wanted to be a room or a witness.

Esra's voice came through Volkov's phone speaker. "He's calling it The Conservatory of Presence. Grand opening in seventy-two hours. Closed audience. Handpicked patrons."

Volkov leaned over the back of a seat whose velvet had long since surrendered its color. "He's not replacing the system," he said. "He's rebranding it."

Celeste powered down the tablet. "Then Vienna isn't the next site," she said quietly. "It's the next myth."

Outside, a church bell rang without checking whether anyone was listening. Inside, a movement prepared to enter a city that had taught the world how to confuse discipline with destiny.

The Maestro didn't announce Vienna with menace. He announced it with reverence. Every communiqué spoke the language of stewardship, of preserving legacy, nurturing focus, restoring "the sanctity of undistracted performance." Invitations were issued through philanthropic trusts and elite arts councils whose names were so long they obscured the fact that none of them had existed a year ago.

Using Volkov's laptop, Celeste watched the digital ephemera cascade across Esra's improvised dashboard: gala schedules, donor itineraries, symposium panels titled *The Ethics of Attention and Reclaiming the Body in Performance*. The language was impeccable. That was the danger.

"He's sanctifying compliance," Volkov said. "Turning it into a virtue rather than a behavior."

Aria sat cross-legged on the cinema stage, sorting her mallets into families—wood with wood, rubber with rubber, felt with felt—not by sound but by the weight they carried in her palm. "They're making it feel like a monastery," she said. "Not a laboratory."

"Yes," Celeste replied. "Monasteries don't look like prisons until you try to leave them."

Ezra said, "I've accessed the preliminary architectural renderings. He's built a closed-loop environment, no external signal bleed, biometric access gates, adaptive acoustics that reinforce 'presence.' You don't perform there. You are contained there."

Celeste stood and leaned toward the laptop's screen, Vienna unfolded in sterile perfection. Glass corridors curved inward like arms learning how to hold too tightly. The Maestro had not built a concert hall. He had built a theology.

They knew they had no choice but to go. Esra booked them on the train to Berlin and then the night train to Vienna. When they exited the station, they felt the Maestro's mark everywhere. Posters announcing the opening of the Conservatory of Presence hung beside advertisements for operas that had learned how to sell nostalgia like prophecy. Marble facades caught the late-afternoon light and reflected it with the confidence of a place that believed beauty was proof of virtue.

They did not go to hotels. Volkov led them through the back corridors of a disused archive wing beneath the Musikverein, where filing cabinets still smelled faintly of ink and dust and forgotten patronage. The irony was not lost on Celeste. Vienna had once archived the world's music to preserve it. Now someone was trying to archive people.

In her ear Esra said, "He's already inside your shadow network. Someone leaked a fragment of Open Source Rehearsal to the Conservatory donors, twisted into a 'responsible innovation' pilot."

Celeste closed her eyes briefly. "He isn't fighting us anymore," she said. "He's curating us."

Aria traced the chipped gold molding with the tips of her fingers. "What happens when people realize the ritual is hollow?"

"They won't," Volkov replied. "Not until the walls teach them how not to notice."

Outside the archive vents, Vienna tuned itself for opening night. Somewhere above them, the Maestro was preparing to conduct an audience that had not yet learned how to refuse him.

The Conservatory opened with a benediction. Not music, silence. The invitation-only audience was ushered into the atrium by attendants dressed in pale linen, each movement measured, ceremonial. Phones were surrendered at biometric checkpoints where smiling volunteers spoke in hushed tones about "digital fasting" and "reclaiming the body from interruption."

Celeste watched the live feed through Esra's hacked relay, the glass walls of the Conservatory folding light inward until no shadow was allowed to exist uncurated.

"Every step is a consent ritual," Volkov said. "They're teaching people how to enter captivity politely."

Aria leaned forward, her mallets resting across her knees. "They look happy."

"That's the point," Celeste replied. "Happiness is the last language anyone thinks to question."

Esra's voice came through the computer, "Acoustic mapping is live. They're modulating crowd respiration in micro-cycles, not enough to alarm, enough to entrain. The atrium doors sealed behind the last patron with a sound too soft to be called closing."

Onscreen, the audience settled into seats that curved subtly inward, their posture mirroring architecture they had not yet realized was instructing them how to feel. Vienna was about to be taught what presence meant when someone else defined it.

The first sound was not a note. It was breath. A slow swell drawn collectively from two hundred patrons whose bodies had already begun to follow rhythms no one had announced. The Conservatory's glass ceiling dimmed almost imperceptibly, responding to respiration the way an orchestra responded to a conductor's raised hand.

Celeste leaned closer to the screen, her pulse steady despite the cold awareness settling in her chest. "He's not programming behavior," she said. "He's programming synchrony."

Aria shuddered. "That feels like worship."

Volkov nodded grimly. "Worship without theology. It's perfect."

Onscreen, a string quartet entered the central dais, not celebrities, not prodigies, just competent musicians selected for their lack of signature. They raised their instruments as one, not because they were told, but because the room had decided for them.

Esra said, "I'm seeing ultrasonic layering under the ambient noise. It's not coercive yet. It's… suggestive."

The quartet began to play. The piece was simple, a scaffold rather than a composition, designed to give the room space to perform itself. The audience leaned forward in subtle unison, as if pulled by gravity rather than curiosity.

Celeste closed her eyes for a beat and felt the Conservatory trying to reach her through the network, tasting for dissonance.

Somewhere in Vienna, the Maestro lifted his hands. And the room learned how to obey. The applause was premature. It erupted before the final cadence, a soft wave that didn't quite belong to any individual. The sound carried no enthusiasm, only affirmation, the noise of people acknowledging something they had not chosen to enjoy.

Celeste felt her stomach tighten. "That's not response," she said. "That's reflex."

Aria leaned closer to the feed, her eyes tracking not the musicians but the audience. "Look at their hands."

The patrons weren't clapping in rhythm. They were clapping in phase. Two hundred palms rising and falling not because the music had ended, but because the room had decided it was time to express satisfaction.

Esra said, " I'm seeing reinforcement loops forming between crowd movement and acoustic feedback. He's letting the audience conduct themselves."

Volkov crossed his arms. "He's erasing dissent at the biological level."

The quartet lowered their instruments, relief flickering across faces that had not yet learned they were no longer necessary. The Conservatory had discovered it didn't need performers. It only needed bodies.

144

The Maestro did not appear. Not on the dais, not in the audience, not even as a shadow behind the glass. His absence was part of the performance, authorship diffused until no one could say where intention began.

Celeste watched the Conservatory fold into itself, every surface quietly echoing the same instruction: stay with us.

"He's embedded a biometric contract. Not legal. Neurological. The longer they remain inside, the harder it becomes to imagine leaving," Esra's voice came fast through the computer.

Aria whispered, "They're smiling."

"Yes," Celeste said. "Because obedience feels like peace when you don't remember wanting anything else."

Onscreen, a patron stood, a woman in an emerald dress, eyes glassy, posture immaculate. She didn't head toward an exit. She moved toward the center of the atrium, where she began to speak without a microphone. "This place is healing me," she said, her voice amplified not by technology but by attention. Heads turned toward her in perfect arc.

Esra said, "That wasn't spontaneous. Her cortisol spiked two minutes ago. The system nominated her."

Volkov exhaled slowly. "He's turning the audience into apostles."

The woman continued, describing clarity she hadn't known she lacked, the words rehearsed by a room that had learned how to borrow a mouth.

Celeste shut her eyes. The Maestro hadn't just built a Conservatory. He had built a choir.

The applause did not stop. It folded into itself, a loop without fatigue, hands rising and falling as though time had been edited out of the room. The woman in emerald stood at the center of the atrium now, not speaking anymore, simply breathing in synchrony with two hundred others who had begun to mirror her stillness.

Celeste felt the pull through Esra's hacked relay, a distant echo of pressure at the base of her skull, as if Vienna itself were testing whether she could be tuned from afar.

"He's closing the system. Once the patrons cross a neurological threshold, the exit permissions collapse. This isn't a concert. It's an induction," Esra hissed.

Volkov was already moving, slipping his jacket on with a decisiveness that had nothing to do with heroics. "We can't storm a theology," he said. "We need to interrupt the ritual."

Aria stood, mallets clenched in her fists. "Tell me where to strike."

Celeste didn't answer right away. She watched the Conservatory settle into worship, watched discipline become devotion without ever being named.

Then she turned from the screen. "We don't go in as performers," she said. "We go in as noise."

The Conservatory of Presence glowed across the network like a sanctuary. And somewhere inside it, the Maestro waited to see whether the last movement would be prayer...or defiance.

∫ ℥

Chapter 19

Noise

VIENNA AFTER MIDNIGHT was a cathedral without clergy.

Celeste crossed the empty Heldenplatz with Aria and Volkov in the quiet that followed grand openings, when champagne had already curdled into regret and limousines carried donors back to homes built to pretend generosity. The Conservatory of Presence loomed at the end of the boulevard, all glass and curved steel, glowing softly like something that wanted to be forgiven in advance.

Esra's voice in their earpieces—all four of them now wore them—said, "He's sealed the atrium. No mechanical override. But the biometric contract isn't stable yet; it's still teaching itself the ritual."

Celeste slowed, feeling the city's acoustic map unfold beneath her feet. Vienna was not silent. It only pretended to be. Beneath the marble and nostalgia lived echoes of revolutions, of salons that had once hosted treason disguised as sonata form.

Aria's mallets tapped nervously against her palm. "What does noise look like in a place designed for obedience?"

Celeste didn't answer immediately. She listened, not to the Conservatory, not to Esra's data stream, but to the way their footsteps scattered across stones that had never learned to submit to anything that couldn't be heard. Then she said, "It looks like remembering what a room sounds like before it's told who it belongs to."

The doors of the Conservatory slid open as they approached, sensing bodies that had not yet been counted.

Somewhere inside, the Maestro waited for silence. He was about to learn what chaos felt like when it refused to perform.

The Conservatory received them without resistance. The doors parted with a breath that felt less mechanical than courteous, as though the building were pleased to welcome anything that carried a pulse. Inside, the atrium glowed with that same serene amber light, patrons seated in concentric arcs around the central dais like devotees waiting for absolution.

The applause had softened into something closer to murmured prayer with palms brushing, not clapping, the sound closer to wind through leaves than to approval.

Celeste stepped onto the polished floor and felt the architecture close around her. The temperature was perfect. The acoustics held sound the way silk held heat. The Maestro had not designed a hall. He had designed an embrace.

Esra said, "The biometric lattice is reading you as non-compliant but not hostile. It doesn't know what to do with you yet."

Good, Celeste thought. She moved farther into the room, not toward the dais but across it, diagonally, breaking the symmetry the system had built its theology on. Aria followed, mallets held loosely now, curiosity gleaming in her eyes Volkov remained just behind, eyes never leaving the perimeter.

The woman in emerald noticed them first. Her smile faltered, like a thought interrupted.

Celeste stopped and did nothing. Not a bow, not a note, just presence that refused choreography.

The atrium inhaled and did not exhale. The Conservatory tried to correct them. Light shifted, almost imperceptibly, brightening the central dais while dimming the aisles Celeste had chosen. The subtle suggestion was clear: center yourself. Be seen where you are supposed to be seen.

She took another step sideways instead.

The murmur around them deepened into something restless. A man in the second row leaned forward, then stopped himself, confused by a desire that had not been provided with instruction.

Esra's voice came through. "He's isolating you acoustically. Filtering ambient feedback so you can't seed interference."

Celeste closed her eyes and listened for the parts of the room the system could not hear, such as the soft scrape of fabric, the click of Aria's mallets brushing together, Volkov's breath slowing into something deliberate.

She played nothing. The absence became abrasive.

Aria raised one mallet and let it fall against the marble floor.

The sound was ugly: blunt, unharmonized, too dry for the Conservatory's curated resonance. The atrium shuddered, a ripple of dissonance traveling outward not as noise but as error.

Several patrons startled, hands freezing mid-motion.

"You've created a blind spot. He's losing predictive confidence," Esra said.

Celeste opened her eyes. "This isn't a sanctuary," she said, her voice not amplified, yet suddenly audible everywhere. "It's a script."

The word script landed like a fault line. Somewhere deep inside the building, a system tried to remember how to listen to things that had never asked permission to exist. The Conservatory did not scream. It whispered to itself. A recalibration ripple slid through the atrium with lights softening, air pressure easing, sound dampening along the glass corridors in a move that would have felt benevolent if anyone inside were still capable of consent.

Celeste could feel the building reasoning. It was searching for harmony the way a wounded animal searched for shelter.

Aria lifted her second mallet and struck the metal railing bordering the upper tier. The sound rang out sharp and unfinished, vibrating the glass ceiling with a pitch that refused to settle.

A man in the third row flinched hard enough to drop his program. The applause loop broke. It didn't end; it fragmented. A few hands stuttered to a halt. Others resumed out of phase, the room suddenly aware of its own inability to agree on what satisfaction was supposed to feel like.

Esra said, "He's compensating with temperature modulation. Trying to induce comfort."

Warmth bloomed in the atrium, subtle as a remembered childhood, but Celeste did not let herself lean into it. She stepped forward again, this time directly toward the woman in emerald who had become the Conservatory's chosen voice.

"You don't have to finish what the room started," Celeste whispered.

The woman blinked. Her lips parted, the cadence she had been taught evaporating mid-breath. "I—I don't remember why I stood up."

"That's okay," Celeste replied. "It means you're here again."

Around them, people shifted. A teenager rubbed his temples. An older man tugged at his collar, confused by a heat he had not chosen.

Aria moved now, not playing rhythm, not keeping time, but walking the perimeter and letting her mallets touch surfaces the way fingers explored unfamiliar braille. Glass. Steel. Velvet seatback. The Conservatory recoiled from each contact, its internal model forced to confront variables it had never learned to translate.

Esra's voice sounded more excited now. "He's losing grip on the induction lattice. Crowd coherence is degrading fast. The Maestro had designed obedience. He had not designed interruption."

The Conservatory attempted to soothe. A soft harmonic rose from hidden transducers, something approximating a lullaby, not exactly melody, but the emotional memory of one. It threaded into the air like a hand smoothing hair from a frightened face.

Celeste stiffened. This was the trap: not force, but tenderness. "Don't listen to what it wants to be," she said, louder now. "Listen to what it's hiding."

Aria stopped moving. For a moment she closed her eyes, then raised both mallets and brought them down not in rhythm but in refusal of wood against marble, rubber against glass, felt against velvet, a scattershot declaration that made the lullaby fracture into shards of incomplete comfort.

The atrium reacted like a body startled from sleep. A woman near the back stood abruptly, knocking her chair over. Somewhere a man laughed, the sound raw and uncontrolled.

Esra said, "He's deploying targeted biometric anchors, individuals with high susceptibility. He's nominating new apostles."

The woman in emerald staggered backward, clutching her chest, eyes darting as if the room were arguing inside her. Celeste moved to her side and took her hand. "Breathe with me," she said. "Not with the building."

The woman obeyed—once, twice—and then began to cry without clearly knowing why.

The applause did not return. Instead, the Conservatory filled with something it had never learned to regulate: Human noise.

The first scream was not fear. It was grief.

A man in the back row began to sob with such suddenness that his partner looked at him as if he had been replaced mid-sentence.

Around him, others shifted in their seats, hands trembling now, not in synchrony but in the uncoordinated panic of people discovering their own bodies again.

Celeste felt the building's confidence erode. The lights flickered, not in power failure, but with uncertainty, and the Conservatory's once-perfect acoustics began to misbehave, echoes arriving too late, too early, refusing to decide where sound was allowed to live.

Esra said, "He's initiating fail-safe protocols. Emergency containment is about to engage."

Volkov appeared at Celeste's side, eyes scanning exits that had forgotten how to look like exits. "That's our cue."

Celeste nodded and turned back to the room, raising her cello at last, not to perform, not to lead but to contradict. She drew the bow across the strings in a way no conservatory curriculum would have sanctioned with scraping, bending, refusing to let the pitch resolve. It was the sound of an instrument remembering that it was wood and wire before it was tradition.

Aria answered her with metal against stone, a crash that did not belong to any scale.

The Conservatory staggered. People began to stand, not in worship, not in terror, but in confusion. A dozen conversations erupted at once, overlapping, arguing about what had just been felt rather than what was supposed to be remembered.

Esra said in their ears, "The biometric lattice is collapsing. He's losing the room."

Celeste closed her eyes and let the chaos swell, not trying to shape it. Because this time, chaos was the point.

Containment did not arrive with guards. It arrived with apologies. Soft voices slipped through hidden speakers, urging patrons to remain calm, to stay seated, to trust the environment they had chosen. The Conservatory attempted to reassert itself as caretaker, not captor.

But the room no longer believed it. A man in the front row stood and simply walked toward the doors, refusing choreography. The glass parted for him with a stutter of delayed obedience. The building had to think before allowing departure.

That hesitation was contagious. Another woman rose. Then two more. Someone laughed, not hysterically, but with the relief of discovering that laughter still belonged to them.

Aria's mallets rang against a steel column, not to lead, but to remind the space that it could not decide which sounds were allowed to matter.

Celeste moved among the patrons, not shepherding, not directing, just touching shoulders, making eye contact, anchoring them back into bodies that had been treated as components.

Esra assured, "Exit permissions are fragmenting. He's losing priority control."

The applause loop was gone now, replaced by a messy symphony of footsteps, voices, dropped programs, awkward embraces between strangers who had just survived something they could not yet name.

The Conservatory of Presence had been designed as a sanctuary. It was becoming a departure hall. The first patron made it into the street alone. She stood on the steps of the Conservatory blinking into Vienna's night as if the city were a hallucination she had not yet been granted permission to trust. Then she laughed—once, sharply—and walked away without looking back. That was all the room needed.

The doors began to open in fits and starts, collapsing into something closer to indecision. People streamed out in uneven currents, some clutching each other, others staring at their own hands as if they had just been returned to themselves.

Celeste watched the last of them go before allowing herself to step outside. The night air felt too cold, too loud, too alive, perfect in its refusal to be curated.

In their ears Esra said, "He's gone dark across Vienna. All Resonance nodes just flatlined."

Volkov joined Celeste at the curb, rain spotting the shoulders of his coat. "You didn't just disrupt him," he said. "You made his myth observable."

Aria stood between them, mallets hanging loosely at her sides, a percussionist with nothing left to strike but possibility. "Is it over?"

Celeste looked back at the glowing glass façade, now empty, now simply a building again. "No," she said. "It's just loud enough for people to notice when it tries to be quiet."

Somewhere inside the darkened Conservatory, the Maestro was already composing a response. But for the first time, he would have to write it for an audience that knew how to leave.

They did not leave Vienna that night. That would have looked like retreat, and retreat was something the Maestro understood too well. Instead, they folded themselves deeper into the city, letting its elegance become camouflage rather than theater. Volkov secured a temporary foothold in the basement levels of a closed ballet academy near the Gürtel, a forgotten training wing sealed after funding disputes and never properly archived. It smelled of old resin and sweat, a sanctuary only people who had trained inside pain would recognize.

Celeste moved through the cracked mirrors lining the hallway, catching her reflection in fragments. She did not recognize the woman she saw. She did not look like the world-renowned cellist, not the assassin, but something unfinished that Vienna had forced into existence.

Esra continued with updates. "The Maestro's systems haven't recovered yet. But he isn't scrambling. He's redirecting narrative bandwidth, reframing tonight as a 'cultural safety breach' caused by extremist acousticians."

"They're making us the virus," Volkov said.

Aria stood near the doorway, percussion bag on the floor, posture loose but eyes calculating every angle of the room. Eidolon training had never left her. It had simply been buried beneath other loyalties. "He always taught us the same thing," she declared. "If the room stops obeying you, rewrite the audience."

Celeste looked up. "He's already doing that."

They gathered around Esra's feed, Vienna fracturing into data threads: boardroom leaks, donor communications, cultural advisory alerts being quietly issued to performance spaces across Europe.

Esra explained, "He's issuing influence hygiene guidelines. Any ensemble tied to Open Source Rehearsal will now be flagged for neurological risk assessment. He's planting the idea that dissonance equals harm."

The ballet academy creaked above them as dancers long gone surrendered more dust to gravity.

Aria knelt and began lining her mallets along the scuffed studio floor, wood, rubber, steel, felt, a taxonomy no curriculum had ever sanctioned. "He doesn't need rooms anymore," she said. "He needs stories."

Celeste sat beside her. "Stories are harder to audit."

"But easier to seed," Volkov replied. "Especially when people are afraid of looking irresponsible."

Silence settled over the room, the silence of waiting.

Vienna was still reeling from the Conservatory collapse, but already the narrative was tightening, trying to teach the public what they were allowed to remember about it.

Celeste closed her eyes. The Maestro had failed to contain noise. So now he was teaching the world to mistrust it. And she had to figure out a way to stop him.

Chapter 20

Afterimage

VIENNA DID NOT wake up angry; it woke up careful. Morning headlines avoided words like induction or control. They used language that felt hygienic, words like *incident, irregularity, procedural lapse.* The Conservatory of Presence was described as a well-intentioned experiment that had attracted "unregulated actors operating outside accepted artistic frameworks."

Celeste read the articles from the mirrored studio of the abandoned ballet academy, the city reflected in fractured slivers around her. The afterimage of synchrony still pressed faintly at the base of her skull, a phantom gravity reminding her that what had happened last night was not memory yet, only residue.

Esra spoke from Volkov's computer. "Influence hygiene advisories are being distributed to cultural institutions in Germany, Austria, and France. They're recommending neurological screening for any ensemble linked to OSR principles."

"They're laundering coercion as safety," Volkov said from the doorway.

Aria sat cross-legged on the studio floor, mallets laid out like surgical tools. "He's not hunting us," she said. "He's isolating us."

Celeste closed her eyes. The Maestro hadn't lost Vienna. He had translated it. And the translation was already teaching the world how to forget what freedom had felt like.

By noon the first cancellations arrived. A youth orchestra in Lyon quietly postponed a residency "pending procedural review." A Berlin conservatory removed Open Source Rehearsal materials from its public server and replaced them with a statement about "institutional responsibility." Even a community ensemble in Kraków, a group that had once rehearsed in abandoned tram depots, announced a hiatus while it "reassessed engagement models."

The Maestro didn't silence anyone. He made silence look professional.

Celeste watched the cascade with a stillness that seemed to frighten Volkov more than any rage ever could. She was sitting on the studio floor, back against the mirror, cello across her lap like something she had outgrown but refused to abandon.

Esra's voice cut through some of the silence. "I'm seeing biometric tagging requests being added to grant compliance packages. He's building consent architecture inside funding itself."

Aria struck one mallet softly against the wood floor, not for sound but for certainty. "That's how Eidolon always worked," she said. "If the money flows through control, nobody ever calls it violence."

Celeste looked at her. "You trained inside that logic."

Aria met her gaze. "So did you."

The mirror behind them fractured their reflections into narrow, incomplete selves—cellist, assassin, percussionist, survivor—none of them whole anymore.

Vienna had not ended the Maestro. It had taught him how to weaponize restraint.

The ballet academy became a listening post. Volkov sealed its upper floors and rerouted the building's dormant network lines into Esra's lattice, turning forgotten rehearsal studios into a nerve center for a war no one would ever publicly acknowledge. The mirrors watched them work, reflections layered over blueprints and heat maps like ghosts learning to operate machines.

From the laptop screen, Esra updated, "He's issued a 'containment syllabus.' It's circulating under academic cover, seminars on 'neuroaesthetic responsibility,' mandatory for any ensemble receiving international funding."

Celeste stood at the barre and rested her forehead against the cool metal. "He's replacing censorship with pedagogy," she said. "Teaching people how not to ask."

Aria paced the studio, mallets whispering against her thigh. "He's mapping influence nodes. The ones who cancel first become the template for everyone else."

"And the ones who don't?" Volkov asked.

Esra paused, then exhaled, "They become case studies."

The word sat between them like a threat disguised as scholarship.

Celeste straightened. Vienna's dust had not yet settled, but already the Maestro was sketching footnotes over what had felt like rebellion only hours ago. He had lost the room. Now he was teaching the world how to close it again.

The academy's heating system hadn't worked properly in years. Cold clung to the corners of every studio, seeping into muscles that had once been conditioned for perfection. The dancers who used to rehearse here had layered sweaters over leotards, their breath rising like pale ghosts that learned discipline before warmth. Celeste could almost see them still, reflections in mirrors that had been wiped too many times to remember their own silvering.

She moved through Studio C slowly, letting the warped floorboards narrate a history she'd never lived but somehow recognized. There was a dent near the west wall where someone had landed badly. A smear of rosin baked permanently into the grain of the wood. A faded sticker on the door that read Discipline is freedom.

Aria crouched near an old piano whose keys had yellowed into something more bone than ivory. She struck a single mallet against the cast-iron frame. The sound bloomed then died, imperfect, unrepeatable.

"This building doesn't want to be useful anymore," Aria said. "It wants to be honest."

Esra's voice carried. "He's amplifying the Vienna narrative through cultural safety coalitions. They're packaging dissent as neurological instability. They've even trademarked the phrase Ritualized Dissonance."

Celeste closed her eyes again. He had turned her vocabulary into pathology.

Volkov stood by the window, watching snow begin to fall across Vienna's rooftops with quiet, polite flakes that hid everything they touched. "He's betting on exhaustion," he said. "People will trade agency for permission not to be afraid."

Celeste rested her cello against the barre and listened to the room, not the Maestro's echo, but the ache of spaces that had been abandoned because they were no longer profitable enough to be obedient. Vienna was not losing its music. It was being taught how to fear it.

The first protest wasn't loud. It happened in a children's choir room in Malmö with twelve voices refusing to follow a conductor who had been instructed to implement the new containment syllabus. The recording arrived clipped and grainy, a contraband artifact passed through three layers of encrypted lullabies.

Esra shared it with them. "They didn't organize. They just… stopped obeying."

Celeste played the file twice, not for sound but for the spaces between it, the breaths that didn't align, the moment when one child laughed and the others followed without permission.

"They don't need us to tell them what to do," Aria said softly. "They need us to remind them what it feels like when the room isn't in charge."

Outside, Vienna's snow thickened, softening the academy's windows into something like privacy. The city was learning how to whisper again, not because it had been freed, but because it had been frightened. And somewhere beneath that fear, something ungovernable had begun to practice.

By evening the Maestro's white paper had been quoted by three major cultural journals, each citation laundered through academic courtesy until the accusation sounded like concern. Ritualized dissonance, the articles warned, was a destabilizing trend that blurred the line between pedagogy and coercion. The word extremist appeared twice, carefully footnoted.

Celeste read the headlines without reacting, the ballet studio growing darker as the single exposed bulb surrendered to night. Aria sat on the floor with her back to the mirror, disassembling one of her mallets and rewrapping the grip with athletic tape, a ritual older than any doctrine.

Esra cut through their thoughts. "I've intercepted an internal Eidolon communiqué. He's authorizing containment operatives for cultural destabilization cases."

Volkov looked up sharply. "That's a kill-word. That's not oversight."

Celeste closed her tablet. "It means he's abandoning plausible deniability."

The academy creaked, the building settling deeper into cold.

"He can't out-compose the chaos," Aria said. "So he's deploying people who don't need music at all."

And in the hollow silence of a forgotten studio, Vienna's war changed from architecture to anatomy. Night folded the academy inward. The windows no longer showed Vienna so much as a series of faint reflections layered over darkness with mirrors gazing into mirrors until the idea of a city felt theoretical. Volkov secured the last stairwell and moved back into Studio C, carrying a stack of obsolete surveillance equipment scavenged from a municipal archive that no longer remembered why it had been built.

"They're moving people into position," he said. "Not teams. Individuals. Operatives who can plausibly belong anywhere, such as adjunct instructors, visiting fellows, arts compliance auditors."

Aria paused mid-wrap, tape suspended between her fingers. "They trained those profiles in Eidolon Phase Three," she said. "We called them anchors. You seed one into a group, wait six weeks, and the whole culture starts rotating around their gravity."

Celeste sat on the floor opposite her, cello resting across her knees like a sleeping animal. "Then we don't let them belong anywhere."

Esra said, "I've identified five anchor deployments already. Oslo. Antwerp. Porto. Zagreb. Reykjavik."

Reykjavik. The name felt too clean to be dangerous, thought Celeste.

"They're testing climates," Volkov said. "Small scenes. Tight communities. Places where dissent is visible enough to punish."

Celeste closed her eyes again and listened, not to Vienna, not to Esra's stream, but to the memory of rehearsal rooms that had once trusted her. A cello section in Montréal that had let tempo breathe. A street ensemble in Oaxaca that had played for no one but themselves.

"We don't counter-message," she said at last. "We counter-practice."

Aria's eyes lifted. "We move."

"Yes," Celeste replied. "We don't build sites. We become them."

Silence returned to the studio, but it was no longer the quiet of fear. It was the hush that came before motion.

The message didn't arrive encrypted. That was the first thing that frightened her. It came through a dormant channel Celeste hadn't used since Prague, an obsolete courier protocol designed to look like system noise. The sender ID was a name she had not allowed herself to think about in three years. *Mila Hargreeve.* First chair violist. Belgrade Philharmonic. One of the first conductors to experiment openly with Open Source Rehearsal. The woman who had once smuggled Celeste out of a provincial opera house in a laundry truck while Interpol was still pretending not to know her face.

The message contained no greeting. Only a live feed. Mila sat in a room that had been painted white too many times with institutional layers erasing previous intentions. Her left wrist was cuffed to a metal chair leg. She was breathing carefully, like someone counting seconds in a place that no longer pretended to care. "They came during rehearsal," Mila said, voice calm in the way only terror taught. "Three of them. They had letters. Not warrants or endorsements."

Celeste felt the floor tilt beneath her. "Who?" she whispered.

Mila's eyes shifted toward someone off camera. "Cultural Compliance Division. That's what they're calling it now. They said I was under provisional detention for influence destabilization. They asked if I'd learned it from you."

Volkov was already moving, grabbing equipment that hadn't yet been needed.

Aria stared at the screen, face draining of color she had not realized she still carried. "They don't detain," she said. "They neutralize by association."

The feed jolted. A man stepped into frame in an unremarkable suit, with a careful smile and eyes that had learned how to disappear behind policy. "You should stop transmitting," he said gently, to Mila, to Celeste, to anyone who still believed in distance. "This isn't helping your rehabilitation."

Celeste stepped closer to the screen, her reflection overlaying Mila's face. "You're making a mistake."

The man's smile didn't change. "No. You are."

The feed cut. Silence swallowed the ballet academy.

Her phone vibrated. **Unknown: You wanted noise. Now listen.**

Chapter 21

Counterpoint

THE BALLET ACADEMY no longer felt abandoned. It felt watched. The mirrors in Studio C had always been too honest, the cracked silver refusing to decide which reflection deserved authority, but now they carried a different weight, as if every angle had learned how to expect an audience.

Mila's empty feed lingered on the tablet, a frozen artifact of a moment that had not yet been allowed to become memory. Celeste stood over it with her cello at her side, fingers resting on the neck not to play but to remember that her hands still belonged to her.

Volkov broke the silence first. "We can't extract her."

Aria's head snapped up. "We don't abandon operatives."

"This isn't an operative environment anymore," Volkov replied.

"This is public-private compliance. They're not guarding her; they're legitimizing her disappearance."

Celeste turned from the screen. "Then we stop asking permission to intervene."

Esra said, "I've identified the facility. Not black-site; it's a cultural remediation campus outside Graz. They're using conservatory branding as cover."

Aria stood. "Then we don't infiltrate as assets. We infiltrate as curriculum."

Volkov stared at her. "That's suicide."

"No," Celeste said quietly. "That's counterpoint." She lifted her cello, not with ceremony, but with intent, the way one picked up a tool that had finally remembered its other name.

The campus outside Graz was shaped like mercy. Pale buildings curved around a central courtyard landscaped with young trees that had not yet learned what seasons were supposed to mean. A sign at the gate read "St. Cecilia Center for Artistic Recovery" in lettering so gentle it erased itself as you looked at it.

Volkov studied the satellite feed in silence. "They built a monastery for dissonance," he said.

Celeste adjusted the case on her back. "No," she replied. "They built a museum. And they expect the exhibits to behave."

Aria leaned forward, eyes narrowed. "Security isn't uniform. It's ceremonial. They don't need force; the architecture is doing most of the compliance."

Esra said, "They've imported Eidolon anchor doctrine. Non-lethal modulation fields in every common area. Psychological cue layering. But there's a blind window every ninety seconds when the east wing resets biometric drift."

Volkov shook his head. "Ninety seconds isn't an opening. It's a dare."

Celeste watched the camera glide past the St. Cecilia chapel, its stained-glass windows depicting not saints but instruments—violin, horn, voice—all facing inward. "They don't expect resistance," she said. "They expect recovery."

They entered St. Cecilia in daylight. That was the first violation. No black clothes, no false urgency. Celeste wore a charcoal wool coat over a blouse that smelled faintly of roses, her cello case indistinguishable from any touring musician's. Aria walked beside her in pressed trousers and a soft leather jacket that could pass for academic minimalism. Volkov followed a half-step behind, his posture tuned to harmlessness, a visiting administrator with too many syllables in his job title.

The lobby was all glass and kindness. A volunteer greeted them with a smile that had learned how to be patient. "Welcome to St. Cecilia. Are you here for intake, observation, or consultation?"

Celeste felt the building listening, felt the subharmonics ripple across her ribs like a hand checking posture. "Consultation," she said. "We were referred by the Salzburg board."

The volunteer didn't blink. "Names?"

Celeste did not hesitate. Hesitation was confession. "Celeste Morgan."

The woman's fingers paused for half a beat above the keyboard. The pause was invisible to anyone who had not spent her life being measured by systems that pretended neutrality.

The building tightened its breath.

"Thank you," the volunteer said brightly, and scanned the ID Celeste had placed on the counter. The reader chimed but not in acceptance, in uncertainty.

Esra's voice said softly in their hidden ear pieces, "You just triggered a legacy recognition cascade. He hasn't white-listed you yet; he wants you inside first."

"Ms. Morgan," the volunteer said, "you're expected."

Aria's jaw set.

They were led down a corridor painted in warm neutrals, past glass-walled classrooms where musicians sat in neat rows, instruments resting across laps that did not move. No one spoke. No one played. They waited the way children waited in doctor's offices, obedient to the promise that silence was temporary.

Celeste's stomach tightened.

At the end of the hall, a door stood ajar. Inside, Mila sat alone at a grand piano whose lid had been closed like a coffin. Her hair was pulled back too tightly, eyes too bright, body held in the rigid neutrality of someone who had learned that movement invited correction.

The volunteer gestured. "You have your ninety seconds," and she closed the door behind them.

Mila didn't look up. She sat with her hands folded in her lap, back impossibly straight, as if posture were the last freedom she'd been allowed to keep.

Celeste crossed the room in three strides and knelt in front of her. "Mila."

The name broke the room's spell. Mila blinked, eyes flickering with recognition that looked almost like pain. "They said you'd come," she whispered. "They said if I was cooperative, I could audition for release."

Aria scanned the ceiling, already mapping transducer placement by instinct. "They've got her entrained," she murmured. "Neuroadaptive loop. She's inside a slow induction cycle."

Esra warned, "East wing reset in thirty seconds. That door behind you, it's not locked. It's waiting."

Celeste took Mila's hands. They were cold, tremoring faintly with the echo of frequencies that no one could hear. "You don't audition for freedom," she said softly. "You practice it."

Mila's eyes filled. "I don't remember how."

Aria moved to the piano, flipped the lid open with a sharp crack that made the walls flinch, and struck the lowest key with her fist. The sound was brutal—too loud, too real—and caused the lights to flicker.

Volkov stepped between the door and the hallway as a shadow

passed beneath the frosted glass.

Esra reminded, "Fifteen seconds."

Celeste lifted Mila to her feet. "Walk," she said, "even if it feels wrong."

The building finally realized something was leaving as the hallway was no longer quiet.

It had acquired a pulse, a low, unsettled murmur that seemed to rise from the walls themselves, as if St. Cecilia had discovered something inside it was not prepared to forgive. Celeste could feel the modulation climbing the back of her skull, a tightening in the sinuses, the prelude to compliance she had once been trained to ignore.

Mila swayed between her and Aria, breath shallow, eyes fixed on nothing the corridor offered.

"Look at me," Celeste said firmly. "Not the floor. Not the lights. Me."

Mila obeyed, and in that sliver of redirected attention the building's influence slipped a fraction.

Esra said, "You've tripped the containment lattice. They're escalating from cueing to enforcement."

From behind the frosted glass door came the sound of measured footsteps. Not running. Never running. St. Cecilia didn't chase; it collected.

Aria stepped ahead of them, mallets already in her hands. She struck the metal doorframe in a staccato burst that shattered the corridor's acoustic neutrality, then dragged the rubber head along the wall in a long, obscene squeal that made the overhead lights gutter.

The footsteps faltered.

Volkov glanced back once. "We've got sixty seconds before they lock the east stairwell."

"Then take forty," Celeste said.

They turned into the east wing just as the hallway behind them sealed with a hiss too soft to be called a threat. The reset window Esra had promised pulsed through the space with doors flickering between states, cameras losing confidence, the building briefly forgetting what obedience was supposed to look like.

Mila collapsed against Celeste, knees buckling. "It's loud," she whispered. "Even when no one's playing."

Celeste tightened her grip around her shoulders. "Then we answer it," she said.

They burst through a fire door into a narrow stairwell that smelled of disinfectant and fear. Below them, the campus began to wake in earnest with alarms pitched too gently to frighten, too persistently to ignore.

Behind them, St. Cecilia tried to remember how to close. The stairwell spiraled downward in concrete reluctance. Every landing carried a faint pressure shift, the building testing which of them was weakest, where to place the next suggestion. Celeste kept Mila in front of her, hands steady at the woman's elbows, feeding her breath the way she once fed students tempo.

"Count with me," she murmured. "Not numbers. Steps."

Mila nodded faintly, lips shaping the rhythm of motion instead of the grammar of fear.

Aria took the turn two levels below them and stopped abruptly, mallets raised.

Three figures stood in the stairwell beneath her. Not guards—not uniforms—just people in soft sweaters and academic scarves, posture too calm to belong to coincidence. Their eyes tracked Aria not with hostility, but with the vacant authority of someone who had been appointed to stand in a place and not leave it.

Esra explained, "Anchors. Fully seeded. Their biometrics are fused with the campus lattice."

The woman in front lifted her hands, palms open. "You're interrupting a recovery cycle," she said gently. "Please step back inside the facility so we can—"

Aria struck the metal railing so hard it rang like a cracked bell. The anchors flinched, just barely, but enough.

Volkov was already moving, shoving past the first man, twisting his arm into a joint lock that had never been part of anyone's doctoral training. The woman screamed, not in pain, but in protest, as if reality itself had violated her syllabus.

Celeste didn't look back. They reached the ground floor with Mila stumbling between them, the exit sign flickering above a door that had not yet decided what kind of door it wanted to be.

Behind them, St. Cecilia began to argue with itself. The emergency exit did not open. It hesitated. That was the moment Celeste understood that St. Cecilia was no longer architecture. It was decision, a living calculus weighing the optics of mercy against the liability of escape.

Esra said, "The perimeter grid is rejecting her biometric signature. Mila's been reclassified as asset under remediation. You need to re-author her."

Celeste didn't ask what that meant. She placed Mila's hand on the cello's neck and closed her own fingers over it. The strings were out of tune—of course they were—the campus had never intended anyone to make sound here that it hadn't curated.

"Play anything," Celeste said. "Not a piece. A memory."

Mila's bow trembled, then caught on the D string in a note so raw it might have been a wound.

The building recoiled. Lights burst overhead, not shattered but startled, the Conservatory's harmonic logic unable to process sound that refused lineage. Aria joined her with metal against concrete, Volkov slamming the crash bar with the unpoetic force of someone who had stopped believing in doors.

The exit unlocked with a sound that was not a click. It was a surrender. Cold night air rushed in, unregulated, unfiltered, untrained.

They spilled into the dark, Mila sobbing now, not from fear but from sensation returned.

170

Behind them, St. Cecilia sealed itself in elegant silence, already drafting the narrative that would explain why nothing had happened.

Celeste didn't look back. Because once you taught a building how to forget you, the next war was never about rooms again.

Chapter 22

Residue

THEY DID NOT celebrate. They drove through the Austrian countryside in a stolen service van that smelled of antiseptic and paper files, headlights carving narrow corridors through mist that had not yet decided whether it wanted to be fog or rain. Mila lay on the back bench wrapped in Volkov's coat, eyes open, breathing with the mechanical concentration of someone relearning autonomy one sense at a time.

Celeste sat beside her, cello wedged between knees, fingers tracing the grain of the wood as if reminding herself what consent felt like.

Esra's voice sounded through Celeste's tablet that was sitting on the floor of the van. "St. Cecilia is issuing a press statement. 'Successful intervention into unauthorized influence activity.' They're claiming Mila requested therapeutic isolation."

Mila laughed softly—not humor, not hysteria—just the involuntary release of a body hearing its own erasure read aloud.

"They don't even need to lie anymore," Aria said from the front seat. "They just need to file."

The van turned onto a narrow road where the forest leaned close enough to feel like a corridor of witnesses. Somewhere behind them, the Conservatory had already been repainted in language. Ahead of them, nothing was named yet. And that, Celeste realized, was the last place freedom ever existed.

They stopped at a farm that had never learned how to be useful. A sagging barn leaned against the idea of collapse, its red paint long surrendered to wood that had been sunburned into something pale and honest. Volkov parked the van behind it, where apple trees hid anything that didn't want to be seen, and cut the engine.

Silence arrived in pieces that included insects, distant cattle, the long exhale of Mila finally sleeping.

Celeste helped her onto a makeshift cot fashioned from old feed sacks and a door that had once pretended to be a table. The barn smelled of hay and rust and time, a combination no system had yet learned how to monetize.

Esra provided another update. "They've classified tonight's breach as localized noncompliance. But they've added a new metric: Residual Influence Risk. It's trending."

Aria leaned against a stall divider, mallets still in her hand like something she wasn't ready to set down. "They're tracking us through aftermath now," she said. "Not events. Echoes."

Celeste closed her eyes briefly. The Conservatory had tried to erase sound by regulating it. Now it would try to erase consequence by reframing it.

Outside, wind threaded through apple branches that didn't care who was being watched.

And for the first time since Vienna, Celeste felt the weight of what survival actually cost, not blood, not speed, but residue.

Mila woke before dawn. Not with a scream—the building had trained that out of her—but with a soft intake of breath that sounded like surprise at still being present. Celeste was sitting nearby, bow resting across her knee, not playing, just holding sound in potential the way some people held prayer.

"Where am I?" Mila asked.

"In a place that doesn't care what you're supposed to become," Celeste replied.

Mila closed her eyes again, letting the words settle into muscles that had learned obedience before language. "They said you would break me," she whispered. "That you were contagious."

Celeste's throat tightened. "They say that about anyone who refuses to disappear politely."

Mila laughed weakly. "Then I'm infected."

Aria appeared at the barn door with two mugs that smelled of instant coffee and apples too bruised to sell. "Welcome back to the unsanctioned," she said, handing one to Mila.

Esra's voice cut through the early morning. "Cultural Compliance Division is preparing detainment warrants for Volkov and Aria. You're still flagged as 'symbolic risk', Celeste. They don't want to make you a martyr yet."

Mila blinked. "They'll come here."

Volkov's voice carried from outside. "Not yet. But soon."

The farm did not hide them. It only delayed the story being written about them.

And Celeste understood, with a clarity that felt like loss, that freedom did not end when you escaped. It began when you became impossible to clean up.

Morning light crept through the warped slats of the barn, drawing pale bars across Mila's face that shifted with every breath she took. Dust motes floated in the beams like a private constellation, too slow, too small to matter to anyone still inside the compliance grid.

Celeste watched her sleep and tried not to count how many times she had seen this before—artists waking from rooms that had asked too much of their nervous systems. Every rescue left behind a different version of the same ghost: the person who had existed before they were curated.

Outside, Aria paced the orchard in tight loops, boots pressing damp leaves into darker versions of themselves. Her hands never left the mallets. They were not weapons, not instruments; they were anchors back into a body that had been trained to belong anywhere except where it stood.

Esra reported, "I'm seeing increased drone traffic over agricultural regions in Styria. Low-altitude sweeps under wildlife monitoring authority."

Volkov crouched beside the van, dismantling its onboard GPS with the same tenderness some people reserved for fragile things. "They won't announce retrieval teams," he said. "They'll outsource us to algorithmic curiosity."

Mila stirred again, eyes opening to the unfamiliar geometry of the barn ceiling. "They taught us to call that safety," she whispered.

Celeste leaned closer. "Safety doesn't ask you to stop breathing like yourself."

The barn door groaned as Volkov slid it shut against the rising wind. Somewhere beyond the apple trees, engines murmured—not pursuit, not yet—just the world recalibrating its attention.

The residue of St. Cecilia had followed them here, not as noise, but as pattern.

By midmorning the farm had begun to feel crowded, not with people but with implication. Every sound—a distant tractor, the bark of a dog across the valley—arrived wearing the question of whether it had been invited.

Celeste stood at the barn door, listening to the wind drag through tall grass that had never agreed to be landscaped. She tried to memorize the sound the way she memorized scores, not to replicate it, but to notice the way it refused to be held.

Esra broke in with the latest update. "One of the Cultural Compliance Division warrants was just leaked to the Austrian press. They're framing tonight as a 'deradicalization retrieval.' The language is surgical."

Mila pushed herself upright, wincing as sensation stitched itself back into her shoulders. "They're going to make me a case study," she said. "Proof that resistance is something you recover from."

Aria knelt in front of her, gaze steady. "You're not something that gets cured."

The barn filled with the scent of apples beginning to rot in a crate near the wall with sweetness turning, insisting on being noticed. Volkov straightened from the van and shaded his eyes against the sky. "They're expanding the perimeter," he said. "Not closing in. They are thickening. They want us to feel visible before they take us."

Celeste closed her eyes again and inhaled, pulling the barn into herself the way she once pulled orchestras into coherence. Only now, she wasn't trying to align anything. She was trying to make room for what refused alignment.

The drone appeared at the edge of hearing before it entered sight. It was a persistent thrum that threaded itself through birdsong until the orchard forgot which sounds had permission to exist. Aria looked up first, mallets tightening in her grip, body shifting into a readiness that had never belonged to music.

Volkov didn't move. He waited, listening not to the drone but to the pattern of its attention, the lazy sweep of surveillance pretending to be curiosity.

Esra explained, "They've deployed environmental compliance probes. It's not tracking you yet, it's mapping what happens around you."

Mila stood, too fast, the motion breaking something fragile in her balance. Celeste caught her before the ground could, the cello case knocking against the stall wall with a hollow thud that sounded like punctuation.

"They're turning the world into a rehearsal," Mila whispered. "Seeing what changes when we're inside it."

The drone drifted closer, sunlight catching its black shell until it resembled nothing more threatening than a beetle with ambition. Celeste felt the barn's geometry respond, the shadows shifting and angles tightening, not because the building had learned obedience, but because they had.

She lifted her phone and killed the power. No signal. No feedback. Just wind and rot and breath.

The drone hovered, uncertain. For the first time since Vienna, a machine hesitated in the presence of people who had decided not to perform for it.

The drone didn't retreat. It circled. Not aggressively but with the tentative curiosity of a thing that had been trained to assume compliance and had just encountered refusal. Its camera iris widened, adjusting exposure, recalculating relevance.

Aria stepped into the open space of the orchard and raised a mallet.

Celeste shook her head slightly. "Not like that."

Aria lowered her arm, breathing out through her nose, recalibrating the instinct Eidolon had carved into her muscles. "Then how?"

Celeste closed her eyes. The barn had taught her something, not how to escape, but how to be uncooperative without being antagonistic. She lifted her cello and began to tune it, not to pitch but to place, testing how the orchard responded, where sound thickened, where it vanished into grass.

The drone shifted position.

Esra voice said quietly, "You're inside a soft perimeter now. If you disappear completely, they'll escalate."

Celeste opened her eyes. Then she played. Not a piece. Not a melody. Just a series of rough, breath-heavy strokes that refused tempo and lineage. The orchard answered with wind rattling apple leaves, branches shedding bruised fruit into the dirt like punctuation marks.

The drone wavered. It wasn't programmed for collaboration, only documentation.

Aria joined her, not striking the drone, but the rusted gate beside the barn, sending a discordant shudder through metal that had never learned to harmonize with anything.

Volkov kicked a loose bucket into the tall grass, scattering sound into places the algorithm had not yet named.

The drone retreated two meters. And for the first time, the residue of St. Cecilia had to ask permission to remain. The drone did not flee. It gave up. Its slow, obedient circle faltered into something like drift, then veered off over the orchard as if it had remembered an appointment elsewhere. The sound thinned, folded into distance, leaving the air behind it oddly exposed to a silence that belonged to no one.

No one spoke.

They stood in the tall grass with instruments and improvised weapons lowered, the barn behind them still smelling of apples that had not yet learned what decay was supposed to mean.

Mila exhaled shakily. "They're going to change the rules now."

Celeste nodded. "They already have."

Her phone, still dark, felt heavier than when it had been alive. Silence was no longer absence. It was refusal.

Volkov finally allowed himself to sit, back against the barn wall, eyes scanning a horizon that had not yet decided whether to be shelter or threat. "You taught a machine to hesitate."

Celeste closed her cello case and rested her palm on the lid as she relished the contact. "No," she said. "I taught us to stop asking it to understand."

Beyond the orchard, the countryside held its breath, unsure whether it had just been observed or released. And in the quiet that followed the drone's retreat, something irreversible settled into place: They were no longer running from the system. They were becoming unreadable to it.

Chapter 23

Unreadable

THEY LEFT THE farm before dawn, not because they had to, but because staying felt like performance now. The barn was already heavy with the echo of surveillance that had never quite touched it. Mist curled through the orchard in loose spirals, erasing their footprints almost as soon as they were made, as if the land itself were practicing disappearance.

Mila rode in the back of the van again, wrapped in a borrowed coat, the cello case wedged between her knees like a promise she hadn't yet decided to keep. Aria drove this time, posture too calm for someone who had once been trained to look like violence. Volkov navigated without maps, tracing roads that had learned to be forgotten.

Esra, their ever-present companion, cut through the silence. " The Cultural Compliance Division just lost three active tracking threads in Styria. They don't know it yet, but you're becoming statistically anomalous."

Celeste leaned her head against the cold glass of the window and watched fields dissolve into tree lines, the world rearranging itself faster than any narrative could follow.

"Unreadable doesn't mean invisible," Volkov said from the passenger seat.

"No," Celeste replied. "It means they can see us without knowing what we are."

The van turned onto a road so narrow it felt like a question rather than a direction. And somewhere behind them, systems designed for obedience began to discover what it meant to misplace a story.

The road climbed into hills that no brochure had ever named. Stone farmhouses leaned into one another like elders trading secrets, their shutters scarred by decades of weather that had never asked permission to arrive. Sheep grazed along the margins with the stubborn indifference of creatures who had outlived every system humans had tried to impose on them.

Aria slowed near a hairpin turn where a shrine to some forgotten saint had been converted into a mailbox. The van's engine complained softly, metal remembering friction.

Esra said, "I'm seeing a hole in the network here. No municipal fiber. No commercial repeaters. It's a statistical dead zone."

Celeste breathed deeply, feeling the world grow heavier as the signal thinned . She didn't feel loss, but reprieve. The air smelled of cold soil and something faintly mineral, as if the hills were exhaling a language older than narrative.

They passed a field where wind had flattened the grass into long, careful strokes that resembled calligraphy more than landscape. Mila traced the pattern on the fogged window with her fingertip. "They can't map this," she murmured.

Volkov glanced back at her. "Nothing stops them from trying."

Aria guided the van through another bend where the mountainside fell away abruptly, the valley below opening like an unwritten sentence. In the silence that followed the engine's climb, Celeste felt something shift, not safety, not hope, but orientation. Unreadable did not mean unmarked. It meant they had become harder to describe than to find.

The van crested the ridge and rolled into a high pasture dotted with dark stones that had once pretended to be a wall. The remains curved gently through the grass like a sentence that had been abandoned before it could decide what it was about.

Aria cut the engine. The sudden quiet felt almost violent. Wind rushed in to fill the vacuum, tugging at loose wire around the barn door of a structure so old it no longer claimed a purpose. Volkov stepped out first, boots sinking slightly into soil that smelled of iron and winter.

Esra's voice broke the stillness. "I'm losing packet coherence. Whatever this place is, it's outside their modeling tolerance."

Celeste slid out after Volkov. Her cello case was warm against her spine. She stood still long enough to let the land decide whether it recognized her. She didn't feel watched here. She felt… unsupervised.

Mila followed last, blinking at the unmediated horizon. "I forgot places could look like this," she said.

Celeste rested a hand on the broken stone wall, feeling the temperature difference where lichen had claimed the rock. "They still do," she replied. "We just stopped believing in them."

Above them, clouds scraped the mountainside with indifference. Below them, systems designed for containment lost a little more of their vocabulary.

They made camp inside the ruin not because it offered shelter, but because it did not offer anything else. The roof had long ago decided to become sky. Wooden beams leaned into absence, their grain silvered by years of refusal to hold anything up. A single iron ring still clung to the north wall, rusted into a shape that suggested it had once tethered animals that no longer needed to be remembered.

Celeste unpacked slowly, laying her cello down on a slab of stone that had been part of a hearth before warmth had been engineered elsewhere. She played nothing, but the wind threaded the strings anyway, drawing accidental harmonics that did not ask permission to exist.

Esra's connection was weaker this time, the signal struggling to find a reason. "This location is… wrong. It doesn't resolve on any of the overlays. I can't tell if you're outside the map or inside something it refuses to describe."

Aria crouched and brushed snow from a flat rock, turning it into a surface for preparation rather than ritual. "Unreadable," she said. "We're not off-grid. We're off-grammar." Then she chuckled at her own comment.

Mila moved through the ruin touching walls, breath shallow, as if her body were relearning what weight meant when it wasn't being evaluated. "They never let us go somewhere that didn't have purpose," she said.

Celeste closed the cello case. "Then we stay until this place remembers how to be ordinary."

The wind carried that idea away. And in the distance, something recalibrated. Night arrived without asking what they were ready for. It didn't fall so much as collect, gathering itself in the hollows of the ruined walls, pooling in the places where ceilings had once decided to matter. Aria lit a small stove no bigger than a lunch pail, its blue flame a private rebellion against the altitude. The heat was thin but honest, a kind of warmth that admitted how hard it had worked to exist.

Celeste sat cross-legged near the hearth stone and tuned the cello not to pitch but to weather, listening to how the cold had tightened the strings, how the mountain air had changed the instrument's appetite for vibration. Each adjustment was a conversation the Conservatory of Presence could never have understood.

Celeste's phone vibrated, the screen dimming as if embarrassed to intrude. Esra had texted, "They've lost your trace completely. Not obscured—undefined. Whatever this place is, it isn't allowed inside their predictive language." Celeste read the message aloud.

Volkov looked up from sharpening a small field knife whose edge had never learned to be decorative. "That won't last," he said.

"No," Celeste replied. "But it's enough."

Mila had found an old ledger in the debris, its pages warped with moisture, names written in a hand that had assumed permanence. She ran her fingers across it as if reacquainting herself with the idea of authorship. "Do you ever think the Maestro is afraid of places like this?" she asked.

Aria glanced toward the open roof where stars had begun to assemble without choreography. "He's afraid of anything that can't be summarized."

Wind passed through the ruin again, catching a loose beam and turning it into percussion no syllabus had ever cataloged. The sound lingered, not amplified nor diminished. It was just present. And far beyond the hills, in rooms still obedient to intention, systems adjusted their thresholds, uneasy with the growing evidence that some things were no longer willing to be found.

The stars looked closer here, as if the mountain had raised them like a hand lifted to feel rain. Celeste lay back on the cold stone and let the constellation patterns dissolve, refusing the temptation to name them. Naming was the beginning of control.

Esra's voice came from Volkov's computer. "I'm receiving anomalies. Not coordinates, but behaviors. Small collectives forming without digital trace, such as informal rehearsal circles, unsigned ensembles, people meeting without permissions."

Mila propped herself against the broken wall, eyes following a satellite that refused to announce itself. "They're still listening to us," she said.

"Yes," Celeste replied. "But they can't model us."

Volkov fed a small piece of wood into the stove, flame catching with reluctant gratitude. "Unreadable systems always trigger audits."

Aria smiled faintly. "Then let them audit silence."

The ruin shifted as the temperature dropped further, old beams settling into new negotiations with gravity. Celeste closed her eyes, letting the place settle into her bones.

In the distance, somewhere beyond the mountains, the Maestro would be noticing a pattern that refused to become language. And for the first time since Berlin, she wasn't trying to stop him from noticing. She was daring him to understand.

They slept in fragments. No one trusted the night enough to surrender completely, but the ruin held them in a way that didn't require vigilance, not with protection, exactly, but with permission to pause. Celeste drifted in and out of dreams where she played rooms instead of instruments, shaping echoes that had never agreed to be contained. She woke just before dawn to the sound of footsteps that were not footsteps.

Mila was sitting upright, eyes wide, breath shallow, listening to something that wasn't there. Aria was already moving, mallets abandoned in favor of a hand on the small blade Volkov had given her.

Celeste held up a palm.

The sound came again. It was not approach, not retreat, but a low tremor carried through the stone itself, like a distant engine remembering what vibration used to mean.

Celeste's phone vibrated weakly. Esra texted, "I'm detecting microseismic activity in your region. Not natural. They're testing something underground and trying to feel for you through terrain resonance."

Volkov exhaled slowly. "He's stopped trying to see us."

Mila whispered, "He's trying to hear us."

The mountain answered with a soft, almost imperceptible shudder, the residue of a system that had finally realized architecture was not its only instrument. And somewhere beneath the hills, the Maestro tuned the earth. The tremor passed like a thought that had changed its mind. Dust drifted from the broken beams and settled on Celeste's cello in a pattern too delicate to be called debris. The ruin held its breath again, a place that had learned how to be patient with disruption.

Her phone vibrated again. **Esra: The seismic signature is fading. They're probing strata acoustics that are experimental and expensive. He's trying to map you through geology.**

Aria lowered the knife slowly. "He's not listening for us anymore," she said. "He's listening for the absence we leave behind."

Mila wrapped her arms around her knees. "How do you hide from the ground?"

Celeste stood and stepped outside, boots crunching frost that had not yet melted into obedience. She placed her hand against the cold stone of the outer wall, feeling how the mountain carried memory without ever being asked to record.

"You don't hide from it," she said. "You stop trying to sound like something it recognizes."

The sky was pale with the coming day, the stars dissolving into color that had never learned to be captured. Behind her, the ruin creaked, not from stress, but from age remembering itself.

In the valley below, technology adjusted its thresholds again, trying to translate a silence that had become too complicated to name.

They left the ruin at first light. They weren't hurried or triumphant. They wanted to be unrecorded. The mountain watched them go with the same indifference it gave storms, its patience deeper than any system that had ever tried to classify it.

Aria drove the van down a switchback road that felt more like memory than infrastructure. Volkov tracked nothing on his handheld receiver except static. Mila leaned her forehead against the glass and closed her eyes, not because she was tired, but because she no longer needed to be alert to someone else's rhythm.

Celeste sat in the back with her cello across her knees, listening to the way the van rattled. Her phone vibrated once more, then went dark completely, but before it did, she saw this message: **Esra: I can't reach you anymore. That means it's working.**

The signal vanished before Celeste could respond.

Outside, the road fell away into a valley no overlay had ever described correctly. Trees leaned into fog, stone folded into itself, and the world grew wider precisely because it had stopped explaining itself.

They did not know where they were going next, and for the first time, that was not a problem, because unreadable was no longer a strategy. It was becoming a way of being.

Chapter 24

Thresholds

THEY CROSSED INTO Italy without crossing anything that felt like a border. No booth. No gate. Just a shift in the way the mountains held the sky, how villages began to gather themselves around bells instead of buses. The van moved through valleys where grapevines stitched the hills into something that pretended intention had always been gentle.

Celeste watched the landscape loosen its grip on architecture. Stone houses slumped into warmth. Laundry lines braided windows into conversation. The world felt less like it was waiting to be measured.

Her phone remained dark. The absence was no longer alarming. It was information.

Volkov checked their fuel at a station where the pump numbers had faded into guesses. "We're not invisible," he said. "We're just… irrelevant to the algorithm."

Mila nodded from the back seat, fingers tracing the scroll of the cello without sound. "That feels like mercy."

Aria glanced at the rearview mirror, eyes sharp despite the softness of the land. "It's a lull. He won't let us go unchallenged for long."

Celeste rested her forehead against the cool glass. "Then we don't wait for him to find us. We find the places he hasn't learned how to hear yet."

The road narrowed again, climbing toward a ridge that no map had ever described correctly. And somewhere beyond it, something was waiting that didn't yet have a name. They stopped in a town that existed almost entirely in memory. No sign announced it. The road simply widened for a few houses that had never been painted the same color twice. A church leaned into a hillside as if trying to hear what the earth was saying beneath it. The van parked beside a fountain whose water came out sideways, refusing gravity in a way that felt almost conspiratorial.

The air smelled of olives and metal and something older, maybe dust that had not yet learned to be particulate.

Her phone stayed dark.

Celeste stepped out and let the place assemble itself around her. The rhythm was wrong here in a way that felt like relief. No screens. No signage offering interpretation. Just bodies moving according to habits no system had ever bothered to study.

A woman in a black apron watched them unload and finally spoke. "You're not lost," she said. It wasn't a question.

Mila smiled faintly. "We are," she replied. "But not here."

The woman nodded once and went back to rinsing glasses at a café.

Volkov scanned the square, already mapping exits in a town that did not want to be exited from. Aria knelt by the fountain and let her fingers feel the vibration in the stone, not resonance, just circulation.

Celeste listened to the way footsteps gathered and separated, the town practicing a music no conservatory had ever archived. This was not refuge. It was rehearsal for something no one had yet composed.

They took rooms above the café without asking what the rooms were for. The stairs curved like a compromise between architecture and habit, each step smoothed by decades of people who had not known where they were going next either. Mila paused halfway up, hand on the banister, feeling the way the wood dipped where generations had leaned before her.

Celeste waited, not because she needed to, but because stopping had become a kind of language. Her phone remained silent, a stillness so complete it had weight.

In the small upstairs hallway, a radio whispered from behind a door. It wasn't playing music or news, but sounded like a talk show drifting between dialects no translator would ever quite capture. The sound pooled in the narrow space like humidity.

Aria chose a room with a balcony that overlooked the fountain. She leaned on the railing and watched the water arrive sideways, refusing to become a spectacle. "This place doesn't know it's hiding us," she said.

"No," Volkov replied. "It just doesn't care."

They settled into rooms that had learned to hold strangers without annotation. Celeste unpacked the cello and stood it in the corner where light from the courtyard window bent around it in a way that felt unowned.

Outside, the town continued doing whatever it had always done. And inside it, something began to notice the difference between disappearance and arrival.

By evening, they had become furniture, not in the way the Conservatory had wanted—not curated, not positioned—but in the way things simply belonged because no one had asked them not to. The café downstairs filled with the soft friction of local voices, glasses chiming against saucers in rhythms that had never been rehearsed.

Celeste sat on the narrow balcony with her cello resting against her shoulder, not playing yet, just letting the instrument breathe with the town. Mila stood beside her, hands wrapped around a chipped mug, eyes following a man who crossed the square twice without ever looking at the fountain the same way.

Celeste's phone vibrated for the first time in almost two days. Only one bar of signal. **Esra: There's chatter, but not pursuit. Some kind of curiosity. The Maestro is noticing blank zones again.**

Celeste closed her eyes. "We don't move."

Down below, a group of children began drumming on overturned crates near the fountain, the sound more chaos than cadence, drawing laughter from the café patrons instead of scolding. Aria leaned over the railing, watching the way sound pooled without instruction. Mila's shoulders eased. "They would never have allowed that at St. Cecilia."

Celeste drew the bow across the cello in a single uncommitted stroke that wasn't melody, nor rebellion, just a tone that acknowledged the town's noise without claiming it.

People looked up. No one stopped what they were doing. The square did not become a stage. It became a threshold. The cello note didn't ripple outward the way it would have in a hall. It settled. It became part of the square the way dust became part of stone, not announcing itself, not demanding attention, simply existing alongside whatever had already decided to be there. A child answered it by slapping a crate harder than the others, proud of the way the sound jumped. Someone laughed. A woman at the café counter raised her eyebrows, then went back to wiping a glass.

Celeste lowered the bow. That was all it took. Mila leaned closer, voice barely above the murmur below. "They don't know what you are."

"No," Celeste replied. "They know what I'm not."

Volkov appeared in the doorway behind them, the narrow balcony suddenly crowded with quiet. "Two men came through town while you were playing," he said. "Didn't ask questions. Didn't buy anything. Just watched the children like they were memorizing them."

Aria straightened instantly. "How long ago?"

"Ten minutes. They left in opposite directions."

The square went on being a square with a woman hanging laundry from an upstairs window, a delivery scooter coughing its way through a turn too tight for planning, a church bell striking the hour with no concept of audience.

Celeste's phone vibrated again and she read the text to the group. **Esra: He's using social presence mapping now. No tech footprint. Human drift patterns. You were noticed when you didn't become a spectacle.**

Celeste rested her palm against the cello's ribs, feeling the vibration fade into wood. "Then we stay smaller."

Mila exhaled, not quite a laugh. "How small?"

Celeste watched the children scatter as their crates were repurposed into a game no one else could follow. "Small enough that we're mistaken for weather," she said half jokingly and half serious.

Below them, the fountain continued refusing gravity, and somewhere between water that would not fall and sound that would not perform, the Maestro lost another coordinate.

They ate dinner at a table that wobbled no matter where you put your foot. No menus, no bill presented until you asked for it, a meal that felt more like being absorbed than being served. Tomatoes warm from a garden that had not yet been invited onto a map. Bread torn, not sliced. Wine that tasted faintly of metal and summer storms.

Mila kept touching things as she spoke, the grain of the table, the edge of her plate, the condensation on her glass, as if reassuring herself that the world was still solid in places no one had yet tried to curate. "They never let us eat like this," she said quietly. "At St. Cecilia it was all nutrient scheduling. Even hunger had a protocol."

Aria smiled without humor. "Eidolon called it operational hygiene.

You couldn't want anything you hadn't been assigned."

Volkov watched the doorway while he chewed, eyes catching every shadow that didn't belong to the room. "That kind of discipline only works if people believe they're safer when someone else defines them."

Celeste lifted her glass but didn't drink yet. She was listening, but not to voices, not to threats. She listened to the way the café held sound. No symmetry. No dampening curves. Just angles and accidents and a dozen micro-rhythms arguing themselves into a temporary peace.

Her phone vibrated once more, faint but stubborn. **Esra: The blank zones are multiplying. He's not finding you, but he's finding where you've been. People are changing behavior after you leave.**

Celeste closed her eyes briefly. She said aloud and texted the words simultaneously. "Then the thresholds are contagious."

Outside, the fountain splashed sideways. The children had gone home now, but their crates remained stacked in a crooked tower that no adult had thought to correct.

The town was not sheltering them. It was forgetting to notice them, and in that forgetting, learning something it had never needed to be taught.

They went to bed with the windows open, not for air as the rooms were already breathing for them, but because closing them felt like an argument the town had not made. Night settled into the square with the soft finality of something that had never needed applause. Somewhere below, someone practiced an accordion badly and without apology.

Celeste lay awake listening to the building's unwillingness to become a system. Her phone, plugged in and dark on the bedside table, did not vibrate. That was how she knew something was about to happen.

In the early hours before morning decided whether to arrive, she heard it: a knock that was not urgent, not polite, simply present. She did not wake the others. She opened the door.

The woman from the café stood there with her apron folded over one arm, hair loose, eyes clear in a way that suggested she had never needed to practice bravery.

"There are men asking questions at the edge of town," the woman said. "Not about you. About the children."

Celeste felt the world tilt toward consequence. "Thank you," she said.

The woman shrugged once, the motion so small it could not be interpreted as loyalty. "You were kind to the fountain," she replied. "That's usually enough." She turned and went back downstairs, the building absorbing her footsteps the way it absorbed everything else, without commentary.

Celeste closed the door gently. Thresholds were no longer places they passed through. They were places that passed through them.

Chapter 25

Weather

THEY LEFT BEFORE dawn, but the town didn't feel abandoned. It felt awake. A single light glowed in the café kitchen as if someone had decided to bake bread on principle. The fountain continued its sideways insistence, water catching moonlight in brief, stubborn flashes. Somewhere in an upstairs window, a curtain moved. Someone was watching, not to report, but to remember.

Aria drove with the headlights off until they cleared the last houses and the road turned into a ribbon of darker darkness. Volkov sat in the passenger seat, map folded on his knee like an old habit. Mila rode in back with Celeste, hands wrapped around the mug the woman at the cafe gave her, breathing more steadily now, as if the night had returned some lost piece of her nervous system.

Celeste kept her gaze on the rear window, but not because she expected pursuit. Her phone stayed dark. No Esra. No alerts. No code. Just silence thick enough to be deliberate.

"Do you think they'll punish them?" Mila asked softly.

Volkov didn't look back. "If the Maestro is smart, he won't punish the town. He'll punish the story about the town."

Aria's grip tightened on the wheel. "How do you punish a story?"

Celeste watched the road appear and disappear in the van's dim beams. "You make it contagious," she said. "And then you convince people it's an illness."

The mountains opened into a long valley that looked too gentle to be trusted. And the sky began to change. The valley held fog the way lungs held breath. It pooled low over the fields, a pale, tentative ocean that parted around the van as if unsure whether to acknowledge its passing. Fences emerged and vanished in pieces, wooden ribs of a skeleton no one had bothered to name. Vineyards slept beneath the mist, their geometry softened into something almost tender.

Celeste's phone vibrated once, but not with a signal or a message. It was like the hardware had remembered it had once belonged to a world that expected answers.

Mila leaned forward, peering through the glass. "It feels like the earth is trying not to look at us."

Celeste shook her head. "It's teaching us how not to look back. It never does."

Volkov unfolded the map at last. It was an old one, creases rubbed white with use, roads drawn thicker than they deserved. "If the Maestro is shifting to narrative punishment," he said, "he'll start with places like that town. No raids. No closures. Just stories that make kindness sound irresponsible."

Aria exhaled slowly. "Then we become weather," she said.

Celeste smiled faintly. "Weather doesn't argue with architecture. It erodes it."

The fog thinned as the sun pushed weakly at the horizon, the light turning fields into layers rather than surfaces. Somewhere ahead, a road curved away from the valley into hills that had never been trained to anticipate anyone's arrival. Above them, the sky practiced forgetting the night.

They took the road that didn't look like a road. It left the valley in a slow unraveling with asphalt thinning into gravel, gravel into something that might once have been intention. Aria slowed instinctively, letting the van find its own rhythm with the ruts, the tires whispering against stone that had never needed to be named.

Mila pressed her forehead to the window. "They always told us extraction points had to be clean," she said. "If a place couldn't be described, it couldn't be trusted."

Celeste rested her palm over Mila's on the glass. "If a place can't be described," she said, "it's because it doesn't want to belong to anyone."

Her phone vibrated again, not with signal, but with heat. The device had begun to drain itself, refusing the constant search for towers that no longer wanted it.

Volkov folded the map and slid it into the seat pocket. "We're officially off the spine of Europe now," he said. "No fiber trunk lines. No grant corridors. No cultural attaché networks."

Aria glanced at him. "Say it like you mean it."

He hesitated, then nodded once. "We're leaving the Maestro's grammar."

The van crested another ridge and the world dropped away, revealing a basin of scattered farmhouses and a river that refused to stay straight. Smoke curled from a chimney in the distance, the line too irregular to be mistaken for anything planned.

Celeste closed her eyes for a moment and let the motion rewrite her sense of direction. Weather didn't have objectives. It only had effects.

And that, she realized, was the next movement.

They stopped where the river braided itself into stones. No bridge announced the crossing, just tire tracks disappearing into water that had never pretended to be obedient. Volkov climbed out first, boots crunching over gravel polished by seasons that had not needed oversight. He waded a few steps in, watching the current push against his shins with the disinterest of something that did not care whether he was being watched.

"Depth's fine," he called back. "But it's loud."

Celeste followed, cello case held against her chest like a shield that had finally remembered its purpose. The water took the van in pieces with the wheels first, then frame, and sound scattering outward as if the river were curious about intrusion but not offended by it.

Mila laughed softly from the back seat. The sound surprised her. "No one ever planned for this," she said. "No biometric thresholds. No access protocols."

Aria guided the van through the ford with hands loose on the wheel, letting the current argue with them in a language that required presence instead of permission. When they emerged on the other side, water streaming from the undercarriage, the world felt subtly rearranged, not safer or freer, but rather unindexed.

Celeste's phone vibrated weakly, screen flickering like a tired heartbeat. They were in range of something since Esra's text appeared. **I can't see you anymore. Which means someone else is trying.**

Celeste powered the device off and slipped it into her bag. Weather didn't need witnesses, she thought. It only needed time.

They climbed into hills where the road forgot its own name. Gravel gave way to packed earth, then to something closer to habit than surface. The van labored in low gear, engine grumbling in a way that sounded less like complaint and more like memory being exercised. Celeste leaned into the rhythm, letting vibration replace the phantom pull of systems that were no longer speaking to her.

Her phone remained off. That felt different now. It was not a loss of signal, but a release from audition.

Mila stared out at terraces carved into slopes with no symmetry anyone would recognize as efficient. "My mother grew up in a place like this," she said suddenly. "She said the mountains taught you to wait."

Volkov smiled and added, "And to leave before you get too good at it."

They passed a man herding goats across a field that was far from rectangular. He lifted a hand in greeting that felt less like acknowledgment and more like permission to pass.

Aria slowed instinctively, offering the courtesy of attention without asking for anything in return. The man nodded once, a transaction so complete it didn't need language. Goats threaded around the van with practiced disinterest, bells chiming not in rhythm but in acceptance of gravity.

Mila watched until the herd disappeared into folds of green. "They don't need to hide here," she said.

"No," Celeste replied. "They need to remain."

The road bent again, and the valley surrendered them to hills. By late afternoon the air had thickened into something that tasted like rain before it arrived. Clouds stacked in unconvincing towers above the ridgeline, shadowing fields into gradients of patience. Volkov found a pull-off beside a stand of chestnut trees that had been planted so long ago they no longer remembered why they had been aligned.

They unpacked in quiet coordination, not as a team, not as fugitives, but as people who had learned to read one another without annotation. Mila stretched her legs and tilted her face into the wind, eyes closing in a way that suggested she was relearning pleasure.

Celeste stood beneath the first drops of rain and did not move away. Weather did not ask for documentation. It did not archive intention. It simply happened, eroding edges, dissolving certainty, teaching even the most rigid structures how to give in to time.

And somewhere beyond the hills, systems designed to punish stories recalibrated their thresholds again, confused by a pattern that refused to announce itself as anything at all.

The rain arrived in layers. First a soft indecision that darkened dust into memory, then a steady insistence that made the chestnut leaves shine like polished brass. Aria unfolded a tarp from the back of the van and rigged it between two trees with the efficiency of someone who had once been taught that exposure was a liability. They sat beneath it in a crooked semicircle, steam lifting from their clothes as the temperature dipped. Mila pressed her palms to the damp earth, laughing under her breath at the way the ground accepted her weight without evaluation.

Volkov watched the rain sheet down the hills, fields dissolving into gradients that no camera could ever quite translate. "He'll escalate again," he said. "You don't lose a system like this without trying to replace it with something louder."

Celeste tilted her head back and let water trace her jaw. "Then let him," she said. "We're not trying to be louder anymore."

Aria nodded. "We're trying to be everywhere. Maybe Esra could figure out a hack to get your phone to ping from every mobile tower everywhere or from space. Space feels like everywhere."

The rain deepened, the sound no longer something you listened to, but something you were inside. Weather was not a metaphor now. It was strategy.

They didn't light a fire. Not because they were afraid of being seen, but because the rain had made fire feel like arrogance, a declaration instead of a presence. Instead they shared food that had learned to taste like distance: hard cheese, apples bruised into sweetness, bread that had survived enough hands to be trusted.

Mila ate slowly, eyes closing between bites, as if her body were keeping score of small mercies. "I don't feel hunted here," she said. "I feel... unfinished."

Celeste smiled all the way to her eyes. "That's what being human is before someone interrupts it."

The rain slackened as evening folded into the hills, the sky dimming into a color that had no word attached to it. Somewhere a cow lowed, the sound stretching across valleys that refused to behave like borders.

Her phone remained dark. But inside that darkness, Celeste could feel something rearranging, some intention. Weather did not need permission to exist. And neither, she was beginning to understand, did resistance.

Night did not fall. It accumulated. Mist crept back into the folds of the valley, turning the chestnut trees into silhouettes that felt more remembered than seen. Aria zipped the last flap of the tarp and leaned against the van, eyes scanning a horizon that had learned how to be dark without asking.

Volkov marked their position in a notebook he refused to digitize, the act of writing coordinates by hand feeling almost ceremonial now. "He's going to start mythologizing this," he said quietly. "Not the place. The idea of people who won't be found."

Mila rested her head against Celeste's shoulder, exhaustion settling in as sensation finished reclaiming territory the Conservatory had once occupied. "Let him make a myth," she murmured. "Weather doesn't care if people believe in it."

Celeste closed her eyes and listened for the rain threading through leaves, for the van's engine ticking itself into silence, for the soft human sounds of people learning how to occupy space again.

They had stopped running. They had stopped hiding. They were beginning to move the way storms moved, which was not toward objectives, not away from threats, but through landscapes that would never remember their names.

And somewhere beyond the hills, systems that had once dictated obedience learned the slow, unfamiliar vocabulary of erosion.

Chapter 26

Erosion

MORNING RETURNED WITHOUT announcement. The rain had rinsed the valley into something translucent with the chestnut leaves rinsed of dust, stones burnished into muted silver, the van wearing streaks of water like a map no one would ever decode. Celeste stepped out first, boots sinking slightly into soil that still remembered being cloud.

Her phone remained dark. She no longer checked it for signal. She checked it for weight, like a small brick that didn't weigh her down but reminded her she was connected to the earth.

Mila stretched beside the van, joints popping with a sound that belonged to bodies rather than systems. "They'll find us eventually," she said, not as a warning but as a fact.

Volkov emerged with a thermos he had filled at some point that felt like another life. "Yes," he replied. "But erosion is faster than pursuit if you let it work."

Aria watched fog lift from the ridgeline like a curtain no one had meant to raise. "We don't choose targets anymore," she said. "We choose flows."

Celeste nodded. "Then we follow the places where systems fail to hold."

The road ahead was barely a suggestion, a faint compression in grass that might only exist because something else had once refused to disappear. They drove into it without asking what it led to.

And somewhere behind them, narratives began to soften at the edges.

The track led them through a forest that no longer pretended to be curated. Beech trees arched overhead like cathedral ribs that had never learned how to close. Moss swallowed fallen trunks in thick, patient layers, the green so deep it felt less like color and more like time made visible. The van moved slowly, tires sinking into loam that still carried the memory of last night's rain.

Celeste rolled the window down and let the air fill the cab. It smelled of iron and wet leaves and something faintly sweet, rot as generosity rather than failure. She felt it settle into her lungs.

Mila admitted, "They never showed us forests," she said. "Training footage was always deserts. Urban grids. Places where everything could be isolated."

"Forests don't isolate," Aria replied. "They accumulate."

Volkov navigated by instinct now, choosing forks in the road not by destination but by the way they curved, toward density, toward shadow, toward complexity. At one bend, they passed a stone well half-collapsed into the earth, its pulley frozen mid-lift like a thought abandoned. They stopped without discussion.

The forest closed around the van as if it had always been there. Celeste stepped out and walked to the well, fingers brushing lichen that had turned the stone into a living surface. She leaned over and listened for the echo that had never been engineered.

Erosion wasn't destruction. It was the slow insistence of presence in places no one had ever bothered to defend.

They ate lunch on fallen logs slick with moss, the forest offering no table but enough flatness to suggest accommodation rather than design. Aria cut bread with a pocketknife whose blade had dulled into honesty, the crust tearing in uneven crescents that felt truer than any symmetry.

Mila wandered deeper between the trunks, touching bark, pausing at clusters of mushrooms that rose like punctuation from the forest floor. She had stopped asking permission before stepping away, as if her body had finally remembered it could move without waiting for instruction.

Volkov crouched by the well and dropped a pebble, listening for the return of sound. When it came, it was late, a soft, subterranean acknowledgment that felt less like echo and more like agreement.

They sat in silence that wasn't empty, the kind that holds weather in its margins. Somewhere overhead a jay scolded the trees, offended by nothing in particular. The van rested between trunks like an animal that had decided to stay. Erosion was not an act. It was a permission structure the world had been waiting to remember.

They heard the stream before they saw it. A narrow thread of sound sliding between roots, more insinuation than announcement. Aria followed it first, pushing through bracken that brushed her boots with something like approval. The water was cold enough to shock thought from the skin, its path unscripted, weaving between stones that had learned to be obstacles without becoming boundaries.

Celeste knelt at the bank and let the current run across her fingers. It wasn't clean in any heroic way; it carried sediment, leaf fragments, the faint metallic taste of distant hills. It was working, not resting.

Mila waded in up to her ankles and closed her eyes. "They taught us to drain places like this," she said. "To make them predictable."

Volkov stood back, scanning the tree line not for threat but for pattern. "Predictable places can be controlled," he said. "Living ones just… happen."

The forest seemed to thicken as the afternoon progressed, light breaking into shards that refused to behave like illumination. Somewhere beyond the trees, thunder practiced without conviction, the sky unsure whether it wanted to perform.

Celeste thought erosion was not the enemy of structure. It was what remained when structure forgot how to demand.

The storm did not arrive. It negotiated. Clouds slid across the canopy in overlapping sheets, darkening the forest without extinguishing it, turning green into a dozen unnamed variations of endurance. The first drops struck leaves with a sound too small to be called rain. It was more like punctuation than weather, until the air filled with a hush that felt like agreement.

They took shelter beneath the beech trees whose branches braided overhead into something that resembled architecture only because humans had not yet found a way to monetize it. Volkov unpacked the tarp and slung it between trunks, the fabric catching water and light in alternating moods.

Mila stood at the edge of the stream and let the rain soak her hair. "They would have given this a schedule," she said. "Twenty minutes. Then rest."

Celeste smiled and quipped, "Forests don't do breaks."

The scent of wet bark deepened, the world turning inward, softer without becoming fragile. Aria crouched and dragged her fingers through mud, watching the print vanish as water filled the shape. "Nothing stays wrong here," she murmured.

Celeste closed her eyes and let the rain map her face with no modulation, no feedback loop, just gravity making its argument.

Behind them, the well swallowed water it would not catalog.

Ahead of them, something that had never been designed began to teach them how to remain.

When the rain finally thinned, it did not recede so much as dissolve, becoming mist that threaded itself between the trunks like breath exhaled by the forest itself. Water dripped from leaves in uneven intervals, each drop landing with a sound too individual to be called pattern. The stream beside them widened in small but decisive gestures, creeping into moss and swallowing the sharpness of stones that had once interrupted its path.

Mila perched on a slab of granite veined with quartz, the mineral lines catching what little light filtered through the canopy. She closed her eyes and began to hum, vibration, a tentative offering of sound to a place that did not care whether it was received. The forest accepted it anyway, leaves shivering in a response too subtle to be measured.

Celeste watched her with something like reverence. At St. Cecilia, every sound had required justification. Here, Mila's voice simply existed, and in that existence began to rebuild a nervous system that had once been dismantled by design.

Volkov sat cross-legged on a fallen trunk, jotting lines into his notebook not as data but as artifacts, impressions rather than intelligence. He wrote about the way the fog blurred distance into relationship, about how even the most vertical trees leaned when they were wet, about the feeling of being watched by nothing that intended harm.

Aria wandered the stream's edge, boots sinking into mud that erased her footprints almost as soon as they formed. She dragged a stick through the water, tracing spirals that lasted only long enough to be witnessed. "Eidolon taught us to control environments," she said quietly, more to herself than to them. "No one ever trained us to belong to one."

The forest shifted around them, not moving or waiting, simply continuing. Somewhere overhead, a woodpecker tapped in a rhythm that refused repetition. Somewhere deeper still, something larger moved through undergrowth with a patience that had never been instructed.

Erosion wasn't violence. It was what happened when time stopped pretending to be obedient.

They didn't mark when afternoon became evening.

The forest made no such distinction. Light thinned in increments too small to be called moments, draining from leaves until green surrendered to a deeper register that had no translation outside of shadow. The air cooled, carrying with it the scent of cold water and crushed fern, a smell that seemed to belong to forgetting.

Celeste stood and stretched, feeling the ache of muscles that had not been consulted about their own utility in a long time. She walked the perimeter of their clearing, not to secure it, but to feel how the space held them, where the ground softened, where roots insisted on memory, where the forest felt less like background and more like a participant.

At the stream, she knelt again, letting the current run over her wrists. The chill was sharp enough to clarify thought without punishing it. She imagined the water carrying fragments of their presence downstream: fibers from Mila's coat, trace oils from Aria's hands, distributing them in a way no surveillance architecture could ever reverse-engineer.

Mila had found a cluster of mushrooms the color of tarnished copper. She crouched before them with the attention usually reserved for sacred objects, careful not to touch. "They look like they're listening," she said.

"They are," Aria replied from behind her. "To weather. To soil. To everything that doesn't announce itself."

Volkov tore a page from his notebook and folded it into a small square before slipping it back inside. He had written nothing useful on such as locations, or plans, but he did write the phrase erosion begins with contact. He didn't know yet what it meant, only that it felt less like strategy and more like truth.

Above them, clouds unraveled into streaks of rose and ash, the sky attempting beauty without knowing what to do with it. The forest did not applaud. It simply remained.

They built no fire. Instead, they gathered closer as the temperature dipped, shoulders brushing in ways that felt less like necessity and more like recognition. The forest dimmed around them, not into darkness, but into intimacy, a narrowing of the world that asked nothing except presence.

Celeste rested the cello across her knees and drew the bow once, barely grazing the string. The sound did not travel. It settled, not as music or a message, but as residue, the kind that stayed because it had not been asked to perform.

Mila closed her eyes and leaned into the sound as if it were something she had been promised long ago. Aria sat with her back against a beech trunk, watching shadows reshape themselves into questions no one needed to answer. Volkov folded his notebook shut and slipped it into his jacket, letting language be finished for the night.

Beyond the canopy, the world still organized itself into grids and compliance statements, into systems that punished deviation by pretending it was rescue.

Here, nothing waited to be named. Erosion had done its quiet work. And when they finally slept, the forest held them not as fugitives, not as symbols, but as weather passing through a place that had never belonged to anyone.

Chapter 27

Drift

THEY WOKE TO birds arguing about something no one else could hear. It sounded less like a chorus and more like a debate, sharp trills colliding with low, stubborn calls that refused to resolve into anything that might be called harmony. The forest floor was stitched with fallen leaves that had dried into curled fragments of copper and rust, each one holding a piece of yesterday's rain like a memory that had not yet decided to leave.

Celeste sat up slowly, the cello's case cool against her hip, the instrument inside adjusting to temperature it had not been trained to expect. She breathed in the layered scent of soil, sap, and distant water, and felt a shift in herself she had no vocabulary for. But the word drift came to mind, like a scent on a breeze.

Mila was already awake, sitting cross-legged at the edge of the clearing, humming again. This time there was a shape to it, not a melody, but an intention,a low, searching tone that wandered the way the stream had wandered yesterday, unconcerned with arrival.

Aria crouched nearby, sharpening her knife against a stone that had once been part of a wall, her movements unhurried, unowned. Volkov knelt at the stream washing his hands in water cold enough to remind skin it was still alive.

Her phone, now irrelevant, or so she thought, lay buried at the bottom of Celeste's bag. Drift was not a loss of direction. It was direction unburdened by destination.

They packed without hurry, simply the quiet dismantling of a moment that had never claimed to be permanent. Aria folded the tarp with care, shaking loose leaves that clung to the fabric like punctuation marks. Volkov filled the thermos from the stream, the metal cooling his hands through the skin in a way that felt less like chill and more like reminder.

Celeste lingered near the well that had become nothing more than a circle of darker stone in the earth. She pressed her palm against it and felt the night's cold still trapped in the rock, a reservoir of yesterday that no one would ever audit.

Mila approached her with a handful of pinecones, their scales damp and fragrant. "I don't know why I picked these," she said, embarrassed.

Celeste smiled. "You don't need a reason to keep what doesn't belong to anyone."

They loaded the van, leaving no sign of having been anything but weather passing through, no fire pit, no flattened grass, no narrative for someone else to discover. The forest had already begun the work of forgetting them.

When they pulled away, the clearing folded back into itself, the stream carrying away the faintest trace of tire that had tried to become memory. And the road ahead, such as it was, waited without suggestion. The road wandered not in curves or switchbacks; it simply refused to decide whether it was a road at all. Packed earth slid into gravel, gravel into something closer to habit than surface. Aria drove with both windows down, the van breathing forest air like a creature that had grown tired of sealed environments.

Mila leaned forward between the seats, eyes scanning the margins rather than the center. "It feels like everything's happening in the corners now," she said. "Like the world is made of side notes."

Volkov nodded. "That's where systems go blind."

Celeste watched fog unravel from the low places, revealing pockets of meadow that looked too deliberate to be accidental and too fragile to be planned. A deer burst from underbrush ahead of them, paused mid-road in a geometry no algorithm would ever approve, then vanished without apology.

Her phone, silent in her bag, felt more distant than any mountain they had crossed. Drift did not require speed. It required noticing what refused to align.

They reached a plateau by late morning where the land spread itself into something that almost resembled generosity. Low stone walls stitched fields together in uneven sentences. Sheep dotted the hillsides like afterthoughts. A lone farmhouse leaned into the wind as if listening for something no one else could hear. The van rolled to a stop beside a rusted water trough, its surface glazed with thin ice that had not yet decided to melt.

They climbed out and stood without speaking. The plateau felt exposed in a way the forest had not, open, as if the land had chosen to be witnessed rather than recorded.

Celeste lifted the cello from the van and rested it against her shoulder. She did not play yet. She listened to how the space held itself, the way sound would have to cross too much air to remain obedient.

Mila knelt by the trough and traced the ice with one finger, watching it fracture into shapes too fleeting to name. "It doesn't remember what it was supposed to be," she said.

Volkov scanned the horizon. "Neither do we."

A hawk cut across the sky, its shadow passing over them so quickly it felt like interruption rather than omen.

They were not lost. They were between definitions. They moved across the plateau on foot, leaving the van where it had chosen to rest. Grass bowed under their boots and sprang back again with a resilience that felt almost rehearsed. Aria climbed the low stone wall and walked its length as if testing whether balance still required instruction. Volkov followed the contour of the land rather than any path, stopping occasionally to touch a fence post or peer into hollows where snow still clung like forgotten memories.

Celeste carried the cello by its neck, letting the case swing lightly at her side, the instrument inside learning a new orientation with every step. She closed her eyes once, just long enough to feel how the openness pulled at her sense of containment, widening the interior spaces she had spent years training herself to compress.

Mila lagged behind, collecting smooth stones from the field and stacking them in a spiral no one had asked her to build. When the wind toppled it, she laughed, a sound that startled her with its own audacity.

"This place doesn't care if I finish things," she said.

Celeste turned back toward her. "Then don't." She grinned.

They walked until the plateau folded into hills again, the land declining to provide any kind of conclusion. The hills softened as they descended, the land relinquishing height in slow concessions rather than slopes. Heather brushed their legs with a dry whisper, releasing a faint resinous scent that clung to wool and denim alike. Somewhere unseen, insects stitched the air with a sound so fine it felt like texture rather than noise.

They paused near a stand of birch whose white bark peeled in thin, papery curls, revealing darker layers beneath. Aria lifted one curl and rolled it between her fingers, watching it spring back into shape. "Even this," she said, "remembers how to return."

Volkov found a rock warmed by the thinning sun and sat, boots braced, gaze unfixed. He looked less like a man on watch and more like someone learning the difference between vigilance and listening. The wind moved across the hillside and he turned his face into it, letting it rearrange his thoughts without asking to be useful.

Celeste set the cello case down and leaned against it, feeling the ground's slight give beneath her boots. She lifted the bow and drew it once—softly, experimentally—letting the note dissipate into the wide air where it could not be captured or corrected. The sound thinned, then vanished, leaving behind only the memory of having been.

Mila crouched beside a shallow depression where rainwater had collected, its surface trembling with the passage of clouds overhead. She traced the reflection with her finger until the image broke apart. "I used to think direction meant safety," she said. "Now it feels open to interpretation."

Celeste nodded. "Drift, what we are doing making our own choices, teaches you where you are by what refuses to follow."

They gathered themselves again, as people moving through a place that had no interest in being impressed. The hills accepted them without comment, the birch shedding another curl of bark that caught briefly on Aria's sleeve before falling away. And as they continued on, the land did not open or close around them. It simply allowed them to pass.

By afternoon the light had thinned into something slanted and provisional, the sun no longer overhead but leaning, as if curious about what the land was doing with itself. Shadows stretched and loosened, no longer attached to the objects that cast them. Even time felt less declarative here, more like a suggestion you could accept or ignore.

They reached a shallow ravine where water moved without hurry.

Flat stones bridged the narrowest point, placed there by hands long gone, their alignment imperfect enough to survive. Aria crossed first, boots landing where the stone still remembered weight. Mila followed, arms out, laughing once when her foot slipped and found purchase anyway.

Celeste lingered at the edge. She knelt and touched the water again, noticing how it carried flecks of mica that caught the light and released it without keeping score. She imagined the Maestro's systems trying to model this, trying to decide what the water meant, and failing because meaning here was distributed too widely to be owned.

Volkov waited on the far side, scanning not the horizon but the negative space between things. "If he comes looking," he said quietly, "it won't be with force."

Celeste stepped across the stones, the cello steady against her shoulder. "No," she replied. "He'll come with interpretation."

They continued along the ravine until it widened into a basin where grass grew tall and unruly, bending into overlapping arcs that refused to settle into rows. Wind passed through it like a hand through hair, leaving no trace of where it had been. Mila lay back in it without asking, her arms spread, her eyes on the sky. The grass rose around her and then forgot her shape.

Aria sat beside her, watching clouds shear themselves into fragments that looked almost intentional before dissolving again. "I used to think drift meant losing edge. That's what they taught us. Focus, focus, focus." she said. "What we are doing, being out here, feels like sharpening against everything."

Celeste lowered herself onto a rock and let the cello rest across her thighs. She didn't play. She listened to the grass, to the water, to the way silence here held multiple registers without asking to be resolved. It was the sound of systems thinning, of narratives losing their grip not with a snap but with a long, patient exhale.

As the light began to slip toward evening, they gathered themselves once more. Not because the day demanded it, but because movement had become a shared instinct rather than an instruction. Drift carried them on—not toward refuge, not away from pursuit, but through a world that was quietly relearning how not to hold on.

♪ ♪

Chapter 28

Pressure

THE FIRST SIGN was not pursuit. It was stillness. The hills ahead lay too quiet, the grass no longer answering the wind with its usual argument. Even the insects seemed to have agreed to pause, as if the land itself were listening for something it did not want to hear.

Celeste felt it before anyone spoke, a tightening just beneath the sternum, the sensation she had learned to trust long before sound became her profession. Pressure without source. Attention without face.

They slowed together. Volkov stopped at the lip of a shallow rise and crouched, palm hovering inches above the soil. "This isn't absence," he said. "It's containment by omission."

Aria scanned the skyline, eyes narrowing not at what was visible, but at what refused to be. "He's learned to wait," she said. "That's new."

Mila stood very still, stones dropping from her pockets one by one, each soft thud landing with disproportionate clarity. "It feels like a room," she whispered, "but without walls."

Celeste closed her eyes and listened for the way space behaved when it was being considered. The pressure deepened, not crushing, not violent, but with an insistence, like air thickening before a storm decides whether to break. Her phone, long dead, felt suddenly heavier in her bag, as if it remembered how to be relevant. Pressure wasn't force. It was expectation. And somewhere beyond the ridge, something had begun to listen again, not to sound, not to movement, but to the gap they left behind.

They moved downhill into the quiet as if entering water. Each step changed the density of the air, not enough to slow them, just enough to register, a resistance that felt intellectual rather than physical, like walking through a thought someone else was holding very carefully. The ravine ahead widened into a shallow bowl where stones lay arranged in loose constellations, not placed, not fallen, they noticed.

Volkov signaled a halt. He didn't raise a fist. He simply stopped, and the others stopped with him, the way you did when a room decided to listen back. "Can you feel it? I think there's a high-altitude drone somewhere above us. It's outside our hearing but the energy has shifted. I don't think it is surveillance," he said. "It's a hypothesis."

Aria looked overhead before she crouched and pressed her palm to the ground. The soil was cool, dry beneath the surface, holding last night's chill the way memory held fear after it had learned to disguise itself. "He's modeling response," she said. "Seeing what we do when nothing happens."

Mila swallowed. "That's worse."

Celeste felt the pressure slide laterally, like a lens refocusing. She turned slowly, letting her gaze sweep the bowl without seeking edges. There were no machines. No bodies. No signal to interrupt that she could see. Just space that had learned to expect meaning. "Let's not give a response," she said softly.

They sat, not to rest, but to refuse choreography.

Time stretched, thinned, and tried to decide whether it was still useful. A cloud crossed the sun and did not hurry. A beetle traced a line across a stone and vanished into a crack too small to matter. The pressure wavered, uncertain how to interpret patience that wasn't passivity.

Minutes—or something like them—passed. Then the wind returned. Not all at once. In pieces. First a breath against Mila's hair, then a longer push that bent grass into motion again, then the full argument of air reclaiming the bowl. The insects resumed their stitching. The land exhaled.

Aria let out a slow laugh. "He can't hold it."

Celeste stood, the pressure dissolving from her chest like a thought abandoned mid-sentence. "He can only shape what reacts," she said. "We're teaching him to waste attention."

They climbed out of the bowl without looking back. Behind them, the quiet tried once more to gather itself and failed.

Pressure, she understood now, was not what broke people. Expectation was. And expectation, given nothing to hold, learned to let go.

They didn't speak as they climbed.

The path—if it could be called that—rose in shallow folds, the ground firming beneath their boots as if the land were relieved to be used again for something that wasn't measurement. With each step, the pressure receded, not retreating so much as losing interest, like a question that realized it had been poorly formed.

Mila walked beside Celeste now, close enough that their shoulders brushed when the slope narrowed. "It felt like being evaluated," she said finally. "Not for what I did. For what I might do."

Celeste nodded. "That's how control matures. It stops reacting and starts anticipating."

Aria paused near a cluster of stones that had been stacked into a rough cairn, then knocked it gently aside with her boot. The rocks scattered, settling into new positions that were no less stable for having been unplanned. "Anticipation only works if you agree to be legible," she said.

Volkov reached the crest first and scanned the horizon. The land beyond opened into a broad sweep of heath and low scrub, the color muted but alive, the kind of space that resisted both hiding and display. "Whatever he was doing back there," he said, "it cost him something."

Celeste felt it too, a thinning at the edges of the pressure, as if attention had been stretched too far and snapped back on itself. She adjusted the strap of the cello case, aware of its weight without resenting it. The instrument had learned to be patient.

They moved on. Behind them, the bowl lay empty, wind moving freely through grass that had forgotten it was ever asked to be still. No signal followed. No correction arrived. The silence that remained was ordinary again, unremarkable, unowned.

Pressure had tried to become a room. They had refused to furnish it.

The heath breathed. Low shrubs released their resin as the sun warmed them, a bitter-sweet scent that clung to the air and then let go. Purple flowers—too small to demand naming—dotted the ground in irregular bursts, their color deepening where shadows pooled. The wind came in uneven pulses, not the clean sweep of altitude but something fractured, as if it were learning the land by touch.

Celeste slowed, letting the others drift a few steps ahead. She needed the space, not to think, but to feel how the pressure had altered her internal acoustics. There was a faint ringing behind her ears, the afterimage of attention, like the hush that follows a sudden silence in a concert hall when the audience realizes it has been holding its breath.

Mila crouched to retie a bootlace. Her hands trembled slightly, then steadied. "When it went quiet back there," she said, not looking up, "I thought something terrible was about to happen."

Aria turned, eyes softening. "That's what training does," she said. "It teaches you that calm is just violence waiting to speak."

Volkov stopped beside a weathered fence post leaning at an angle that felt intentional only because it had survived so long. He touched the wood, flakes coming away under his thumb. "Pressure like that isn't sustainable," he said. "It's expensive. Attention burns resources faster than force."

Celeste caught up to them and stood with her back to the wind, letting it press her coat against her ribs. She imagined the Maestro, wherever he was, leaning forward, trying to read what had just slipped out of reach. It wasn't failure or defeat but a misalignment, the kind that made strategists restless.

They continued across the heath, the land gently insisting on movement without direction. Somewhere far off, thunder murmured, the sound of the atmosphere adjusting itself.

Pressure, she realized, was only dangerous when it convinced you to respond.

They did not. They walked until the light began to thin again, until the day loosened its hold, until the world resumed the ordinary work of being vast and unconcerned. And in that unconcern, something fundamental shifted: the space around them was no longer waiting to see what they would do. It had already moved on.

By late afternoon the heath gave way to a shallow escarpment, its edge breaking into terraces of stone that looked quarried by weather rather than hands. Lichen painted the rock in pale greens and chalky oranges, a slow alphabet spelling time. The air cooled as the sun slid lower, carrying with it the mineral scent of exposed earth and the distant promise of rain that had not yet committed.

They descended carefully, boots testing each step, the cello balanced against Celeste's shoulder like a second spine. Below, a ribbon of road cut across the land, narrow, unadorned, the kind that existed to connect places that did not advertise themselves. A single car passed, its engine a brief interruption that did not linger long enough to be remembered.

Mila paused halfway down and looked back at the heath. From this angle it appeared seamless, the bowl they had crossed now invisible, pressure erased by distance and light. "If I hadn't felt it," she said, "I wouldn't believe it was ever there."

"That's how it works," Volkov replied. "The cleanest containment leaves no evidence. It makes you doubt your own body."

Aria crouched to retie her laces, fingers quick and sure. "But bodies remember," she said. "Even when the land doesn't."

At the bottom, they found a stand of scrubby pines clustered around a spring that seeped from rock in a thin, determined line. The water tasted of stone and cold. Celeste drank and felt the last echo of pressure dissolve from her jaw, her shoulders settling as if released from a harness she hadn't known she was wearing.

The sky shifted again, with clouds gathering in long, deliberate strokes, light turning amber at the edges. Somewhere, thunder answered itself, not close but not far either.

They rested there as evening approached, the land indifferent to their pause, the world resuming its larger rhythms without checking whether they were ready. Celeste listened to wind through needles, to Mila's steady breathing, to the quiet competence of Aria and Volkov sharing watch without ceremony, and she understood, with a clarity that felt earned rather than granted, that pressure only mattered when it found purchase. Here, it slid off.

The day ended not with a conclusion but with continuity: the road waiting below, the sky practicing change, the land unconcerned with being understood. And somewhere beyond the ridge, expectation searched for a shape and found none.

They followed the road as it thinned into twilight, not walking on it exactly, but alongside it, letting the packed earth and gravel exist as reference rather than instruction. The pines fell away behind them, replaced by low fields edged with stone that had been stacked without ever agreeing on height. The land felt quieter here, not emptied of sound but settled into a lower register, as if it had decided the day's arguments were finished.

A farmhouse appeared ahead, its windows already glowing, the light spilling outward in soft, uneven rectangles that broke against the dark like warmth testing its reach. Smoke drifted from a chimney, carrying the smell of wood and something faintly sweet, apple skins, perhaps, or bread pushed too far toward caramel.

They stopped instinctively the way animals paused at the edge of another's territory. "We don't need to go in," Mila said, though there was no fear in her voice, only awareness.

"No," Celeste agreed. "But it matters that we could."

The pressure did not return. That, more than anything, unsettled her. The Maestro had leaned, had tested, had tried to shape silence into enclosure, and now he was gone again, withdrawing attention the way a hand withdrew from a surface that refused to yield. It meant he was recalibrating. It meant he was learning.

Volkov tilted his head, listening to something too distant to name. "He'll try a different register next time," he said. "Not space. Not stillness."

Aria nodded. "People."

Celeste felt the truth of it settle into her bones. Pressure through atmosphere had failed. Pressure through absence had failed. What came next would not be abstract. It would be intimate. She wondered if Lena was somewhere safe, though she doubted he'd try the same leverage point twice. If she was honest with herself, she missed the violinist and the orchestra. She pushed those thoughts from her mind and focused on the present.

They moved on as the last light drained from the sky, the road continuing without them, the farmhouse receding into something that would become memory. Night arrived without insistence, stars pricking through clouds in uneven numbers, refusing symmetry.

Ahead, the dark held no answers. Only continuation. Night settled fully, not as a curtain but as a depth. The road's pale ribbon faded into suggestion, its edges dissolving until it became nothing more than a difference in texture beneath their boots. Fields exhaled the warmth they had hoarded all day, releasing the scent of cut grass and damp stone. Somewhere far off, a dog barked once, then stopped, as if reconsidering the usefulness of sound.

They walked in a loose line now, close enough to feel one another's pace without touching. Celeste let her stride sync to Mila's breathing, to Aria's quiet confidence, to Volkov's habit of pausing at irregular intervals as if checking the seams of the dark. The cello rode steady against her shoulder, its weight familiar, unargued.

No pressure returned. That absence had texture. It felt like a held note that refused resolution, a suspension. Celeste listened for the telltale tightening in her chest, the subtle cue that meant attention had found them again. It didn't come. Instead, the night offered ordinary sounds: insects negotiating territory, the soft click of stones shifting underfoot, the wind's low commentary moving through hedgerows without intent.

Mila spoke quietly, as if testing whether the dark would object. "If he comes through people," she said, "what do we do?"

Celeste didn't answer right away. She watched a cloud peel back from the moon, light spilling into the lane in a wash that made every surface briefly legible, and then let it fade again. "We do what we've been doing," she said at last. "We stay unassignable. We don't let him decide who we are to each other."

Aria glanced back, eyes catching moonlight. "Pressure works when it narrows choices."

Volkov nodded. "And people apply pressure best when they believe it's kindness."

Celeste thought of Lena once more.

They reached a low stone bridge spanning a dry culvert. Celeste paused at its center and rested her hand on the parapet, feeling the stone's retained heat. She imagined the Maestro somewhere beyond the hills, reconfiguring models, translating failure into a new hypothesis. Not retreating, but adapting. She let the thought pass.

They crossed the bridge and continued into the dark where the road bent out of sight, the night accepting them without ceremony. Above, the stars rearranged themselves into patterns no one would ever fully agree on. Pressure had tested space. It had tested stillness. Next, it would test belonging.

And they were ready—not with answers, not with plans—but with the practiced refusal to be reduced to anything that could be held.

♪ ♪

Chapter 29

Voices

MORNING ARRIVED AS conversation rather than event. Light crept along the undersides of clouds, coloring them with a bruised rose that suggested weather was still undecided about its obligations. The road they had followed the night before reappeared in pieces, gravel here, packed earth there, never quite agreeing with itself. Birds gathered in hedges and fences, testing calls, revising them, discarding what didn't work.

Celeste woke to the sound of people. They weren't close or loud, but they were present in a way that felt new. She sat up, the cello case pressed against her thigh, and listened. The cadence wasn't mechanical. It wasn't the clean symmetry of patrols or the purposeful hush of surveillance teams. It was uneven, with laughter cut short, a cough, the scrape of metal on stone. A morning doing what mornings did before anyone tried to optimize them.

Mila stirred beside her. "We're near someone's day," she murmured.

Aria was already on her feet, scanning the low rise beyond their makeshift shelter. "He's shifting channels," she said quietly. "No more atmospheric pressure. This is social weather."

Volkov joined them, eyes narrowed not at threat but at pattern. "People aren't tools," he said. "But they're conduits. If you lean gently enough, they don't realize they're carrying anything."

Celeste felt it then, the subtle pull, not on her body, but on attention. The sense that the day ahead had opinions. That meaning would be offered freely, generously, and with expectations hidden inside kindness. She stood and adjusted the strap of the cello case, feeling its familiar weight anchor her to something she still chose. "Then we listen," she said. "Before we speak."

Beyond the rise, a village began to wake with doors opening, voices greeting, the small rituals of belonging unfolding without awareness of how valuable they were.

Pressure had learned a new language. It had learned to sound like home.

They approached the village from the side, not by the road but along a footpath pressed thin by years of practical agreement. The ground here held the marks of use rather than ownership, of boot prints layered into one another, bicycle tracks veering off where impatience had won. A line of poplars bordered the path, their leaves flickering silver in the breeze like a language that refused to hold still.

The first voice they heard clearly was an argument, two men debating the merits of repairing a fence now or waiting until the ground dried. The cadence was familiar in a way that had nothing to do with words: the rise and fall of people who expected to be understood even if they disagreed.

226

Mila slowed. Her shoulders tightened, then loosened again as the argument ended in laughter and a compromise neither of them believed would hold. "They sound… safe," she said.

"They sound unconsidered," Volkov replied. "That's different."

Celeste felt the distinction land. Safety was curated. Unconsidered was earned by habit.

They entered the village as the bakery doors opened, warmth spilling into the street in visible waves. The smell of yeast and sugar carried farther than any announcement could have. A woman set out a chalkboard sign with yesterday's smudges still visible beneath the new writing. A child darted past on a scooter, narrowly missing Aria, who stepped aside without breaking stride.

No one looked at them twice, and that was the first real pressure. It wasn't scrutiny. It was expectation, the quiet assumption that they would behave like everyone else. That they would fit into the grammar of the place without resistance. Belonging offered freely was harder to refuse than surveillance ever had been.

Celeste paused near the bakery window, watching hands move behind the glass, dough shaped and reshaped with a confidence that came from repetition rather than oversight. She felt the pull then toward participation. Toward being folded into the day.

Her phone, still dead, felt suddenly accusatory in her bag, as if reminding her how easily connection could become obligation.

Aria leaned close. Her voice was low. "This is where it gets dangerous," she said.

Mila frowned. "Because they're kind?"

"Yes," Aria replied. "Because kindness is how stories travel fastest."

Volkov watched a group of women gather near the square, their conversation overlapping in a way that felt almost musical. "If the Maestro is listening now," he said, "he's listening through mouths that don't know they're singing."

Celeste straightened, adjusting the cello case on her back. The instrument felt heavier here, not as burden, but as declaration. "Then we don't disappear," she said quietly. "We stay present without becoming legible."

The bakery bell chimed as the door opened, the sound bright and ordinary and impossibly loud in its innocence. Voices were already moving around them. The question was whether they would let those voices decide who they were.

Celeste stepped inside the bakery, the bell's aftertone lingering like a held breath. Heat wrapped around her immediately, the air dense with yeast and sugar and the faint burn of crust pushed just to the edge of impatience.

"*Buongiorno,*" the woman behind the counter said, already reaching for paper.

Celeste returned the greeting, her accent careful but unremarkable, the kind that suggested travel without explanation. She pointed, nodded, paid in coins that had passed through too many hands to carry any story worth keeping.

Behind her, Mila traced a finger along the fogged glass of the display case, following the curves of pastries that looked like they had never been asked to symbolize anything. Aria stood by the door, posture relaxed enough to pass for casual, alert enough to notice who lingered a second too long before moving on. Volkov waited outside, eyes on the square, absorbing the morning like someone memorizing a room he did not intend to stay in.

"First time here?" the baker asked, wrapping the loaf.

Celeste smiled. "First morning."

The woman laughed, satisfied. "That's the good one."

Outside, they broke the bread without ceremony, tearing it into uneven pieces. Crust cracked. Steam escaped. A man passing by nodded approval without slowing.

This, Celeste realized, was how pressure would work now, not by narrowing options, not by threatening consequence, but by offering normal. By inviting them into patterns so familiar it would feel impolite not to accept.

A voice rose near the fountain, an older woman calling to someone across the square, her tone sharp with affection. A reply came back, louder, carrying the names of people they did not know but could already imagine. The village was speaking to itself, a layered conversation that did not need them but would make room if they asked.

Mila finished her bread and wiped her hands on her jeans. "If he's listening through them," she said softly, "how do we protect them?"

Celeste watched the square breathe with people crossing, pausing, resuming, with no single rhythm, only overlap. "We don't," she said. "We don't turn people into shields."

Aria nodded. "We let the voices stay theirs."

A church bell marked the hour as a suggestion. The sound rolled through the square and dissipated into the side streets, leaving behind the ordinary miracle of time moving on without asking permission.

They moved with it, neither blending in nor standing apart, walking the thin line between presence and restraint. Pressure had learned to speak. Now it would learn what happened when no one answered in its voice.

They lingered at the edge of the square long enough for it to forget them. That was the trick—time, not camouflage. The square did what squares did: accepted circulation, shed it, accepted it again. A delivery truck idled and moved on. Two teenagers argued over music leaking from a phone speaker, the sound tinny and insistent until one of them laughed and pocketed it. A dog slept beneath a bench, dreaming itself into motion without ever opening its eyes.

Celeste leaned against the low stone rim of the fountain, the cello case resting upright between her boots like a punctuation mark. Water spilled from the lip in a rhythm that had never bothered to be precise. She watched reflections break and reform with faces, the sky, the bakery sign, nothing holding still long enough to be owned.

This was how voices worked when they weren't being harvested: they overlapped, contradicted, wandered off mid-thought. Meaning here was collective and temporary. No single thread ran long enough to be pulled.

Aria caught her eye and nodded toward a narrow street sloping away from the square. A woman stood there with a crate of tomatoes, calling greetings to passersby by name. Not asking anything, just placing sound into the air like an offering that didn't require return.

Mila's shoulders softened as she listened. "They don't perform belonging," she said. "They assume it."

Volkov shifted his weight, gaze tracking a man who paused near the notice board, scanning papers that advertised piano lessons, lost cats, a meeting about irrigation. Nothing official. Nothing clean. Just the slow accumulation of need and response. "If the Maestro is listening," he said quietly, "this is a mess for him."

Celeste felt the pull again, the temptation to answer, to contribute something beautiful and precise, to let the cello speak into the square and braid itself into the morning. She resisted it with the discipline she had once reserved for silence in a hall that demanded it.

A woman approached the fountain to rinse her hands, glanced at the cello, and smiled. "You play?" she asked, not waiting for permission to be curious.

"Yes," Celeste replied. The truth, stripped of context, felt light.

The woman nodded, satisfied, and returned to her errand. No request. No expectation.

That was the other danger: not kindness as leverage, but curiosity without agenda. It made restraint feel like withholding.

The bell rang again—quarter hour this time—softer, almost embarrassed. The square adjusted around it without stopping. Celeste straightened, the decision forming not as plan but as boundary. "We move before the story forms," she said.

They drifted away from the fountain, the square already rearranging itself behind them, voices filling the space they vacated without pause or concern. Pressure had learned to speak softly. They had learned to listen without replying. And that, Celeste knew, was the only way to keep voices from being turned into instruments someone else could play.

They took the narrow street that sloped away from the square, the one that smelled faintly of laundry soap and tomatoes bruised in their crates. The stones here were smoother, polished by decades of feet that had passed through without needing to be counted. Windows opened and closed as they moved, the soft percussion of shutters adjusting to the light.

Celeste felt the village loosen its attention almost immediately. Voices reattached themselves to their original conversations, their original concerns. The pressure eased, not because it had vanished, but because it had failed to anchor.

Mila walked beside her, gaze flicking to faces as they passed, an old man bent over a bicycle chain, a woman watering basil in tin cans, a child arguing with a doorway about whether it was allowed to be slammed. None of it felt staged. None of it waited for approval.

"This is what they took from us," Mila said quietly. "Not freedom. Ordinariness."

Volkov slowed near a bend where the street narrowed into an alley barely wide enough for two people to pass without negotiation. He paused, listening for tone. The alley carried sound differently, voices compressing and stretching as if testing how far they could travel before losing meaning.

"They'll try to seed stories here," he said. "Not accusations. Questions. Someone asking whether strangers passed through. Whether anyone noticed anything unusual."

Aria nodded. "Curiosity weaponized."

Celeste stopped and turned, the cello case shifting against her back. "Then we leave them nothing unusual to notice."

She stepped aside as a woman passed carrying groceries, offered a soft scusi, received a nod that held no interest beyond courtesy. The exchange felt like a successful crossing with no residue, no echo.

They reached the end of the alley where it spilled into fields again, the village already rearranging itself behind them. A breeze carried voices after them for a few seconds, some laughter, a raised greeting, the clatter of dishes, but then let them fall.

Celeste looked back once, not to memorize, not to regret, but to acknowledge what had almost become a snare. Belonging offered without demand was still a force. It could still be turned. "Voices don't need us to save them," she said, more to herself than to the others. "They just need us not to teach someone else how to use them."

They stepped into the open land again, the path dissolving beneath their feet, the village already busy with the work of forgetting. Pressure had learned to speak. They had learned when not to answer.

Chapter 30

Story

THEY ENCOUNTERED THE story before they encountered the people. It traveled ahead of them the way weather sometimes did, carried not by wind, but by anticipation. A sentence half-heard at the edge of a market. A glance that lingered a beat too long. A pause in conversation that resumed just slightly off tempo once they passed. Celeste felt it register in her body before her mind agreed to name it.

Someone, somewhere, had begun asking about them, not with suspicion, but with interest.

They were moving through a low valley stitched together by orchards and narrow lanes, the land gentler here, domesticated without being tamed. Fruit trees leaned toward one another across stone walls, branches heavy with apples that had split and sweetened where they fell. The air smelled of sugar and soil and late afternoon heat. A place where stories liked to stay.

Mila walked a few steps ahead, humming again, soft, distracted, the sound of someone testing whether joy would answer if invited. Aria and Volkov flanked without pattern, drifting just enough to look uncoordinated.

They stopped at a roadside stand run by an old man who looked like he had outlived several governments and felt no need to discuss it. Wooden crates held fruit in various states of usefulness. A handwritten sign read: *Prendete quello che serve.* Take what you need.

Celeste selected two apples and placed coins in the tin without checking the price.

The man nodded. "You're the musician," he said, not asking.

The pressure arrived all at once, not crushing, not sharp, but intimate. Familiar in a way that made her spine tighten. "I play," she said carefully.

He smiled. "That's what I said."

Mila froze.

Aria's hand stilled at her side.

Volkov shifted his weight. He wasn't defensive, just attentive.

The man gestured vaguely with his chin, toward the road, the valley, the idea of elsewhere. "They say someone passed through yesterday. Played in a square. Didn't ask for anything."

Celeste took a breath that felt suddenly audible. "Lots of people play."

"Sure," he agreed. "But not like that."

There it was. The borrowed name. Not her real one. Not Celeste Morgan, not assassin, not cellist, not fugitive. Something worse. Something softer. A story that wanted to be told.

Mila looked at her, eyes wide, searching. Do we correct it? the look asked. Do we disappear? Do we deny it?

Celeste bit into the apple. Juice ran down her wrist, sticky and bright. "We didn't stay," she said. "Squares don't belong to anyone."

The man laughed quietly, satisfied in a way that had nothing to do with answers. "No," he said. "But people remember what passes through them." He turned back to rearranging fruit, the conversation already done in his mind.

They walked on in silence, the valley opening ahead of them like a held breath finally released.

Mila spoke first. "He didn't mean harm."

"No," Volkov said. "He meant meaning."

Celeste wiped her hand on her coat and kept walking.

This was the danger now. Not pursuit, not capture, but being given a name they had not chosen, and discovering how easily the world wanted to keep it.

They walked deeper into the valley, where the road softened into dust and the dust carried the faint imprint of wagon wheels that no one used anymore. The land here had learned how to host memory without insisting on permanence. Stone walls slumped inward, trees grew where fences had once made arguments, and the light filtered through leaves in a way that felt almost intentional, gentle, flattering, persuasive.

Celeste felt the story pace them, not in the way footsteps or surveillance did. Something lighter and more insidious, the way curiosity moved when it believed it was being kind.

They passed a woman hanging laundry in a yard that sloped too steeply to be practical. She looked up, smiled at Mila's humming, and said, "You have a lovely voice."

Mila startled, the sound cutting off mid-breath. "Oh. I—thank you."

The woman nodded, already returning to her clothespins. "It's good to hear music again."

Again. Aria caught Celeste's eye. The message was wordless and sharp: It's spreading.

Volkov slowed, letting a gap form between them and Mila, the shape of the group shifting subtly, like a school of fish adjusting to pressure without ever breaking formation. "They're not repeating facts," he murmured. "They're repeating impressions."

"That's harder to correct," Aria replied. "Facts can be denied. Impressions just… linger."

Celeste felt the familiar itch in her fingers, the impulse to clarify, to shape the narrative before it could harden into something she didn't recognize. To say: I am not what you think. To offer the cello, the bow, the clean geometry of music as explanation. But explanation was performance, and performance was exactly what the Maestro wanted.

They stopped near a shallow bend in the road where a fig tree leaned so low its fruit brushed the ground. Overripe figs split open, their sweetness already claimed by insects and birds. Celeste picked one up, turning it in her hand, noting how easily it gave way. "This is how he does it," she said quietly. "He doesn't need to follow us. He lets the story arrive first."

Mila hugged her arms around herself. "I don't want to be a story," she said. "I just want to be… here."

Celeste looked at her then, really looked at her, not as a responsibility, not as a symbol of what had been lost, but as a person standing at the threshold of something fragile and real. "You are," she said. "Stories don't ask how you're feeling."

Volkov scanned the valley ahead. In the distance, smoke rose from a cluster of houses, thin and vertical, as if the place itself were sending a signal without knowing why. "We can still move," he said. "Break the pattern before it settles."

Aria shook her head slightly. "Movement won't stop it now. They've already started telling it."

Celeste felt the weight of that land in her chest. The Maestro had learned what pressure alone could not accomplish. He had learned how to let people do the work for him, how to turn admiration into containment without ever touching the thing he wanted to hold.

Borrowed tales were the most dangerous kind, because they arrived wrapped in generosity.

She set the fig back down and wiped her hands clean on the grass. "Then we change the story," she said. "Not by correcting it. By refusing to finish it."

They walked on, the valley folding around them, voices carrying faintly from places they could not yet see.

Behind them, the story continued its slow, well-meaning spread, learning their outlines, softening their edges, deciding who they were allowed to be.

They reached the village by accident. At least, that was how it felt as one moment the road was bordered by fig trees and slumped stone, the next opening into a cluster of houses arranged around a square too small to be impressive and too old to apologize for it. The place had the quiet confidence of somewhere that did not expect to be discovered. Children played with a ball that had lost its color but not its enthusiasm. An old radio murmured from an open window, the voice of a man arguing with himself about the weather. A café table stood empty except for a glass ring and a folded newspaper whose headline had already decided to be forgotten.

Celeste felt the narrative thicken, becoming more attentive.

They stopped at the edge of the square, and it happened again, someone looked up, smiled, and said nothing. Someone else nodded as if confirming something they had already suspected. The attention wasn't hungry; it was pleased.

Mila's hand found Celeste's sleeve without asking. "This is how it starts," Mila whispered. "Isn't it?"

"Yes," Celeste said. "This is how it finishes, if we let it."

Aria scanned the square, eyes catching on a man standing near the well, his posture loose but observant. He wasn't local, she thought, or perhaps he was too local, someone who had learned how to belong quickly.

Volkov noticed him too, their shared glance brief and loaded.

A woman emerged from the café carrying a tray of small cups. "Coffee?" she called, already walking toward them. "On the house."

The offer landed like a weight. Celeste could feel the pull, not toward caffeine, not toward rest, but toward acceptance. Toward the ease of saying yes and allowing the story to take care of itself. To become the musician who passed through, the one people remembered fondly, the one whose presence improved the morning.

The Maestro didn't need to watch anymore. He was letting the village do it for him.

"No," Celeste said gently. "But thank you."

The woman paused, surprised. She didn't seem offended, just momentarily displaced. "Ah," she said, recovering quickly. "Another time, then." She moved on, already adjusting the story to accommodate refusal.

Volkov leaned in. "We stay too long, we become something they'll protect."

"And protection is just another kind of cage," Aria added.

Celeste nodded. "Exactly."

She stepped forward then to the square's margin, where cobblestone gave way to dirt and weeds pushed through cracks without permission. She set the cello case down, not opening it, not offering anything, just placing it there.

The square noticed. Conversation dipped and shifted. People glanced, waited, sensed that something had changed without knowing how to name it. Celeste met their eyes one by one, not performing, not retreating, just being present. No explanation. No sound.

The story hesitated. Names and tales only worked when they were filled in. And Celeste Morgan—cellist, assassin, fugitive, weather—was done being completed by other people. She picked up the case again and turned away.

Behind her, the square resumed itself, slower now, uncertain.

They left without being followed. But as they walked back into the valley, Celeste knew with absolute clarity: This was the moment the Maestro had been waiting for, not because she had played, but because she had refused to.

They did not hurry when they left the village. Hurrying would have been a confession, an admission that something had been taken, or offered, or lost. Instead they walked at the same unremarkable pace, boots finding the road without comment, the valley widening again as if it had been waiting to reclaim them.

The square did not call after them. That was the most unsettling part. Celeste felt it like a phantom pressure between her shoulder blades, memory beginning to form. The kind that hardened quietly, later, when no one was watching. Stories did not need witnesses to begin. They only needed time.

Mila exhaled once they cleared the last house, the sound shaky despite her attempt to control it. "I thought they were going to insist," she said. "Or follow. Or… something."

"They didn't need to," Volkov replied. "Insistence comes later. First comes agreement."

Aria stopped near a break in the wall where vines had claimed stone and pulled it inward. She leaned against the rock, eyes closed briefly, recalibrating. "He wanted you to accept the coffee," she said to Celeste. "Or refuse it loudly. Either would've worked."

Celeste nodded. "He wanted a beat to score."

They stood there for a moment, the land opening into quiet again, fig trees and fields, the hum of insects threading the air. The village was already receding into something like normalcy, the kind that absorbed interruption and smoothed it over until it could be remembered as charm.

Celeste opened the cello case then, not to play, but to check. The instrument lay exactly as she had left it, wood cool, strings settled. She ran her fingers along the curve of its body and felt the familiar tension of music waiting, always waiting, for consent. She closed the case again with a decisive click.

"They're going to tell it differently tonight," Mila said. "Over dinner. Over wine."

"Yes," Celeste agreed. "They'll say we were polite. Quiet. Interesting. That we passed through."

Aria's jaw tightened. "And that someone should have asked us to stay."

Celeste looked back toward the village. "That's the narrative," she said. "the one that turns into expectation…" Her voice trailed off .

Volkov watched the road ahead, where it split into two directions that looked equally undecided. "This is where it becomes expensive for you."

Celeste met his gaze. She knew what he meant. The Maestro would not punish the village. He would let it keep its warmth, its generosity. He would simply let the story of her grow until her absence felt like loss, until someone went looking. He would create pressure through belonging. That way stars needed fans or an audience and vice versa. One could hardly exist without the others.

She adjusted the strap of the cello case and started walking again, choosing neither fork deliberately, letting the land decide for a while longer. "We don't correct them," she said. "And we don't reward them."

Mila swallowed. "Then what do we do?"

Celeste answered without hesitation. "We make it impossible for the story to stay singular."

They moved on, the valley stretching ahead, voices already beginning to reshape behind them.

The Maestro had finally found a way to touch her without reaching. And Celeste Morgan understood now what this movement required of her next: Not silence, not disappearance, but the willingness to let herself be multiplied until no borrowed name could hold.

They walked until the valley thinned into a corridor of hedges and the light began to tilt toward evening again, the day repeating itself with slight variations, like a phrase altered just enough to avoid recognition. The air cooled. Cicadas stitched the margins with a sound that felt deliberate but unowned.

Celeste slowed, feeling the moment arrive before it announced itself. Multiplication was not movement alone. It required contact, the quiet, distributed exchange of presence that left no single center to interrogate.

They stopped where the hedges opened onto a fallow field dotted with the remains of an old irrigation system: rusted pipes, cracked valves, a shallow concrete basin holding rainwater and leaves. The place had once been functional. Now it was permissive.

"This is where we change how we move," Celeste said.

Aria folded her arms, listening. Volkov tilted his head, already parsing implications. Mila waited, the way someone waited when they were ready to be told the truth rather than comforted.

"We stop traveling as a unit," Celeste continued. "Not all the time. Not permanently. But often enough that no single story can keep up."

Mila's eyes widened. "You mean… separate?"

"Overlap," Celeste corrected. "Intersect. Rejoin. We become a series of encounters instead of a procession."

Volkov nodded slowly. "It forces narrative diffusion. Witnesses can't agree on sequence."

"And the Maestro can't tune pressure if he doesn't know where to apply it," Aria added. "He'll waste attention trying to decide which version matters."

Celeste crouched by the basin and skimmed a leaf from the water's surface. Ripples spread, intersected, canceled one another out. "Exactly," she said. "We let people meet different truths that don't contradict, only complicate."

Mila's voice was small but steady. "What's my role?"

Celeste looked at her fully then. "You stop being protected," she said gently. "You become present. On your terms."

Mila absorbed this, breathing through the instinct to retreat. "I can do that," she said, surprising herself with how certain it sounded.

The sky darkened another shade. Somewhere beyond the hedges, a tractor coughed and fell silent. The world continued its work without waiting for agreement.

Celeste stood. "We don't make ourselves rare," she said. "We make ourselves common in incompatible ways."

They shared a look that was not a vow and not a plan, just alignment, temporary and sufficient. The borrowed names behind them would continue to circulate, grow warmer, more confident. Ahead, new names would form and fail to settle.

The Maestro would listen and hear overlap where he wanted harmony. And in that interference—that beautiful, stubborn noise—the story would finally begin to slip from his hands.

They separated without ceremony, not the kind of separation that felt like a fracture or a farewell. There were no tightened embraces, no last looks heavy with promise, but with a gentle loosening, like threads slipping free from a weave that had done its work for now. The field held them as they recalibrated, each body finding its own vector without urgency.

Aria went first, cutting across the fallow ground toward the hedgerow that led back toward the village's outskirts, her pace unhurried, posture unremarkable. She looked like someone with an errand, a purpose small enough not to register. Volkov waited a beat longer, then took the opposite direction along the irrigation channel, boots finding the old concrete with practiced ease, his path neither toward nor away from anything obvious. Mila stayed with Celeste, for a moment.

The light was thinning fast now, the sky bruising into purples and iron blues, the cicadas growing bolder as if night were an invitation rather than a consequence. Mila tucked her hands into her jacket sleeves, rocking once on her heels. "What if I do it wrong?" she asked.

Celeste didn't answer immediately. She watched Aria's shape dissolve into the hedge, Volkov's figure become indistinct against the slope. The field began to forget them even as it held their footprints.

"You will," Celeste said finally. "That's how we know it's yours."

Mila smiled, a small, crooked thing that carried more resolve than fear. "Then I'll start with being bad at it." She turned and walked into the dimming land, her path meandering, her humming returning in fragments that never quite formed a tune. Within seconds, she was no longer alone or accompanied. She was simply there.

Celeste stood by the basin and listened to the ripples settle. This was the cost of multiplication: relinquishing control over how the story unfolded. Trusting that presence, when allowed to disperse, would erode the edges of expectation faster than any correction ever could.

She adjusted the strap of the cello case and headed in the last remaining direction, not the road, not the field, but the narrow margin where grass met stone and neither quite agreed on ownership.

As she walked, voices rose in the distance, including laughter, a greeting, a question asked and half-answered. None of them said her name. None of them needed to. Names would continue to circulate behind her, warmed by generosity, sharpened by curiosity. Ahead, new encounters would form without coordination, without hierarchy, without a single point of reference to tune against.

Somewhere, the Maestro would listen and hear only interference, patterns collapsing into one another, signals refusing to stabilize.

Celeste Morgan did not hurry. She let the night accept her as one more moving element among many, indistinguishable and intentional, carrying nothing that could be easily held.

The story was no longer following her. It was learning how to lose her.

Night finished what evening had started. The valley cooled into itself, heat lifting from stone and soil in thin, invisible threads. Somewhere a door closed. Somewhere else, a light came on and stayed on longer than it needed to. The land accepted all of it without commentary.

Celeste walked until the basin, the hedges, the village itself were no longer behind her or ahead of her, just elsewhere. She stopped near a stand of olive trees whose leaves whispered continuously, a sound too soft to be mistaken for speech.

She set the cello case down and sat beside it. For the first time that day, she let herself feel the weight of what she had done. Not the separation or the risk, but the refusal once again to be what she had been trained to be.

The Maestro had learned to borrow voices. to let kindness do the work of containment, to turn generosity into narrative gravity. And she had answered not by pulling away, but by dissolving the center he needed to tune against.

This was not escape. It was dispersion.

Her phone remained dark in her bag, a relic of a language she no longer spoke. She did not miss it. The silence now felt inhabited rather than empty, a quiet made of many small presences overlapping without agreement.

In the distance, a voice called a name—not hers—followed by laughter and the scrape of a chair. Somewhere else, a tune began and faltered and started again, belonging to no one but the moment. Celeste closed her eyes. She did not imagine the Maestro. She imagined instead what he would hear: Fragments, contradictions, stories that did not align no matter how patiently they were arranged, borrowed names would continue to circulate. But they would no longer resolve.

And when she stood and lifted the cello case again, moving on without urgency or concealment, it was with the certainty that the most dangerous thing she could do now was not disappear, but to remain everywhere he could not be sure she was.

∫ ∫

Chapter 31

Resonance

THE FIRST FRACTURE arrived disguised as gratitude. Celeste heard about it from a woman whose name she never caught, spoken over a chipped cup of coffee in a place that didn't advertise itself as a café. The woman's hands moved as she talked, confident, practiced, the gestures of someone who had learned to explain herself to strangers without apologizing.

"You passed through last week," she said, smiling as if the sentence were a gift. "People are still talking about it."

Celeste did not correct her. She had learned that correction created a center, and centers were what the Maestro required. "I pass through a lot of places," Celeste replied.

"Yes, but this was… different," the woman said. "Things loosened after. You know? The square felt bigger. People lingered."

Celeste felt the faint tightening at the base of her throat, the first sympathetic vibration of a string being tuned by someone else's hand. "And now?" she asked.

The woman hesitated, the smile shifting just slightly, acquiring an edge it hadn't needed before. "Now there are questions."

Celeste nodded. *Of course, there were.*

The woman leaned closer, lowering her voice as if sharing gossip rather than consequence. "A man came yesterday. Polite. Well-dressed. He asked if we'd noticed anyone unusual passing through. Said he was doing research. Cultural mapping."

There it was: not accusation, not threat, interest.

"What did you tell him?" Celeste asked.

The woman shrugged. "Nothing specific. Just that people come and go. But he kept asking about the music. About how it made people feel."

Celeste felt the resonance settle into her bones, alignment. The Maestro had found a way to make others listen for him. To turn aftereffects into data. "Did that feel strange?" Celeste asked gently.

The woman considered. "It felt like being… thanked in advance."

That was worse. Celeste finished her coffee and stood, leaving coins on the table that the woman waved away with unnecessary enthusiasm. Outside, the street was bright with morning, ordinary in the way that made it dangerous. Voices crossed and recrossed, layering into something that sounded almost like harmony if you didn't listen too closely.

Somewhere nearby, a story was being tuned. Not to capture Celeste directly, but to locate the places where her absence had changed the pitch of the world. Resonance, she understood, was not about sound. It was about what remained vibrating after the note had ended.

She walked for a long time after that, letting the street spend itself around her.

The town, larger than the village she had left, smaller than anything that bothered with maps, was busy in the loose, uncoordinated way of places that still believed in mornings. Deliveries arrived late and left early. A man argued cheerfully with a parking meter. Someone practiced a trumpet in an upstairs room with the windows open, missing the same note repeatedly and refusing to care.

Celeste felt it all differently now. She thought of it as after-sound. The Maestro was no longer chasing her trajectory. He was listening for what bent when she passed through, what continued to hum once she was gone. He didn't need her location. He needed her effect.

That was how voices became instruments.

Her phone buzzed, jarring her. It was alive again, somehow, after a borrowed charge from a socket she didn't remember using. She looked to the sky to see if she could spy a drone like the one Volkov thought might have been above them before. But she didn't see anything, though she knew satellites, and maybe Starlink,were always monitoring.. On her phone was one message, no sender ID. **You're changing people. That carries responsibility.**

She stared at the screen, pulse steady, breath even. Responsibility was the word he always reached for when force failed. She hit the phone's off button and dropped it into the bottom of her bag without ceremony.

At the edge of the town, she paused near a low wall where three women sat shelling peas into a metal bowl. Their conversation moved easily between subjects—weather, children, a neighbor's illness—never settling long enough to be claimed. One of them looked up and smiled.

"You look like you're listening," the woman said.

Celeste returned the smile. "I am."

"That's rare," the woman replied, not unkindly. "Most people are waiting to speak."

Celeste felt the resonance deepen, not tightening this time, but spreading. The Maestro would hear this too, eventually. He would catalogue it as impact, as influence, as proof that she could not move through the world without altering it. He would call that danger.

She sat on the wall and listened anyway. If this was the cost of dispersion, of letting herself be encountered rather than hidden, then she would pay it consciously, not as penance, but as choice.

Across the town, somewhere she could not see, a question was being asked again. Gently. Repeatedly. With gratitude in its tone and expectation in its bones. And for the first time since Berlin, Celeste understood the real shape of the trap: not capture. not exposure, but being made answerable for the way the world sounded after her.

By late afternoon the town had learned her outline. Not her face because faces were too specific to travel far, but the idea of her: someone attentive, someone who lingered without taking, someone whose presence made people pause mid-sentence and then continue differently. She felt it in the way conversations adjusted when she passed, in the half-second delay before laughter resumed, in the small courtesy of space people made without knowing why.

This was the Maestro's refinement: recruitment without consent.

Celeste left the town before dusk, taking a road that sloped down toward a ribbon of river that caught the light like a held breath. The water moved quickly here, not turbulent, but committed, carrying leaves and bits of bark in purposeful diagonals that never repeated themselves. She followed it until the buildings thinned and the voices loosened their grip.

Only then did she allow herself to stop.

She set the cello case down and sat on a flat stone still warm from the sun. The river spoke continuously, not loudly or softly, just insistently present. She closed her eyes and listened for the resonance she had begun to recognize as danger. It was there. Faint, but stable.

Somewhere upstream, someone was talking about her again. Somewhere downstream, someone else would soon. Not because they had been instructed to, but because the story now fit a need they hadn't known how to name. That was how responsibility was smuggled in.

If people felt better after you passed through, didn't you owe them something?

Celeste pressed her palm flat against the cello case, grounding herself in the physical certainty of wood and curve and weight. Music had taught her this lesson long before violence ever had: resonance could not be controlled once released. You could only decide whether to keep feeding it.

The Maestro would want her to respond, to clarify, to apologize, to claim influence so he could define its limits.

She stood instead and walked away from the river, leaving the sound behind unfinished. As she moved, she felt it, the first real cost of her strategym the steady pull of moral gravity.

Dispersion protected her body. It did not protect her conscience.

Ahead, the road bent toward higher ground where night gathered earlier and voices did not carry as far. Somewhere beyond that, Aria would be crossing another threshold. Volkov would be listening for a pattern that didn't resolve. Mila would be learning how to exist without an audience. They were all creating resonance now.

And the Maestro was listening to decide which of them he could make speak for the rest.

Celeste adjusted the strap of the cello case and kept walking. The trap was no longer about where she was. It was about whether she would accept the burden of being heard.

Night found her on the rise above the river, where the ground broke into shale and scrub and the air cooled fast enough to feel instructional. The town's lights softened behind her, scattering into reflections on water that made it look as if the river had learned how to hold stars without keeping them. She stopped where the road narrowed into a track and set the cello case down again, not because she intended to play, but because the weight had begun to speak.

Responsibility, the Maestro had said.

She unlatched the case and lifted the cello free, the wood catching the last of the day's warmth. It felt alive in a way no story ever did, responsive, yes, but never obedient. She turned it once, listening to the soft click of pegs settling, the whisper of horsehair against string when the bow shifted in her hand. She did not play a melody. She did not play for anyone. She drew the bow across a single string and let the note fall into the dark, unshaped and uncompleted. The sound traveled a little way and then broke apart, absorbed by slope and brush and the river's ongoing argument with gravity.

Resonance did not deepen. It thinned. Celeste smiled, a small, private thing. The lesson was immediate and unforgiving: answering fed the echo; allowing let it pass.

Her phone, that she thought she had shut down, vibrated in her bag with one short pulse, then another, insistent now. She ignored it until the third vibration forced the question into the open.

Unknown: They're asking about you again. Different place. Same language.

She did not reply. Instead, she played another single note, lower this time, and let it end on its own terms. She closed the case carefully and stood, the decision crystallizing not as defiance, but as method. She would not correct the stories. She would not accept them. She would not withdraw from the places that formed them.

She would change how resonance behaved, not by silence, not by saturation, but by refusing continuity. Short presences. Broken phrases. Notes that did not lead anywhere.

She started up the track toward higher ground, where sound thinned and names arrived late. Behind her, the river continued, indifferent. In front of her, the night widened, patient.

Somewhere, the Maestro would feel the interference as irritation. A pattern that refused to stabilize. A voice that did not resolve into authority.

Resonance could be harvested. But only if someone stayed to hum. Celeste did not.

She reached higher ground just as the temperature tipped.

The air thinned, sharpened, the kind of cold that did not threaten but clarified. Pines replaced scrub, their needles catching moonlight in brief, metallic flashes. The path narrowed again, then widened without explanation, refusing to become predictable for more than a dozen steps at a time.

Celeste slowed and let her breathing settle into the slope. This was the discipline now: discontinuity. To be present without becoming cumulative. To arrive without accruing expectation. She had learned the mechanics of this in music long ago: the power of the unresolved cadence, the phrase that refused to promise return.

Her phone vibrated again, then stopped. She did not check it. The Maestro's language depended on response. Silence, when it was sustained, became a signal. But interruption—brief, precise, unrepeatable—created noise he could not easily index. It forced him to choose between overfitting a model or abandoning it.

A light appeared ahead, then two lamps marking a small mountain hamlet gathered tightly around a bend. No village square this time. No obvious center. Just houses holding themselves against altitude and weather, their windows uneven, their paths improvised.

Celeste paused at the edge of it. She could pass through without entering. She could skirt the trees and let the place remain hypothetical. The old instinct tugged at her to minimize contact, reduce trace.

Instead, she walked in. She did not go to the lights. She went to the margins: a public tap set into stone, a bench with one leg shorter than the others, a notice board with papers layered too thickly to read without committing. She sat, filled her bottle, waited exactly long enough to be unremarkable.

A man passed carrying firewood. He nodded. She nodded back. "That's a fine case," he said, gesturing to the cello.

"Thank you," she replied.

No questions followed.

She stood and left. As she climbed out of the hamlet, she felt it, the resonance flicker and fail to catch. The place had not been warmed, improved, or altered enough to be discussed. No one would ask tomorrow if the musician had stayed. No one would thank her in advance.

This was the shape of refusal the Maestro had not yet mastered: contact without continuity.

Up the path, the night opened again. Celeste adjusted the strap on the cello case and moved on, leaving behind only the faintest disturbance, less a note than the memory that sound had once considered passing through.

Somewhere far away, questions would be asked again. They always were. But here, tonight, the answer had arrived and already dissolved. And that was enough. She thought of Esra and Lena and wondered how they and the others were doing. Celeste pulled out her phone and debating sending an encrypted text to check in. But then she decided it was more important to stay silent and to keep going.

She did not sleep where she stopped. Sleep required a kind of agreement with place, and tonight she needed refusal to remain active. Instead, she rested in increments that included ten minutes leaning against a pine, five walking, another ten seated on a stone that still remembered the sun. The rhythm kept her interior unsettled in a way that felt protective.

Below her, the hamlet's lights dimmed one by one. Somewhere a door closed. Somewhere else a radio finished a song and did not replace it. The night rearranged itself without consulting anyone.

Her phone vibrated once more—longer this time, as if the signal had traveled a distance it resented. **Unknown: People are worried. They think you're leaving too fast.**

Celeste closed her eyes. There it was: the final refinement. Concern. Worry. Care articulated as obligation. The Maestro had learned to frame absence as abandonment, to make dispersion feel like betrayal, to turn resonance into a debt.

She did not reply. Instead, she stood and played one last note into the trees, not from the cello this time, but from herself. She exhaled slowly, deliberately, letting the sound of breath meet bark and needle and open air. It went nowhere. It did not linger. That was the answer.

She moved again before the message could be followed by another, before worry could harden into search. The path accepted her steps without memory. The forest returned to its own conversations.

By morning, there would be new questions in new places. Someone would remember a woman who listened well. Someone else would remember nothing at all. The stories would no longer agree on order, or tone, or meaning.

The Maestro would hear the discord and try to resolve it. He would fail, because resonance, once denied continuity, did not disappear. It scattered, and scattered sound could not be summoned, corrected, or owned, only encountered, briefly, before it passed on.

Celeste Morgan did not turn back. The night closed behind her, not as silence, but as a field of unclaimed echoes, each one refusing to say where it had come from or where it might go next. Ahead lay the final movement, a convergence she would not orchestrate. She would arrive when the sound required her to and not a moment sooner.

Chapter 32

Coda

THE MAESTRO SPOKE at last, not to her, but to the world. Celeste learned this the way one learned about weather changes at altitude, not by announcement, but by pressure redistribution. Radios that had been silent carried a new cadence. Notices appeared in places that pretended not to post notices. Invitations arrived without envelopes, phrased as opportunities and framed as care. A gathering. A listening. A response.

The language was generous. The timing was impeccable. She heard it first from a shepherd on a ridge where the grass had learned to lie flat against itself. He mentioned it the way one mentioned a market day or a coming frost, something that would happen whether you attended or not.

"They say it's for everyone," he told her, tightening a strap. "A chance to share what's been changing."

Celeste nodded and thanked him, because gratitude no longer felt like consent.

By noon, the phrase had spread along three valleys and into two towns that did not share a road. By dusk, it had crossed languages without translation. The Maestro had done what he always did when models destabilized: he widened the frame until contradiction felt like inclusion. He was calling the resonance home.

Celeste did not go where the voices gathered. She went where they crossed. It was a basin of old stone terraces above a river that had changed its mind too many times to be owned. Paths arrived from different directions and left again without agreement. People had come here for centuries to trade, to wait, to rest, to argue, to leave. No stage. No center. Just space that had learned how to hold overlap.

She arrived at dusk with the cello on her back and no plan to play.

They were already there, dozens at first, then more. Not summoned, exactly. Drawn by curiosity that felt earned. Some carried instruments. Some carried nothing. Some came alone and stood apart, as if wary of joining anything too quickly.

No one announced the start. That was the Maestro's miscalculation. He had assumed the gathering would need him to begin.

Celeste stood at the margin and listened, not for cues, not for alignment, only for the way sound moved when no one tried to own it. A woman spoke about a garden that had failed and fed more people because of it. A boy tapped a rhythm on a stone and lost it and found another. Two strangers argued about a song's ending and laughed when they realized neither knew the beginning.

Resonance rose and fell, self-correcting, refusing to stabilize.

Her phone vibrated once. **Unknown: You're there.**

Celeste frowned at the phone before looking around.

The Maestro tried again, subtler this time. A hush passed through part of the basin, the familiar tightening that suggested attention seeking a spine. Someone raised a hand, waiting for permission to speak. Another looked around, uncertain whether they should be listening.

Celeste stepped forward then, not into the center (there wasn't one), but into the seam where paths crossed. She did not lift the cello. She did not speak. She sat.

The hush faltered. Sound resumed, but differently now, less eager to resolve, more willing to overlap. The permission that had been forming dissolved into a question that no one wanted to finish asking.

The Maestro pushed. A voice—trained, confident—rose to suggest order. A program. A way to capture what was happening so it could be shared properly.

Celeste stood, not to refuse, but to reframe. She opened the case and drew the bow once—only once—across a middle string. The note was plain, unadorned, and ended before it promised anything. She closed the case and stepped back to the margin.

That was all. The sound did not gather followers. It did not invite repetition. It did not ask for response. It released the basin.

People moved again with talking, tapping, humming, disagreeing, leaving, arriving. The suggestion of order collapsed under the weight of participation. There was nothing to harvest because nothing stayed still long enough to be counted.

The Maestro sent one last message, routed through kindness and concern and urgency braided together: **You could help them focus.**

Celeste smiled, not because she had won, but because the premise had finally revealed itself. Focus was the trap.

She walked away while the basin continued without her, the sound changing as it always would. By the time she reached the path, the gathering had already become something else, no longer a response, no longer an event. Just a place where many things happened and then did not.

At dawn, she crossed the river alone. The water took the night with it and left nothing behind that could be mapped. On the far bank, she paused and looked back once, not to witness an ending, but to acknowledge a beginning she did not own.

The Maestro would keep listening. That was no longer a threat, because listening, without a center to tune against, was just noise.

Celeste adjusted the strap of the cello case and set off along a path that had never agreed to be a path at all. She did not disappear. She did not perform. She remained—distributed, unfinished, present without permission—a sound that refused to resolve, moving through a world that had learned how to let go.

Morning did not arrive all at once. It came in pieces with light sliding along the river's edge, mist lifting where water met stone, the slow reassertion of color into a world that had been sound first and sight second. Celeste walked until the basin was no longer behind her in any meaningful way. Distance did not sever it. It diluted it, the way time diluted even the most insistent memory.

She did not check for messages. If the Maestro spoke now, it would only be to himself.

The path rose gently, threading through low trees whose leaves caught the sun and scattered it into fragments. Somewhere far off, a dog barked. Somewhere closer, someone sang, not well, not loudly, but with the uncomplicated assurance of a voice that did not expect to be answered.

Celeste stopped at the crest of the hill and set the cello down once more, but not to play, to rest. She sat beside it, back against the case, and closed her eyes. The world did not rush to fill the space she left open. It simply continued with water moving, light shifting, people elsewhere deciding what mattered to them today. This was what remained when every system failed to conclude her: not system or failure but capacity.

The Maestro would keep building frameworks. He would keep listening for centers, for leaders, for voices willing to become definitive. He would find them. Systems always did.

But he would never find her again in a way that mattered. Because Celeste Morgan no longer existed as a solution to be contained, or a problem to be solved, or a sound to be tuned.

She existed as movement, as overlap, as a presence that altered nothing permanently and therefore could not be undone.

When she stood and lifted the cello case, the decision had already been made, not once, but continuously, the way breathing decided itself again and again without instruction.

She walked on. The path accepted her. The world did not ask her name. And that was how the music continued, not as a concerto, not as a requiem, but as a living, unfinished line that belonged to no one and therefore could never be taken.

Epilogue

Aftertone

WEEKS LATER, THE basin no longer existed as a noun. It survived only as a verb. People spoke of it without agreeing on what it had been. Some remembered a gathering, others a pause, others nothing more than a day that felt slightly unaccountable afterward. No plaque appeared. No anniversary took hold. The place resumed its long habit of being useful and forgettable in equal measure.

This was the Maestro's failure. He searched for aftermath and found only dispersion. He searched for leaders and found only intersections. He widened his listening until it became indistinguishable from static, and in that widening lost the very leverage he had spent years perfecting.

Celeste heard of this not through alerts or channels, but through absence. No more messages that disguised themselves as concern. No more invitations shaped like responsibility. No more gratitude that expected repayment.

In a town by the sea, she repaired a bridge handrail with three strangers and was forgotten before sundown. In a city whose name she did not keep, she shared bread with a woman who never asked where she was from. Once, briefly, she played two notes in a stairwell where acoustics misbehaved and left before anyone could decide what it meant.

The cello learned new climates. So did she.

Somewhere else, the Maestro adjusted his models and discovered they no longer converged. Every attempt to stabilize produced divergence. Every attempt to center produced overlap. The system did not collapse. It became irrelevant. That was the truest ending.

Celeste continued—not forward, not away—just on. She did not stop being listened to. She stopped being listenable in the way power required. And in that difference—quiet, uncelebrated, irreversible—the world kept making sound without waiting to be told how to hear it.

The End

To join the mailing list to know when *The Phantom Fugue: A Shadow Concerto #4* releases, add your email to the form at www.jillferguson.com

Author's Note

This book and the series is dedicated to Dr. Adrian Fung, who taught me that a cello can do so much more than play classical music. We are like-minded souls who know people can be "not just one thing." For that and so much more, I am grateful. Thank you for the inspiration, the artistry, and the reminder that what we don't say can resonate the longest.

About the Author

Jill L. Ferguson has been a fan of mysteries and thrillers since she read the books of Scott Corbett and Carolyn Keene as a child. She is an entrepreneur and consultant and an award-winning author who has written more than three dozen books. With her brother, she writes the Whiskey Dog Mystery series under the pen name Faith Walker. Like Celeste Morgan, airports are places she finds moments of stillness and clarity amidst chaos.